IN THE HOUSE OF IN BETWEEN

J.D. BUFFINGTON

IN THE HOUSE OF IN BETWEEN / J.D. BUFFINGTON

Praise for other works by J.D. Buffington

41: AN AUTOBIOGRAPHY
"Told with a stark candidness, Buffington weaves a tale filled with hope, through a minefield of a very complex upbringing. An honest portrayal of life with a toxic relative, one filled with layers, discovery and ultimately self-discovery. '41' is a must-read for anyone trying to come to terms with how to navigate life when one of the main people you expect to guide you, isn't."
— Steve Stred, author of 'Mastodon,' 'Churn the Soil,' and 'The Color of Melancholy'

COME HITHER NO MALICE
"A beautifully written re-imagining of the story of Medusa. Captivating and impactful."
— Candace Nola, author of 'Bishop.'

NOTHING BUT THE WILLOWS & OTHER THINGS THAT ARE NOT THERE
"Nothing but the Willows is a poignant, introspective story of tragedy, hauntings, guilt and forgiveness told with compassion and warmth."
— Suzan Palumbo, author of 'Skin Thief: Stories' and 'Countess'

Dedication

This book is for those who *want* to believe, but *need*
to know facts and understand the truth.

And for Irene, always.

Introduction

In the House of In Between is a novel exploring the nature of a haunting. As such, trauma—personal and societal—center in this tale. In this house, you will encounter specters that display malice and malaise. There is reference to death's natural and violent expressions, with depictions of self-harm and self-loathing. Backlund House is haunted, but its inhabitants are often carrying something with them. A haunted house is not just a building, but the homes of our minds and the cages of our hearts. We are our own ghosts, we fall into cycles that feel like we're haunted by the traumas of our pasts and anxieties for the future. Yet, I also wanted to acknowledge that cycles can be broken the more we become aware of the harm they are causing. There is blood and tears in this house, but everyone who walks away from it is changed in some way—for some, for the better. There is hope in fear. Being afraid is a sign of awareness. Being aware can lead to survival, and sympathy. Watch your step, for the ghosts in this house have paths they must follow, ruts they have worn into its floors and walls. Falling into someone—or some-*thing*—else's track can make you lose your own. Backlund House offers a glimpse into the cyclical nature of trauma and fear, and maybe even ways to break free.

If you're ready, Madam Backlund's ledger is ready for your signature.

Foreword

'This place is scary to even think about, but there's no reason it should be like this. It's just a house.'

Why are we so in love with the idea of the haunted house? It has, over many, many years, penetrated both literature and lore, the concept that a house is not just a collection of walls and windows but rather, a living, breathing entity, with its own desires and whims. We like personification, don't we? Projecting our own ideas, thoughts and motivations onto the inanimate. Why is that? Why can a house no longer be just a house?

Perhaps it is the inherent romanticism that is part and parcel of being a human being—which leads us to ascribe personality and meaning and significance to our surroundings. Perhaps it is because a house is so rarely just that for the people who live there—a house is actually a home, something we become attached to from the moment we take possession of the keys and step inside those empty rooms, decorating the place in our minds, rearranging our furniture, imagining ourselves in this space, or that. Perhaps it is a spiritually driven extension of the whole 'bless this house' practice—religions denominations from Christianity to Buddhism all seem to have a version of this ritual, where a house is 'cleansed' and made safe for the inhabitants. The implication being that evil may be living within, waiting to pounce. Maybe it is more simplistic than that. Houses are easy to compare to people. Many have names, rather than numbers, and if we were to push that idea further, we could say that houses have faces—we see windows as eyes, the door as a mouth, the roof as a hat. Whatever the reason, we have been doing it for centuries: painting our houses with a layer of psychology that often leads us, logically, to the notion of something being 'haunted'. When a person is haunted, it is by grief, or trauma, or the memory of a past love, or a tragedy. In literature, houses are the same, and the way they process those traumas is very distinct. Some houses are angry and vengeful. Some are sad and confused. Almost all of them play their trauma out upon their unsuspecting inhabitants.

Think of some of the more commonly known haunted houses: Hill House, the DeFeo house in Amityville, Belasco House, Bly House, the House of Leaves, even the Overlook Hotel. Each of them is a character, and all characters have their distinct personality traits. In these books, it is less about the ghosts that live inside, and more about the building itself. A haunted house is never an empty stage upon which ghostly players merely perform. The house itself is the ghost, a breathing, sometimes timorous thing. The Backlund House in this book is no different. Full of history, it suffers, sitting as a gateway between our world and the next. It has many ghosts, and many stories to tell, but what speaks to you the loudest is the conflict, the atmosphere of tragedy that has infused into the bricks and mortar and become a part of its very architecture.

Houses are where we play out most of our key moments in life. Births, deaths, love affairs, arguments, reconciliations, betrayals, moments of glory, moments of banality. In houses we live the full spectrum of our emotions, and when you read this book, perhaps you can do the same. For there are many stories inside these walls, and as Phoebe Backlund herself says, 'only pain and fire reside'.

Backlund House is ready to meet you, dear reader. I would suggest that you do not keep it waiting for long.

—Gemma Amor, Bram Stoker Award nominated author of *Dear Laura*

1 – PHOEBE BACKLUND

The paper was old and faded. It had been folded so many times that the words were starting to disappear under the wrinkles, just like her face, and who she had been. She had read it countless times. By now she had memorized the letter's entirety, but it still carried all its weight. That was the most important part; the vulnerability had to be present, had to be real. She might be Madam Backlund to the thrill-seekers waiting outside, but in here, in this moment and late at night, all by herself, she was a lonely widow named Phoebe, and she lived in a haunted house.

The door downstairs flung open, and she heard the nervous chatter and the piling-in of feet. Slowly inhaling, she listened for them to settle down, read the notice on the pedestal in the foyer, and sign the registry. She folded the letter carefully and slid it back into the envelope. Straightening her blouse in the bureau mirror, she placed the paper under the empty ringboard of her jewelry box. Without a sound, she stepped into the hall and stopped at the top of the stairs outside her bedroom door.

Of the six people gathered below, four were men, and one of them noticed her first. Her silver hair was pulled tight in a bun, her ruffled white shirt and black skirt were impeccable. She looked more like a schoolmarm than a spooky medium. "Madam Backlund!" he said, almost frightened. "I understand the sign; but that scream—" he searched for the right word. "That was quite *vivid*."

"Indeed," she said, gesturing with her hands. It was cold tonight. Her fingers felt tight, and she was reminded of her age. Reminded of her age, she couldn't help but feel her loneliness rage against the walls of her heart. She could use that, but she wouldn't show it to her guests.

"It was the first thing I experienced almost ten years ago," she continued. "If everyone has signed in, I would like to invite you upstairs. You'll follow me to the door down the hallway. Naturally, you may find yourself looking into the rooms to the left, or the master bedroom here directly next to the stairs. You may see things, such as movement or the presence of individuals. Please ensure you continue to follow only me; for I promise, whom you can see now are the only living souls present."

They looked about at each other as they fell in line to climb the stairs. Of course, curiosity drove them to look around and take in their surroundings. Even if they didn't see anything, Phoebe planting the idea in their heads drove them to look for things that weren't there. Fear, even unfounded, made it more entertaining for them. Whether either of the two young women *truly* saw something is unclear, but one of them shouted and both clung to one man's arm.

"I saw a man," one of them said. "Right there, in front of the window in the bedroom."

"I see nothing." A man's voice argued.

The other girl yelped, complaining that something dripped on her.

Phoebe turned to face the group. "Ah, if I had been prepared, I could have caught the tear of the ghost. Alas, the incorporeal are not always cooperative."

They stared in disbelief. She cleared her throat, urging them on.

The séance room was lit only with candles, which gave the burgundy walls an earthy warmth. A round table with seven high-backed chairs sat in the middle of the room. Phoebe stood in front of one, ready to sit at the table. As the others entered the room, she spread her arms out across the table to invite them to take their seats.

"There is no arrangement," she said. "Please sit where you feel comfortable."

Taking their seats, they glanced around at each other, then returned their attention to Madam Backlund.

"Welcome to my home," she began. "I'm sure many of you have heard stories of how I came by this house and the events that plague it. I invite you to believe what you will. If any events transpire during our attempts to contact the other side, they may well shape the very nature of your beliefs, of this house and its history, and of your notion of the afterlife.

"Many people attend a séance expecting certain events to transpire," she continued. "Table rapping, ectoplasm, and automatic writing are theatrics, formulated to entertain. If you came for entertainment, I cannot guarantee that you will or *won't* be disappointed; but recall the scream you heard from outside. I assure you it was not I who screamed, though I understand doubt could dissuade you from accepting my word."

She noticed one of the men raising his head slowly, showing an increased interest as she explained away the stereotypical séance with what could potentially transpire here.

"In this house, I have learned there are rules. You've followed the first rule, to remain outside until a scream urged you to investigate within. If you read the entirety of the sign upon the pedestal, you will understand that I cannot guarantee you will experience the full force of a haunting. Many have come seeking answers about the great beyond, seeking to contact loved ones who have passed. However, this house gives no answers, it will only raise questions—of that I promise you.

"The fee you paid in advance to attend this evening is not a guarantee of service, and each of you agreed that should absolutely nothing transpire, you will not seek refund. The fee is to help me pay the regular expenses of keeping a home such as this in proper order. I am no charlatan, but I do ask that if you are told to do something by me, you follow my directions; it is for your own safety, but also for your benefit. Sometimes standing in the right place in this house can afford you a view into a greater mystery.

"Soon, you may begin to hear things outside of this room. I will try to allow the house to speak for itself. I must make clear: this is not the spirit of my late husband. Nor was the house built where any stood before. There are no signs this location was ever used as *anything* prior to my purchase of the land and construction of my home. For almost a decade I have endured its lamentations—"

The sound of a door shutting downstairs at the back of the house made the six guests jump.

"This house is somehow connected to another world; one where only pain and fire reside."

Someone ascended the stairs, dragging something heavy that banged with every step. Then they slid across the floor of the balcony over the foyer. Everyone listened intently as silence filled the place.

Madam Backlund sat and let her hands rest on the table before her. She listened along with them for a moment, then closed her eyes. "Though this is no gateway to Hell, it is certainly full of suffering."

Indistinct voices started to fill the foyer. Words were impossible to make out, but the muttering resembled urgent conversation. A shout made the guests jump in their seats yet again. A rushing of someone up the stairs and another cry followed by a hard knock against a faraway wall had them turning uncomfortably in their chairs, expecting the door to crash open. More rushing steps, doors at the opposite end of the house began to slam and bang. The tension had the group pleading with Madam Backlund to offer the spirits some respite or to make them cease, but she only held a finger to her lips. In the room next to them they could hear scuffling, perhaps two people wrestling, followed by a violent shattering of glass.

Madam Backlund stood and eyed them each, taking in their levels of fear and confusion. "Welcome, guests, to the house of in between."

2 - NOAH BENJAMIN

Looking at the monitor at the foot of the camera, Noah Benjamin tugged at the edges of his gray wool coat. He checked his watch, his glasses, and finger-combed the bangs off the right side of his forehead. He looked again, this time obviously reading the banner under the anchorwoman's image. Looking back up and catching Cynthia Morrison's bemused gaze, he chuckled.

"Sorry." He gulped.

The tight red curls of her hair bounced as she shook her head. "Don't worry," she replied, "I'm pretty excited myself."

They sat in reasonably comfortable armchairs under bright lights. Ten feet to their left was the news desk where a chipper woman rattled off the overnight news stories. Noah and Cynthia had met about an hour ago and discussed the topic they'd cover, but he had been in touch with her and the station for months. There was no reason he shouldn't know her name. He looked at the monitor again, but he was checking how much time until they were supposed to go on.

"I blank out when I'm nervous." He apologized. "Especially on names."

She smiled. "I wish I could take credit for your nerves, but I know you're ready to get back on the road."

Letting out a breath, he relaxed a little back into his seat. "I've been on the road since—" he looked at his watch. "I don't know," he laughed, "all night? We drove up from Chicago, looking at several places there, investigating Fort Dearborn, 1893 World's Fair sites, HH Holmes… Promoted the book of course, but I'm almost to my ultimate goal."

His enthusiasm was evident as he started to muse on that final destination. She was glad to see him loosen up, but she was excited herself. Cynthia and a small crew would accompany Noah's team to film a documentary. It was her big break, but even more than that, it was genuinely thrilling to join them.

The ready light above the camera flashed and caught their attention.

"Are you ready?" she asked.

He nodded, straightening his posture and checking his coat again.

The camera man counted off their time on his fingers, the light turned green, and Cynthia flashed a brilliant TV smile. "Visiting with us today is Noah Benjamin, author of *Violent Echo.* He's here to investigate the infamous haunted Backlund House of Grand Marais."

As she held up the book, he smiled quickly, then worried he was showing too much teeth. The interview circuit was the hardest part of this whole book tour. Every time he tried to explain exactly how the Temporal Resonance Activity Profiler worked, he'd watch the host's eyes glaze over and their brains check out as all they registered was *science goes here.*

Cynthia turned to him, "I know a lot of people are pretty excited about your visit and to learn what may have caused all the events that have been fabled surrounding the Backlund House. But what brings *you* here, specifically? Of all the famed haunted places in America, why document Grand Marais?"

Noah smiled more naturally now and let out a nervous laugh. "Well, first, Grand Marais is beautiful.Getting out of big cities and stuffy hotels is a nice break. But the Backlund House is one of those ghost stories you happen upon as a kid that sticks with you. I've looked into it as I've learned more about hauntings and tried to solve its mysteries. Yet, it always manages to defy logic. It is truly one of the most inexplicable hauntings I've learned about. I've never been able to visit before now, but my book has afforded me that opportunity."

Cynthia nodded politely. "And from what I understand from your book, you believe the Backlund House may still defy you, despite your device?"

"I'm excited to see what I see," he remarked. "Eric Svendson, Charles Brimer, and John Dale discovered a particle we've come to call a chronoton. This particle seems to be directly connected to entropy, the flow of energy in everything in space, and it can be *tracked*. We use the Temporal Resonance Activity Profiler, or TRAP, to basically chart the flow of time and see how it affects physical space. We can see the interaction between physical objects, even if they're no longer present. It's opened up awesome avenues for crime scene investigation, archeological digs, and geological surveys.

"How this connects to hauntings is that these chronotons can wear grooves in the fabric of space, and our observations can be influenced by these effects, much the same way an unseen indentation can affect the flow of water. But Backlund House has no correlating stories. It's said to have been haunted from the day it was built. Tracking the chronotons and their influence may defy our perceptions. We'll be attempting to put together a puzzle that has no picture. I hope science and legend can come together and reveal the truth."

Without missing a beat, she followed up with, "And if you can *observe* the culprit of the haunting, will that collapse be like collapsing a *wave function*? In other words, will it make it a reality or forever end the haunting?"

He gave a sheepish smile. He was pleased she had at least looked up some stuff before he'd come along.

"That is a possibility," he admitted. "By knowing and understanding the nature of a thing, we can render it inert. If we can learn its secrets, the house might give up the ghost… as it were."

The cameraman gave a hand signal that they needed to wrap it up.

"Thank you so much for your time," she said, reaching out and lightly touching his knee, "but we're not exactly done yet."

She turned to the camera. "We'll be joining Mr. Benjamin and his crew to document their case for a special that will air next year, but we'll keep you posted as events unfold." She flashed her TV smile again and the light on top of the camera turned red and the lights above them dimmed.

She turned back to him, looking much more human. "That wasn't bad!"

They chuckled with each other. "I don't mean any offense," he started, "but I didn't peg you for a physics-geek."

"I'm deeply offended!" she mocked. "Honestly, I love science. A lot of the math flies over my head, but it's astounding to me how deeply interconnected everything is. It's amazing that even what you're seeking is a function of nature. I'm really excited to be coming along, Mr. Benjamin."

"Oh, no." He groaned. "Please, call me Noah, save the formalities for my father."

She smirked. "Already looking to introduce me to the parents?"

He flushed and stammered, "I-I, I'm sorry…" he laughed.

She laughed with him and shook her head. "I'm playing with you."

He shook his head a little, too.

A tall, thin, black man stepped up to catch Cynthia's attention. "Harden's champing at the bit. He wants us on the road already."

Cynthia sighed and rolled her eyes.

The man rolled his eyes, too. "I know. Thom and I have a van half-loaded, so whenever you're ready to go."

She nodded and he left.

"That was Reggie Barker," she explained to Noah. "He's one of the studio's best cameramen; he'll be along with us. But it looks like everyone's really ready to get this show on the road. It's been the talk of the last couple of weeks. We're all pretty excited."

"Well," Noah said with a shrug. "Who am I to hold back anyone's excitement? I'm ready to get moving myself."

They smiled at each other until the moment stretched out into an awkward silence.

"I'll, uh," Noah started, "I guess I'll see you at the house—"

She threw her hands out in front of her to stop him. "Actually— if you wouldn't mind—" she said, "could I ride with you and your crew? Reggie and Thom will no doubt have the news van loaded down with every loose camera and microphone in the studio…"

He didn't want to leap with his response, but "Yes, of course!" came out sounding overly excited anyway.

They laughed with each other again. "I'll let my crew know," he said.

"Great, let me get a few things and I'll meet you outside."

They laughed and nodded, then clumsily stepped away from each other in their own directions.

3 – ANDREW & JOANNA NEWSTED

The leaves were changing, but it was still warm and breezy. The two-story Victorian stood in a clearing surrounded by birches, about twenty yards off the lakeshore. It was a dusty blue and white; the paint was peeling in a few spots, but otherwise it was a beautiful house, albeit one that had stood empty a little too long. It looked like it was hibernating, ready for the winter.

"What's wrong with it?" Joanna *said* more than *asked*.

Andrew laughed, standing right next to her. He wrapped his arm around her and squeezed her shoulder, hugging her to him. "Nothing; I thought it was gonna need some major work myself, but on the walk-through, it only needs some polish. Foundation is in great shape, and it even comes with an antique hutch!"

She knew she *should* be excited—this was a big, beautiful house. Andrew had landed a fishing job out on Superior, and they were in an excellent position to really start a life, a *family*. Something bugged her from the moment they pulled up, though; it was too good to be true.

Maybe it was being so far from home.

Both of them had grown up in Nebraska, met in their last year of high school, married a year after graduating, and here they were—a year and a half later—for all intents and purposes, worlds away. He'd lost his dad in Korea; her father had run off when she was only three. Both their mothers cried and cried when they moved away. For some reason, though, Andrew had it in his head he was going to fish on the

Great Lakes. It was surreal when he finally found an opportunity. With the little money they had, they managed to put a down payment on a house and move up to Grand Marais, Minnesota. She'd never even heard of it before he announced they were moving there.

She resisted at first, but the thought of adventure, owning their own home, and making a life for themselves on their own swayed her. Standing in her new front yard, though, the excitement was waning.

"I mean, look around, Jo!" He gestured to the entire scene.

"I know," she conceded. "It *is* beautiful. It seems—it feels like it's not *ours*; like we're intruders or something."

"What an awful thing to say!" he cried. "It's ours, baby! Look, we'll get all our stuff in, and this will be your pride and joy in no time."

They faced each other, and he wrapped his arms around her waist. "Until we, uh, get one in the oven, anyway."

She shook her head and patted his chest. "Let's at least get moved in first."

He gave her the key with a smile and then walked over to the truck and trailer. She looked at the house again. It didn't *feel* right, but maybe Andrew was right; after they got everything in and they spread out and relaxed, it would feel more like home.

Walking tentatively up to the house, she shook her head. She wasn't going to be silly anymore. This was *their* house, and she shouldn't be afraid of something that was their own. She climbed the couple of steps onto the veranda. Already she envisioned some furniture out here, taking in a cool autumn morning with Andrew and some coffee. She smiled. *Yes*, this could be their home.

She unlocked the door and stepped into the foyer, her footsteps setting off echoes in the emptiness. "Wow. This place is entirely too big for just two people," she said under her breath. The downstairs appeared to be a series of living rooms, one to the right with a fireplace and built-in bookshelves, one to the left with benches under the windows. Straight through the foyer was what must have been a dining room and yet another living room to the left of that. The windows were longer, though, and it had a wonderful view of the trees and even the lake. To the right was the kitchen, and she meandered through there to find a laundry room and a toilet that connected back to the room with the fireplace.

Upstairs she found a long hallway that ran the length of the house. To the left were four doors after the balcony, a set of double doors on the balcony, and to the right, one door beside the staircase. Further down was a door near the end of the hall on the wall she faced, and a closet at the end of the hall. She opened the door immediately to her right. She screamed and slammed the door shut.

Andrew stepped in from outside at the same time carrying a box full of cleaning items. "What is it?" he asked, feigning concern.

She *shushed* him with a finger to her mouth and rapidly descended the stairs on her toes, making as little noise as possible.

"I saw someone in the room right next to the stairs," she said, staring terrified into his eyes. "They were standing in a doorway on the other side of the room."

His mock concern turned real, and his usual jovial expression gave way to something stern. He pulled out a pocketknife—his only defense on hand—and crept up the stairs. Leaning against the wall as if to steady himself, he also tried to listen through the wall for the stranger. Once he reached the top, he looked back down at her, nodded, then threw open the door where he expected to engage in a fight with an intruder.

Instead, his anxious anticipation gave way to confusion. He straightened up and dropped his hands to his side, then looked back down and shrugged.

"Go *in there*!" she seethed through gritted teeth.

He nodded and obliged. The sharp echo of his footsteps broke the silence, announcing his presence to any would-be trespasser. A door opened and closed, perhaps a closet, another door already open swung on its hinges, some shuffling around.

Stepping back into the hall, he said, "Nothing; nobody. It's empty. The bathroom door opens outward, though right in front of a window here, maybe you saw a shadow."

She sighed and straightened up as he came walking back down the stairs. "I swear I saw a man standing in front of the door and window."

He grabbed her and hugged her tightly. "You didn't know what to expect when you opened the door. You saw a shadow; your brain played a trick on you. It's okay."

"It's not okay," she whined. "I'm terrified for no reason, and this is supposed to be our *home*."

"It is okay, Jo. Don't worry about it," he said. "Let's get to work, it'll take your mind off everything. Then you'll be too tired to care about shadows."

She nodded against his chest. They both moved to get to work, but not before she took a quick reassuring glance up the stairs to make sure they weren't being followed.

~

As the day wore on, their boxes and furniture seemed to get heavier with each pass. Joanna began to relax, trusting Andrew's assertion it was a play of shadows in a room she didn't know what to expect. Nothing else caught her attention. She saw no shadows or boogeymen out of the corner of her eye. There was another thing Andrew had been right about: she was too tired to care if she did.

The queen-size bed was the last thing to go in and the most difficult to maneuver up the stairs, back into the upstairs living room, then into the master bedroom. Andrew hadn't even put up the frame. They threw the mattress on the floor and plopped down themselves. They held each other's hands and stared at the ceiling. Light reflections and shadows danced there as the sun started to go down.

"We're gonna need more stuff," Joanna said.

"Huh?"

"For all the crap we hauled in here," she said, turning her head to look at him, "it's still empty."

"It's a lot of house for two people," he agreed. "But I couldn't pass up the deal. Besides… we fill it up with a couple little humans and you'll be complaining we have too much stuff and nowhere to put it!"

"Oh?" she said, raising her eyebrows. "A *couple*?"

"Okay, maybe *three*." He said and rolled over on top of her.

She laughed, and he kissed her. She returned his kiss, and they wrapped their arms around each other, squeezing together. He reached for her waist and slid his hand under her shirt and up her bare back. She could feel his excitement and pressed closer to him. She opened her eyes to meet his, but something caught her eye in the doorway.

"Shit!" she screamed and backed up, scooting out from underneath him and against the wall, her eyes locked on the doorway.

He whirled around on the spot and rose to stand on the mattress to see what had scared her. He crept to the doorway, then stopped short, started to crouch down, and looked back at her. He put his finger to his lips to make sure she stayed silent; she nodded vigorously, and he pointed to the hall and then his ear, indicating he could hear something. He stayed low, which looked odd, like he was ready to spring on someone, and Joanna feared he could see someone in the hall.

When he reached the edge of the doorway, he launched himself upward and into the hall, but then he came to a standstill and looked around. He finally focused down the stairs and quickly descended.

"Hello?" he called. "Who's out there?"

Joanna worked up the courage to go out into the hallway. Once there, she saw they'd left the front door hanging open after bringing up the mattress. Andrew was standing outside on the porch, then he quickly went out into the yard and dashed off to the left to check around the house. She started to shake her head and slinked down the stairs, coming to a sit on the bottom step.

Andrew came around from the right side of the house and strode back in, purposefully shutting the door behind him.

"What did you see?" he asked.

"I thought I saw someone peeking in," she said, "standing in that little space between the stairs and the door."

He put his hands on his hips, hung his head, and sighed. "I didn't see anyone. But I *felt* like someone was there. I swear I could hear someone talking, like it was right out the door like you said; but I couldn't make out what they were saying. I felt, I don't know, *compelled* to get low and jump them. But when I came out, all I saw was the front door hanging open. I must have heard the leaves outside. I bet we both remembered leaving the door open."

She nodded in agreement. "That must have been it. We're exhausted; it's been a very long day."

"You want to get something to eat and call it a day?" he asked.

"Absolutely."

To satisfy both their paranoia, Andrew checked all the windows, the doors, and all the rooms and closets. Finding nothing, he came back down, looking relieved. Joanna, however, only started feeling relaxed once they hit the interstate and were heading back into town.

After cheeseburgers, a couple of beers, and listening to old men bitch about the war, Joanna and Andrew tried to set up a living area in the room with the benches under the windows. Andrew found a decent position for the rabbit ears and they watched CBS for a while. *Mission: Impossible* was playing, and when the news came on leading with the war in Vietnam, Joanna stood up and turned off the TV.

She shook her head. "I've been frightened twice today. I don't need nightmares tonight."

He gave a weak smile and nodded his head in agreement. "I'm tired anyway. *And* I've got to get up at five o'clock in the morning and meet my crew."

It took Joanna a long while to fall asleep. Andrew was snoring before she even felt like dozing off. She was afraid to look toward the restroom and afraid to look out into the hallway. Her fear made her ashamed—ashamed she didn't feel safe, even with Andrew in bed next to her, ashamed she was *this* scared over shadows in a new house. She felt like a child. But sleep came, eventually, and so did the morning without further incident.

4 – CYNTHIA MORRISON

Cynthia and Noah's crews traveled to Grand Marais from Duluth, heading up MN-61 N along the shore of Lake Superior. Being late September, the leaves were changing and set the scenery in pastel flames. The sun had risen, turning the sky, clouds, and a little bit of fog into bright shades of pink. Noah had only been *out* of this van for about two hours since leaving Chicago. At least the scenery was livelier in the daylight.

Driving was Marcus Shepherd, Noah's media man, a documentarian who recorded and logged their investigations. Well-built, darkskinned, and short, he was a well-mannered young man sporting a military haircut. He had recently completed basic training to serve in the Reserve but was preparing to ship off to the Pacific Islands due to rising tensions. Having no immediate family, he stuck with Noah in the meantime, loving his job and experiences.

Serving as copilot for this leg of the trip was Shannon Camp, their technician and engineer. A spindly, waif of a woman with cropped, dusty blonde hair, about Marcus's height. She often acted quite motherly to both Marcus and Noah, though she was reserved in her personal life. Next to Noah, she knew the most about the technology they used in their investigations.

Cynthia and Noah sat in the middle row of the van, and she typed on a tablet, making ready to chronicle the research. "In your book, you discuss how particle physics reveals more and more about how the universe works, but that we can take those lessons and apply them to some unique situations. You're focusing on the paranormal. Why point the lens at such a contentious topic?"

Noah shifted in his seat. "There are very few ghost stories that can really be taken seriously. Consider the Amityville Horror. Everyone likes the picture of the boy at the top of the stairs when the house was supposedly empty. Everyone considers the movie franchise and Hollywood concepts of ghosts and poltergeists. But the scary thing about that house was the murder that took place.

"Ronald DeFeo, Jr. killed his family in the middle of the night with a rifle. He shot his parents, each twice, then his four siblings, once each, and no one got up or tried to get away. How come no one woke up after that first shot? That's at least *abnormal*, if not paranormal. It's those kinds of stories that made me want to give the paranormal a proper scientific eye. Not drafty hallways or faulty wiring, not that architecture and electromagnetics don't lend a lot to some fantastic ghost stories. We're looking for those places that still have question marks and maybe reveal some exclamation points."

Cynthia typed silently. Shannon looked over her shoulder and her eyes darted between Cynthia and Noah's growing, awkward silence. She cleared her throat and said, "I don't think that's quite the answer she was looking for, Noah. Why don't you tell her about the title of the book?"

Noah huffed and shook his head.

Cynthia looked up from her tablet. "I thought it was because your theory indicates these are echoes in time and some of them can be overwhelming. Like a poltergeist."

"Yes," Noah conceded, "but I could have called it a resonance or reverberation, too, and probably more accurately. An echo, per se, is a sound bouncing back at you. You make a sound, those waves hit a surface and come back. You hear your own sound again."

Scratching his temple, he groaned as he committed to sharing his tale. "Okay, when I was younger, there was a set of woods at the end of the neighborhood. Nothing fantastic, mind you. It was *woods* in that there were several trees packed together, there was a retention pond, and on the other side a cul-de-sac of another neighborhood. *Anyway,* some neighborhood kids and I would go and pitch tents on weekends in the summer and tell ghost stories. That's probably when my love of the paranormal began. But one night we all got spooked pretty good and ran home in the middle of the night. None of us ever went camping again. Kid stuff. We got scared and didn't want to tempt fate.

"A few years later, I start hearing these crazy stories about how ghosts have been seen in the woods in the middle of the night—like aggressive ghosts running around, breaking things in the trees; sticks, rocks, rattling cloth and metal. I wondered right then if we'd been chased out of the woods by ghosts. I went back a few nights as a teenager and a young adult. You'd hear something, maybe *think* you saw something, but as you concentrated, there was nothing there. It stayed in the back of my mind for years.

"Flash forward to the discovery of chronotons and the development of the time delineation device, our machine. I got my hands on the technology, getting a grant and a complimentary device on the premise of "speculative forensics". That's the *professional* way of saying *ghost hunter*. I booked it back home on my own to see what I could find out in the woods."

With her hands in her lap, no longer typing, Cynthia stared at Noah. He smiled and swallowed a few times, then took a deep breath and continued.

"And I found *us*. Us as kids. We were the ghosts. Somehow when we all flipped out and ran out of the woods, we made our own indentation on time. So, it really was an echo; I had committed an action that I was now seeing again."

Cynthia's forehead wrinkled as she scrunched her eyebrows. "You could see yourself as a ghost?"

"Well," Noah shrugged. "I figured out it was us. Maybe we'll be able to refine greater detail out of these events in the future, but right now you can tell the basic shape and size of something, see how it's moving. The more movement there is, the stronger the Echo. I could count how many of these child-sized objects there were running from a central point off into the trees; kids running from their tents. Yes, we had created our own 'haunting' and I was seeing myself as a ghost.

"The *violence* of *Violent Echo* comes from the fear we experienced. I can't tell you for sure what allows us to leave these marks on the fabric of space. I'm sure it has something to do with our own physical chemistry, adrenaline, other hormones, whatever; that's part of why we're headed to Backlund House. With no history of violence and no real-life stories correlating to the described events, how did they form?"

Marcus and Shannon in the front seat exchanged a knowing glance, but Cynthia missed it. Noah shook his head.

"And that was probably a lot of letdown for the build-up," he said with a chuckle.

She shook her head. "No, I'm sorry. It's kind of scary to think about. I mean, even if it's not a spirit walking the Earth, an echo in space—hearing, seeing, or feeling these events from some other time still seems… *supernatural.*"

"I don't think that's wrong. It is super," he paused for a beat, "natural."

She smiled and then looked down at her tablet. "With what you've found in mind, are a lot of hauntings, in fact, these echoes?"

"Oh no, I'd say 99% of hauntings can be reasonably explained, if not by natural phenomena within the space, then by functions of our own brains. The mind is terribly tricky, if not downright devious. But there are certain criteria I look for when investigating a haunting, if not professionally, then for my own interest. They can be tricky, too, however. If you can keep to these criteria without finding a source, then you're getting closer to an Echo.

"They all affect our primary senses. One is a rotting smell, or something like sewage, which is one of the easiest to explain away. You can find a dead animal in the walls, or a busted water pipe causing wood rot, but when those things have been checked and explained away and the smell persists, you might have an Echo on your hands. Next are sounds. Sounds are easy to explain away. You can get strange corners in a house causing regular echoes. Something sounds like it's behind you when there's nothing there, but the sound is really from a pipe with a loose fitting, lightly banging inside a wall; the sound is echoing through the attic and back down into a hallway intake vent.

Spooky, but once you know what these things are, you might feel foolish. We've torn up many a floorboard! But sometimes there is nothing to find. These can be the sounds of voices, footsteps, furniture moving or—my favorite—what sounds like a bowling ball going down a lane or billiard balls across a table. That rolling sound, without any other explanation, is one of my favorites."

"In those events where you can't explain it away, your device can then show you what's caused it?" She asked.

"Sometimes. Sometimes it's a result of the Echo and not the spawning event. Like lightning and thunder, for example. The light from the electrical discharge isn't making the sound, it's the sound of displaced super-heated air. For chronotons that have left a deep wrinkle in space, it throws everything off around it, and if you happen to be in the right spot, you can experience any number of things, even being able to perceive the events that caused the Echo as though they were happening in the here and now."

"And you believe the Backlund House is a hub of this sort of activity?"

"Absolutely." Noah beamed. "It's said to have been haunted from the day it was built, over a hundred years ago. Many residents of the house have complained of ghosts, poltergeists, and even physical manifestations. My favorite instance being the staircase completely on fire without burning anything, yet somehow still being hot and smelling smoky."

"That…" she said with a hesitant pause, "that sounds dangerous. I mean, I've heard the stories, too, but if these echoes can in fact affect you…"

"That's one of the other signs of a true haunting: the sense of touch. Physical interaction, being scratched, hit, touched, the case of the fire feeling hot without burning anything it's touching; those are hard to replicate, and often fall into the realm of psychosomatic and become almost impossible to disprove, especially to a scared inhabitant or victim. But by connecting related stories—by people who've never met or don't know about a particular event or its possibilities—you can piece together clues that say that this space, a house, building, *a set of woods*, meet the criteria for a haunting. I suppose a particularly strong Echo could have its physical impact on you, but through all of history, no one has ever been killed or majorly hurt as the result of a paranormal event, so I would rest easy."

She smiled, but it was obvious she was still wary. She looked out her side of the van and stared as brown and red leaves zoomed past.

5 - PHOEBE BACKLUND

On such occasions that the events played out in their entirety, Phoebe found varying responses from her guests. Some would laugh, satisfied with the mysterious entertainment. Others would question what they had heard and seen. A few were truly shaken, disturbed by sounds and visions of another world. Rarely was someone upset with either the lack of a performance or getting more than what they bargained for. She could see it on many of their faces, but the rules were always made quite clear before any money exchanged hands.

There had been something strange about a solitary man who said little during the transaction, or the night of the séance. She noticed the intent with which he listened to her stories, how he paid attention to subtle details others overlooked. He paid attention to the mechanics of the events. He was spying.

Seeing him standing before the house the following morning did not surprise her in the least. Rather, she expected him. She wrapped a shawl around her shoulders, despite the unusual warmth of this late September morning, and stepped through the front door. "Mr. *Eric Cardo*, was it?"

The man was fit, though short, not even five and a half feet tall, but he commanded attention. His face was as sure as it had been the night before, slightly triangular with how he wore his black, burly hair. His eyes were blue and piercing; even now, he studied every detail, looking for answers without questions.

"Madam Backlund." He said and bowed his head.

"You don't look like a *Cardo*, though," Phoebe said, taking slow, deliberate steps down the stairs of the veranda. "No, I would think you look more like a… *Weiss*. Or shall I call you Mr. Houdini?"

"Harry's fine, Madam Backlund," he said. "I was quite impressed with your show last evening. I had the chief of police with me and a reporter from Duluth. I *was* ready to expose you, but this was magnificently bizarre. I hope that I might take a look again—with your permission, of course."

She pursed her lips and nodded. "In the beginning, there were those who thought what I did was indeed a cruel joke, taking advantage of terrible circumstances. But I am no medium and have never claimed to be. The title of Madam was put on me and it sells tickets. I'm sure you understand, Mr. *Houdini*."

He laughed, a kind and genuine laugh. "A valid point. And true to your word, never did you claim to be controlling what we saw and heard, and I saw no conjurer of tricks. Except for maybe this house. I was genuinely disturbed."

They stood in front of each other now. She was only about an inch shorter than him, and in her day, she may have even been an inch taller. He was in his mid-forties, and she was firmly in her sixties. It reminded her of her lack of children.

He was handsome and mature, and seeking things he didn't understand. It was that ignorance that excited him; she could see it painted on his face. A true mystery was far more exciting than exposing a fraud.

"You are welcome in my home, Harry," she said with a nod. "In fact, I *invite* you to try and discover its secrets. I would welcome an explanation. But I cannot promise that you will experience anything. Circumstances must be met. Criteria that I avoid when I am home alone."

Before he followed her inside, he took in the house's exterior. It was light gray with bright white trim, pillars, and railing that wrapped around the veranda. The decking was warm, natural wood and the awnings over the upstairs windows were painted a dark blue. The trees around the house were still green thanks to the warmth of summer extending into fall. The house sat close enough to Lake Superior that it could be seen shimmering through the trees as the sun had yet to top them.

For ten years the house stood, well out of the town of Grand Marais, but everyone knew of it. Old Lady Backlund cried to anybody in town who would listen that some evil force occupied her home. It terrorized her nieces and nephews the few times they stayed. Her dream home had become a nightmare house. There were those that accused her of inviting the Devil in by building something so lavish for herself alone, while in the same vein, others believed that her husband, dead in a logging accident, was haunting her; exacting revenge for her selfish use of his insurance money.

Phoebe Backlund was not a sinister and selfish woman, though. Harry had looked into it. The local paper had reported on the home's construction, built with savings and the earnings of a life insurance policy her husband had purchased himself, understanding the risks of his profession. The house was built with family in mind. They never had children of their own but were close to their siblings' children. They enjoyed the company of their surviving, aging parents. The house was built with the intention of being a warm and happy place filled with generations of family. However, the house seemed to be occupied before Phoebe ever set foot inside.

"The story goes," she said as they stepped into the foyer, "that the contractors working on the interiors could hear footsteps running up and down the stairs when no one was walking on them. That they could hear voices when no one was talking. That, of course, is bullshit."

Harry looked surprised at her rancor.

"Come now, Harry, I was married to a logger. I'm sure you've heard and said much worse in show business."

He laughed again. He may not believe she had a house acting as a portal between worlds, but he certainly could grow to like this woman.

"Nothing happened until the house was complete." She continued. "I visited the construction regularly. It was the day the foreman gave me the key and drove off, leaving me standing outside my new home. I stood there the right amount of time. There came a loud pop, like one single clap of the hands, followed by what sounded like a woman's scream. I knew no one was in the house; I had completed the tour with the foreman before seeing him off. But terror got the best of me and I rushed in. There was nothing. After exhausting myself looking for a stranger in my house, I searched the outside, I called out into the trees; still nothing.

"And that's how it started. That first night was nothing but dread. I feared the rumors before they even started. Was this my husband, or the Devil himself? Shadows lurked and leapt; there were the voices— never saying anything directly, but speaking adamantly. The doors moving on their own was difficult to handle, but the breathing—*oh* the breathing. It is the labored breathing of someone who has done something terrible, and it persists in nearly every room. Each room has its share of sights and sounds under the right conditions. The only safe places are what I had converted into my séance room and the two eastern rooms downstairs. Even the closet outside the séance room has its own form of malice it puts on display."

Harry was still looking around, taking in every detail; the angles of the archways; the banister on the stairs; the pedestal that had been in the middle of the foyer now moved to beside the front door, re-signed to holding a set of keys like any table found inside of a door.

He looked at her directly. "Even your bedroom offers torment?"

"This whole house does." She sighed.

Fatigue belied her stoic façade. She continued, humbly, "I'm afraid to be in my own home. This house was *built* for me, but it was not *meant* for me. Whatever happened here, this house belongs to that event."

Harry showed sympathy, and it looked sincere, but he was decidedly more fascinated with what was happening in this house.

6 – JOANNA NEWSTED

Andrew would be gone all day, out on the boat from sunup to sundown. They expected this. With winter coming soon, it would make for extremely grueling work, and he'd probably be beat most of the time. He had fished the rivers in Nebraska with a degree of skill, though, and being on the water seemed to make up for the hours. At least to him.

Joanna needed—felt *compelled*—to supplement their income. As nice as the deal on the house had been, they still had to make the payments and keep the lights on. Finding a job was not so much what she *needed* to do, but after that first day, something she *wanted* to do. She headed into Grand Marais and went into nearly every business, hiring sign or not. She talked to a lot of people and shook a lot of hands and told her situation countless times. Most were polite, especially when they said no.

A handwritten sign seeking waitresses hung in the window of a diner. She thought for sure she could get on there. The wage might not be good, but if she could be friendly enough, maybe the tips would make up for it. The manager, a stereotypical fat man in a greasy apron, listened to her, determined she wasn't local, thanked her and sent her on her way. She walked out, distraught, feeling her leads dwindling, when a middle-aged black woman walked followed her outside.

"Excuse me, Miss," the woman said.

Joanna turned and smiled. "Yes?"

"I heard you in there. You're looking for a job?"

"I am," Joanna said, not trying to be short but fearing she suddenly sounded rude.

"My name's Loretta," the woman said, not seeming to take notice. "I own my own business. It's not much, but the work is steady and I can promise a paycheck."

"Wow," Joanna laughed. "I-I'm, uh, my name is Joanna Newsted, and, well—what is it?"

Loretta smiled. "Cleanin' houses. Sounds bad, sometimes it is, but the houses are usually empty when I go in. It's quiet, and not much different from what you might do in your own home."

"Why would you offer me a job?" Joanna asked.

"I saw how he shrugged you off just because you don't sound like you're from around here. I know that feeling," she said circling a finger around her face. "But I do a damn good job and people pay me well to do what they're too lazy to. With an extra hand, I could take on more work in a day, make more money, we both come out on top. 'Sides, looks like you need more than a job. Maybe you need a friend in a town full of uptight fat bastards like him."

Joanna smiled and laughed. "*Okay*… When can I start?"

"I was on lunch," she said. "You can follow me to my next job if you want. I work in cash, you don't like it, I'll cut you what's fair on the spot. You want to stay on, I'll pay you tonight when we're done."

Joanna shook her head, surprised by her luck and impressed with her new employer's tenacity. She hopped in her truck and followed Loretta's Dodge sedan to the next house. Heading north, they came close to a beautiful park and some big houses, until Loretta pulled into the driveway of a house twice the size of Joanna's. The bushes were all well-shaped and the lawn meticulously cared for, even as autumn was setting in.

"This is gorgeous!" Joanna exclaimed.

"Oh, thank you!" Loretta crooned. "I needed to stop by and pick up some extra supplies for you."

Joanna's jaw dropped. "This is *yours*?"

Loretta let out a belly laugh. "Hell no! But to see your face right now!"

She kept laughing and grabbed a laundry basket full of supplies from her backseat, then waved for Joanna to follow her. They stepped up to the front door and Loretta took out some keys, still snickering at her own humor. "I wouldn't live here even if I *could* afford it. Too much house for me, I'd be fine with a shack if it was warm."

They walked in and the interior was as exquisite as the outside. A large circular Oriental rug adorned the floor between two arched staircases. A far cry from her own home, but she could see what Loretta meant; the place was massive.

"I don't *live* in a shack, though," Loretta said as if trying to save face. "I've got a nice two bedroom in the middle of town."

"I didn't think you were serious," Joanna reassured.

"I know," Loretta said. "I'm thankful for what I've got and I'm not about to jinx myself saying I'd be happy with a shack."

"I don't know," Joanna said. "I think I might be happy with a shack."

"Oh? You move into a dump trying to get yourself situated in a new town?"

"No, but sort of like what you were saying, too much house."

Loretta handed Joanna two rags and some wood cleaner. "You can do the wood tables. They're easy; smear 'em down with one rag and polish 'em off with the other."

Joanna nodded, looking around and seeing several little display and end tables in sight.

"Where'd you move into?" Loretta asked walking off. "I know most the houses 'round here."

Joanna approached a table, poured a little solution on its surface and started wiping in circles. "Um, it's an older two-story down highway 61; entirely too many rooms. We don't even have enough furniture to place one piece in each room!"

"How'd you afford something like that? You all get an inheritance?" Loretta called from some unseen room.

"No. Andrew—my husband—came up for a week earlier in the summer. He looked for a job and a house. He found both. We got the house for next to nothing, didn't even have to make a down payment.

He said with his wages out fishing he'd probably be able to afford it all on his own."

"What?" Loretta cried. "There's no way. What's wrong with the house?"

"That's exactly what I asked when I saw it!" Joanna laughed. "It's a pretty house, great physical condition. Has a room with no windows on the inside, but there's windows on the outside of the house, so that's a little weird. It's in tiptop shape, otherwise." She thought about mentioning what she had seen, but she still wasn't *sure* of what she had seen. Anxiety in a new house far from home still cast doubt.

Loretta's foot falls came quickly from a hallway stretching behind the stairs. "Off 61 you said? Few miles out of town?"

Joanna scrunched up her eyebrows. "Yes."

"Is there a big-ass hutch in one of the rooms, couldn't possibly be removed without taking it apart?"

Joanna raised the rag she was holding to her chest. The look in Loretta's eyes was a mixture of fear and disbelief. "*Yes*. But, how did you—"

"How did I know?" Loretta asked. She shook her head and looked at the floor. "I think everybody here knows about the Backlund House."

The way Loretta said the name—that the house even *had* a name—made Joanna feel both more comfortable with what she had seen, but also terrified of what it might mean.

~

"Please don't tell me something terrible happened here," Andrew said, rubbing his temples.

He was still happy to see her and excited to share his experiences from his day despite being beat. He asked about her day, too, and the conversation was light until she brought up what she'd learned. They sat at a small table in the kitchen, since they didn't have a dining room table yet.

"No," Joanna said, with an apologetic smirk on her face. "Loretta said no one has ever been hurt here. But somehow the house is haunted, and from what she said, it always has been!"

Andrew leaned back in his chair and sighed. "You say that like you're *excited.*"

"What if what I saw yesterday was a ghost? We're living in a historical house, Andrew, one with stories."

"I still think it was nerves, Jo," he said. "I don't know that we've got ghosts. But I'm glad you've got entertainment in this Loretta during the day. And you said the pay is pretty decent?"

"Don't try and change the subject, Andrew!" Joanna chided. "She said the house was built in 1920 by a widow after an insurance payout. Apparently, this used to be a trading post between the French and Indians, there's a lot of history going on. She built the place up because it was the kind of house she and her husband had always wanted, with land by themselves, but still close to town. She wanted her family to come and stay. Everyone said it was her husband haunting her for being selfish with the money and building a house clearly too big for one old woman.

"But then she started trying to contact whatever spirits were possessing her house by holding séances. And she held them in the room with no windows, boarding it up to shut it off from the rest of the world. Word got out she was regularly talking with spirits…"

"Ugh, Jo," Andrew moaned. "It sounds like tales of a crazy old woman in a crazy old time that we would have made fun of back in school."

She playfully smacked his hand on the table. "Come on now, have some sense of humor!"

"I don't think it was ghosts," Andrew said with a shrug, followed by a yawn. "And I don't think I want to talk about them anymore. I'm hitting the sack."

She nodded. "I'll come with you; I'll get the dishes in the morning. Loretta works three to four days a week, and she said there's nothing for tomorrow."

They headed upstairs, but Andrew stopped before reaching the top. He turned around slowly and put his finger to his lips. Joanna started to feel anxious all over again. Then he made a rictal grin, stuck his arms out, moaned like a restless movie spirit, and acted like he was going to attack her.

She cursed him and swatted at the air, trying to smack him. She chased him into the bedroom and tackled him on the bed. They wrestled and tickled at each other for a moment before starting to undress each other. They made love and then held each other until they fell asleep.

Joanna felt okay. Maybe it was meeting a new friend, maybe she'd gotten used to the house after a night in it, but the previous day's events didn't even weigh on her mind.

7

Moving sucked. They weren't moving far; her friends were still about half an hour away. And there was the satisfaction of seeing her parents finally getting their own home. It would be her home, too, for a little while anyway. Only that little while, though. Then she shipped out, ultimately headed for Afghanistan. It would have been nice to spend that little time at *home*.

Pulling up the long drive, they stopped at a house that could be described as *once* pretty. It was Victorian in appearance, but there was a packaged feel to it; it was too symmetrical. The paint was faded and peeling. The house looked tired. By contrast, the trees surrounding the property were green and healthy. Behind the house, the lake sparkled through the tree trunks.

"It looks like a ghost house," she said as she stepped out of the car. "You know there's a serial killer who hasn't been caught around here, right?"

Her mother got out of the car as well and looked around, not responding.

The moving van pulled up after them and squeaked as it stopped. A few birds chirped their dissatisfaction in the trees. Her father jumped out of the van and strode up beside them, beaming with pride.

"What do you think?" he asked her.

She chewed on her lip.

Her mother finally piped up. "She was saying it looks haunted."

Her dad laughed. "Well, funny you should say so."

Her mother rolled her eyes and went about opening the trunk to grab their bags and take them inside.

"The locals call the place the Backlund House," he started. "Legend says the lady who built the house held séances to contact her dead husband, but she opened a gateway, letting demons through."

"You bought us a *demon* house?" She sneered. "Thanks, Dad."

"C'mon, sweetheart, it's just for fun! The house has stood empty for a few years. It was a bed-and-breakfast once, but the owner passed away."

"Not *here* I hope."

He shrugged. "We got a major deal on it. It's more than we could dare dream of, and even after taxes and insurance, it'll be cheaper than what we were looking at *within* our price range."

He paused a moment, then put his arm around her. "I'm sorry we couldn't do it before you… well, before you *grew up*."

She wrapped her arm around his waist and hugged him from the side. "It's okay. I'm sure it'll feel like home soon enough."

"Aw, now that's a crack," he said.

She sighed and disengaged. "I'm sorry, Dad. I know now's the time to move, you got the house… It's like, I've been away for drill, I'm about to ship out; it's strange place after strange place."

"I know."

They walked around to back of the van, where he opened it up to reveal a bed railing. It came clattering to the ground. A few things had fallen over, their moorings having come loose.

"That's how I feel," she said, pointing at the rails on the ground. She bent over to pick them up. "I feel like I *should* be secure. I've been *assured* I'm secure, then you get to moving around and you're flying all over the place, not sure where you're going to land."

"You get all that profundity from your mother." He pulled the extra bedrail out of the car.

"That's a big word for you, Dad," she teased. "How long have you waited to use that one?"

"A few weeks. It was on the calendar, and I thought it fit you guys perfectly."

They walked towards the house together as her mother stepped out, sniffing at the air like a cartoon dog. "I thought I smelled smoke," she said, "but I didn't see anything, and as I walked around, I couldn't smell it anymore. Maybe it was dust?"

They all stepped in. Her father shook his head. "I don't smell anything. Well, old wood maybe."

With no curtains hung, sunlight poured into the house. Everything was bright, but somehow cold and empty. Dust motes lazily hovered through the rays.

"Any demons or ghosts?" she yelled out.

There was a dull reverberation through the walls, but no answer.

"Why did you even tell her that?" Her mother asked.

Her father whistled, looking randomly about.

"Whose bed am I holding, anyway?" she asked, raising the rails hanging in her arms.

"Uh, *yours*, actually." Her father thought back on how he packed the truck. "There are two small rooms and one good-sized one to the left upstairs. The big one has an antique hutch that's apparently been in the house since it was built. It's pretty, and *big*, I guess no one's had the heart to take it apart. Um… to the right is mom and I's bedroom. There's another room up there but the windows are blocked, so I was going to use it as a darkroom."

"Awesome," she said, but he got the feeling she was only humoring him as she inched closer to the stairs.

"Go," he chided, like he was the one who was annoyed. "Sooner we get done, the better." He handed her the other side of the railing and retreated to the truck.

Dragging the cumbersome metal beams up the stairs revealed how much moving *really* sucked. Also, as cool as a two-story house might be, getting everything up was going to be a nightmare. She maneuvered the rails well enough, though, only bumping a wall once, thankfully leaving no marks.

She claimed the room with the hutch by placing the rails in the middle of the floor. She turned around to look at the hulking piece of furniture. The thing looked to be eight feet tall and five feet wide, maybe two feet deep. Hand-carved nature scenes, plants and animals and whatnot, adorned the panels. The back and sides appeared to be one solid piece of wood, the only way to get it out would be to cut it in half or tear out a wall. It was trapped.

She reached out and touched it. Somehow, the wood felt warm and comforting.

"I think me and you got a lot in common, friend. We want to be outside, but we're stuck in here." She patted the edge of the hutch again and went downstairs to continue helping.

8 - NOAH BENJAMIN

They drove through town. It was a beautiful sight in its own right. On the shores of Lake Superior, it was the perfect tourist trap with its fishing village feel and nature trails off to the north in Judge C. R. Magney State Park. Grand Marais was the perfect setting for a haunted house. The area was centuries old—once a major station of the fur trade—and it would host logging and fishing for years to come. The Backlund House owed its history to the area.

The vans pulled off Highway 61 onto an unmarked, unevenly paved road. They were surrounded by trees and at one point they were so densely packed together that the sunlight was blocked out altogether. At the end of the broken private drive was the two-story Victorian home, its faded blue and white paint cracking. No one had lived there for nearly ten years now, but the bank officer lucky enough to be notified he needed to let yet another curious crew investigate the house was sitting on the veranda.

Despite its infamy, there was no plaque, no historical marker, nothing of note about the house whatsoever. Attempts to have it demolished were always foiled and, despite many long stretches of emptiness, it never crumbled or succumbed to natural disaster. It was as if the house was waiting for something.

Noah hopped out first, marveling at the house. Marcus and Shannon came around and stood next to him. Cynthia made notes and took pictures with her tablet before getting out of the vehicle.

Marcus patted Noah on the back. "We're here. Let's make history."

The bank officer stepped down off the porch and greeted them as the TV crew readied their equipment.

"I'm Dennis Shelby," he said, reaching out to shake Noah's hand. "We're all pretty excited to have you visit one of our landmarks."

Noah smiled back. "I'm Noah Benjamin, this is Marcus Shepherd and Shannon Camp; they're my technicians. I understand power has been turned on?"

Dennis shook each of their hands. "Yes, came on yesterday. I went in and checked everything out. Fast as I could, mind you; this place doesn't much like visitors."

Noah laughed. "I've heard. But that's what we're here for, to find out what's really going on."

Cynthia walked up behind them. "Will you be able to show us around?"

"No ma'am, Ms. Morrison." He said, recognizing her from television. "I already heard footsteps while I was checking the lights. I've had my fill. I'm sure you'll all be able to find your way around well enough. It's a pretty basic floor plan."

Reggie came over. "Harden wants a tease for the evening news."

She touched Noah's shoulder. "I'll be right back."

Noah nodded, then looked back to Dennis. "Have you been in there before?"

"Yeah," Dennis said. "I've come to check on the place a couple of times. Seems like you hear things without anything being there. There are a few pieces of heavy furniture left by the last occupants who couldn't get out fast enough. There's a table in the dining room, straight back from the front doors. An antique hutch in one of the upstairs bedrooms—it *has* been here since the house was built. The primary bedroom, the first right from the top of the stairs, is completely furnished. That seems to be the scariest place for anyone who's lived here or visited. Some kids would have you believe it's Mrs. Backlund's old furniture, but it's from the last couple who lived here."

"No efforts to contact them? The previous owners…" Shannon asked.

"They still own the place, but disappeared after moving," Dennis said. "They pay taxes on the property and any maintenance fines the City might levy. The bank acts as a steward. We protect and respect their anonymity. That arrangement settled before I came on, but from what I understand, the stories they had didn't even scratch the surface of the worst legends. They were ready to be gone and done with it, but took it upon themselves to prevent anyone else suffering. They simply have nothing to do with it."

"Well, thank you very much for letting us in, Mr. Shelby," Noah said. "We'll take good care of the place. Maybe with some better understanding, we can help you get some new owners into it."

"That would be wonderful." Dennis smiled. "But even if you've got a scientific explanation for what's happening in there, Mr. Benjamin, it doesn't change that this house is scary as hell. I wish you all the best of luck, though. I'll be back in the morning."

Dennis shook their hands again and walked to his car, leaving the keys in Noah's hand. The three of them stared at the house.

Shannon clapped and rubbed her hands together. "Let's do this!"

The three of them began to unload their equipment from the back of the van, mostly cables and sensor equipment; they wanted to make sure they got as much ground covered as they could. Cynthia and her crew offered to help, and the entire team worked together to get what seemed like hundreds of feet of cable into the house and strung.

Connectors for the machine that tracked chronotons were spaced every five feet on the cables. After running cables through the house for about two hours, up and down stairs and opening every door, they had all the sensory equipment hooked up and ready to start reading. No one had anything weird to share yet and Cynthia's technicians, Thom Bridgewater and Reggie Barker, seemed disappointed.

"Weren't you saying the bank guy already heard footsteps?" Reggie asked Cynthia.

She nodded, but Noah answered. "With all of our commotion, we could have missed something pretty easily. A lot of a haunting is circumstantial. Are you standing in the right spot? Are you paying attention to the right thing? I honestly don't expect us to see much ourselves. We'll be talking with each other like this, focusing on equipment—"

As if on cue, a heavy thud erupted from upstairs, like a piece of furniture falling hard against the floor.

Noah smiled as everyone else looked around. "Then again, maybe the Backlund House won't disappoint."

Cynthia, Thom, and Reggie all looked far off as they listened to someone in their earpieces. Charles Branson—Chuck—monitored from the van outside. He said he could hear more than the thud, as if someone had moved something and was now walking around in one of the rooms upstairs.

Thom ran up the stairs and went immediately right and through the first door: the primary bedroom. "There's nothing!" he called out.

Chuck insisted he could still hear the footsteps, even while hearing Thom come into the room.

"This is gonna be *awesome*," Reggie said. "Hey, Thom! Let's get the little motion-cameras and set up some traps!"

Thom came back down the stairs, shaking his head. "I don't know what Chuck's hearing, I; it's quiet as a tomb up there."

Cynthia groaned. "Did you have to say '*tomb*'?"

Noah smiled at her. "Don't worry, we'll catch it, expose it for what it *really* is, and set the mystery of the Backlund House to rest."

"We're ready, Noah…" Shannon said.

A big metal box sat on the floor, covered in air vents. An exposed panel on one side connected all the cables running through the house to the box. A complex keyboard with extra Function keys and two monitors were built into the top.

"I'll need to register everyone's wireless devices—cameras, phones, headsets—so we can get a clear signal once we've settled in for the night." Noah said.

He then pressed the power key on the keyboard. The monitors flickered to life; a power indicator light flashed under one of the air vents. The only sound it made was the small whir of a fan.

Cynthia took a step closer and watched the boot sequence stream along the monitors. "That's it? That's the Temporal Resonance Activity Profiler?"

Noah looked at her. "What did you expect?"

"I don't know." She shrugged. "Have you ever seen *Ghostbusters*? When they first turn on their proton packs?"

Shannon laughed. "I love that movie."

"Fortunately for us," Noah answered, "monitoring the movement of chronotons does not require a miniature nuclear reactor strapped to our backs. However, '*it's a trap!*'" He chuckled.

Marcus and Shannon gave him a blank stare and Cynthia shook her head and gave him a courteous, though quiet, laugh.

He sighed, then cleared his throat. "Time is constantly moving and interacts with any and every particle it interacts with. The sensor panels cast out a specialized radio wave, and through this computer we can see where time is moving to and from between the panels, which is why we have them all over the place and in every room. We'll get a three-dimensional map displayed on the screen and be able to see everything that interacts with the radio waves. Once you pick out time's displacement, you can track and chart every chronoton that has passed through here, presumably all the way back to when the house was built. Any further back, we would only see trees."

Reggie and Thom came back in with a couple of duffle bags full of more equipment. They started unpacking and let Noah check out the equipment to enter information regarding all their devices into the TRAP.

"Isn't that a bit of overkill, guys?" Cynthia asked.

They shook their heads.

Noah chimed in, "Honestly, the more monitoring equipment we have, the better. It'll help us to zero in on what's happening here, right now. Perhaps help us focus on anything *para*normal."

"Don't encourage them," Cynthia joked, "they'll get every last camera in four counties."

"You better believe it," Thom exclaimed.

Noah continued, "The séance room is rumored to be—if I may be so bold to use the term—an *echo chamber*. Everything can be heard in that room. A few extra mics won't hurt."

Cynthia shook her head, but Thom gave an enthusiastic, affirmative nod.

Again, a heavy thud sounded from upstairs.

Noah knelt in front of the TRAP and tried to read the situation but looked confused. He motioned for Marcus and Shannon to look.

"Is that… *static*?" Shannon asked.

Cynthia looked at the monitors but couldn't make heads or tails of what she saw. It was a lot of lines and dots that vaguely resembled the house's structure. The image was fuzzy, though, and out-of-focus.

"Is there a problem?"

Noah shook his head. "Not at all. All the readings are fine. I've never seen anything like *this*."

"But that's what you were looking for, right?" Cynthia asked. "The inexplicable?"

"Yes," Noah answered, "but I haven't yet simulated the movement of time. This display is what's happening right now. The chronotons should be moving only as we see time moving, not this chaotic motion. This looks like an earthquake's happening right now."

Noah stood up slowly and took a step back. He stared at the monitor for a moment, then at each person around the house, startled.

"What is it?" Cynthia asked.

He shook his head, sighed, then shook his head again. "Nothing. Well… I don't know. It's like the house isn't sitting still. Like it's dislodged in time."

Cynthia was under the impression he had wanted to find something like this, but the look of concern on Noah's face troubled her. Was he really prepared for something he couldn't explain? She thought she heard footsteps on the landing at the top of the stairs and turned to look, but there was nothing. When she looked back, he was still staring at the machine, but his gaze was as empty as the balcony.

9 – HARRY HOUDINI

In Harry's experience, mediums and spiritualists were frauds. Magicians, like himself. They preyed on the hope and ignorance of their innocent patrons. They pulled stunts, played tricks, and behaved as pranksters. Phoebe Backlund seemed different, though. She never claimed that the oddities in her home were any particular spirit, and she never took credit for calling out the specters.

At first Harry thought he had encountered yet another spiritualist peddling theater effects; sounds from unseen areas and moving objects out of reach. Starting the séance in the low lit, windowless room put Harry immediately on guard, but as he partook, he realized this was a woman who knew what was happening, if not how or why. She was merely guiding guests in her home through unseen doors she had learned to navigate.

As she explained it, the house had been haunted from day one, but the haunting wasn't the storybook type. After ten years in the house, she had learned where the events took place, how severe they were, and what set them off. She could replicate individual events through physical actions and guided Harry to the landing, outside of the master bedroom.

"I do not sleep in here," she said. "It is in here where it starts—the scream you heard from outside. Several events center around this room. If you will, stand against this short bit of wall between the door and the stairs."

She held his shoulders and looked back and forth for herself. "Yes, here. Now, look into the room, then look down the stairs as though you are speaking to someone. Then, look back into the bedroom."

He followed her instructions. As he looked back into the room, he saw the figure of a man standing between the door of the restroom and the window on the far wall. If he had been startled, he controlled himself; he didn't show even the slightest twitch of his muscles. He examined the figure and considered his actions. The act of looking away made him wonder if it was a sheet of clean glass reflecting a silhouette on the opposite wall, but it moved subtly, naturally, as if it breathed. Then the soft chatter of speech—a conversation held with someone out of view—whispered through the room. Phoebe pulled back and let him observe.

He felt compelled to look back down the stairs and noticed a glow of fire. It was much too warm to have a fire burning. A quick recollection of his surroundings as he'd stepped into the house reminded him there had been no flame in the fireplace. There was the faintest odor of smoke and his heart leapt with excitement. He looked back into the room and noticed the shadow had moved closer to the edge of the bed.

There was a depth to the shadow, it couldn't be a reflection. The incomprehensible muttering was directed at him now, but with this recognition came a sense of urgency. Panic threatened his composure. The smell of smoke hammered his nostrils. When he looked back down the stairs, he saw flames advancing out of the room to the left of the stairs. He looked back into the room again. The shadow still stood at the opposite edge of the bed, but a second shadow lunged upward from the floor, and he was knocked to the floor.

He righted himself and prepared to defend himself, as was his instinct, but Phoebe grabbed his arm as he stood and pulled him to the side, deeper into the hallway.

Everything was gone.

The shadows, the smell of smoke and vision of fire—all gone.

He touched her hands on his arm; he was stable again.

"That was... *interesting*," Harry said.

He ran his hand over his head and took a deep, calming breath. Looking at her, he saw that she was completely unfazed.

"You didn't see any of it, did you?" He asked.

"I have seen it many times. I have tried to listen to what they say, I have been in a fight with a woman, and I have been the woman in a fight with an injured man. I have seen fire consume the stairs. I have seen doors slam and blood on the walls and floor. I have caught tears out of thin air."

"Wait," Harry said. "You've *been* the woman?"

"My house is haunted, Harry," she said, "but it is not haunted by a wayward spirit. It is haunted by something that happened, and that thing is happening over and over. You can see it from here, or you experience it there. You can feel it, smell it, and taste it. There is sadness, anger, and malice. You can even feel life extinguishing. All of it, though, is full of fear." She folded her arms. "So, can you explain it?"

He smiled. She had played him. She knew he couldn't explain it, and part of her was proud of that.

He had to admit he was impressed.

"Madam, I believe you know much more about what is happening here than I could hope to explain," he conceded. "I have never found myself at such a loss. But something about your demeanor indicates you yourself even doubt the validity of these events. You called it the *house of in between*. Do you not believe you live in a space between the worlds?"

She shook her head. "I do not know. I share with people something I cannot explain, they cannot explain, and *you* cannot explain. I profit from this house the same way a family might profit from a natural wonder on their property. I know how to make it work, but I do not know why or where it comes from. This house reveals *something*, but I do not know what."

"Then we'll start with where you start," he said. "Explain the rules."

She agreed and beckoned him to follow her down the stairs. "Almost every room experiences some aspect of these events. Someone— *I*—must be inside and six others must be outside. At some point, there will be a *pop!* followed by a startled scream. The timing of these events seems to be different for whatever reason. Perhaps the positioning of the people outside? Once they step in, it's all a matter of timing and position. Observing the events directly can break the chain of events. My séance room is the one room in the house where nothing happens. However, you can hear everything from within the room. Once the events are set in motion, they are difficult to stop as we step out of the room."

"And if the criteria aren't met?"

"Small events like what you saw up there, random and out of order."

"There's an order, then?"

She nodded slowly. "As far as I can tell, the pieces fit together like a puzzle."

"Well, that makes it obvious, then." He said with a wicked smile. "We'll have to gather a few more people and set off the events and find out once and for all what it is."

10 – CYNTHIA MORRISON

A linen closet, presumably, sat at the end of the eastern hallway between the primary bedroom and the séance room. Presumed because, currently, the door was stuck shut. Cynthia and Shannon stood in front of the door for a long time wondering why, of all the doors in this old house that opened with ease, without so much as a *creak*, this one door was jammed.

"Of course, only you would be worried about a closet that doesn't open," Marcus joked with Shannon.

"Hey, call it woman's intuition," Shannon retorted with a punch to his arm. "I don't like it when only one thing sticks out. The rest of the house is a dream, a marvel, really. All these years with next to no maintenance and everything looks great. Why is *this* door stuck and not the washroom downstairs which is in relatively the same spot?"

"I want a camera on this door," Cynthia said.

"You think it might be important?" Marcus asked.

"I've read the official record of the house. Attempts to demolish it in the past thwarted by suspicious means, acts of vandalism leaving next to no damage… It's sat empty all these years and not even a broken window or kicked-in door? But *this* door is stuck. Yeah, it might be important."

Marcus shrugged and walked off, leaving the ladies to ponder the mystery.

Downstairs, still in front of the TRAP, a frustrated Noah tried to plot chronoton courses to no avail.

"What's up, Noah?" Marcus asked.

Noah pointed at the screen, which appeared to be an even sloppier mess than before.

"What does it mean?"

Noah shook his head. "I'm not sure, but I'm scared of the answer. It could be the extra camera equipment. I mean, usually we're in a place with a few handhelds, but we've got a lot of extra wiring and sound equipment. I don't know if it's interfering with the transmitters or what."

"Dorchester?"

"Dorchester was a fluke," Noah seethed.

"Maybe this *is* a fluke, Noah. You said it might be interference. Or, maybe some mysteries aren't meant to be solved."

Incredulous, Noah craned his neck to stare at Marcus.

"But I can check our sensors." Marcus shrugged.

At the top of the stairs, Cynthia and Shannon had stopped short and heard the brief exchange.

"What's Dorchester?" asked Cynthia.

"A neighborhood in Boston," Shannon explained. "We tried to take some readings there and the TRAP couldn't get a fix. It looked amazing at first, like we were seeing something completely unprecedented, a chronoton upheaval of sorts. We charted, graphed, and checked settings over and over for weeks, only to find four of one hundred seventy transmitters hadn't been calibrated to differentiate Bluetooth radio signals. It threw the whole system for a loop, and everything was trash. That's why we had to set permissions for all the communication to the van. He's kinda sore about it. But the problem is, that sort of upheaval is exactly what he's looking for."

Cynthia looked at her curiously.

"He wants to capture the birth of an Echo, ever since his encounter in the neighborhood he grew up in. We can monitor the *results* of these events, but not the *cause*. He wants to see what causes the chronotons to affect the space they occupy. We can see the effects in all kinds of places, and knowing where the Echoes lie, we can even replicate the events to feel the full effects of a 'haunting'. It's fun, in a morbid, *terrifying* way, but we don't know what it takes to create a haunting. Do we influence it? Is it random? Why are there terrifying hauntings and then hauntings which are almost amusing, like pranks? He believes Backlund House is where he can find that event because there's no correlation between the haunting events and any sort of real event throughout history, yet they are quite specific. The fire, attacks, violence, and victimization: this place is scary to even think about, but there's no reason it should be like this. It's just a *house*."

Cynthia walked down the stairs and came around behind Noah. The screens still made no sense to her, but he pored over diagrams and computer jargon as though he were watching an intense movie.

"What does it mean?" she asked. "Maybe if you walk me through it, you'll figure something out. Maybe it's a mundane step you may have overlooked."

Noah looked up and smirked. "Everything on the screen here is everything I can read; especially after *Dorchester*." He shot Marcus a glance.

Marcus sighed and walked off to check the sensors.

Noah stared over the top of his monitors for a moment, then said, "Say, you're in a sales meeting. You get a graph up where you see broadcast times and viewership. You want to see viewership go up around your time slot. Advertisers want to buy airtime around those spikes. High spike is good for you and for them; you want to see it high and steady. You see those spikes and you understand what that means. Regardless of how they display the graph, the information is the same. You can get more complex with raw data. You can break it down. Is it kids? Is it women? Is it fishermen? It's similar here. I know what these numbers mean, and the graph is an easy visual equivalent to get a generalization of the data."

He pointed several times at different aspects displayed on the two monitors, but the numbers and graphs didn't look like they could sit still. Like Shannon had said earlier, it almost looked like static.

"And until you can find a stable common denominator, you can't be sure of exactly what you're looking at," Cynthia said.

Noah nodded. "Exactly. And I'm definitely introducing you to the parents."

Cynthia, standing next to a sitting Noah, kneed him in the back.

Reggie came in from outside with Thom and grabbed Cynthia's shoulder. "Chuck's still hearing the footsteps, like someone's pacing in the primary bedroom. We're gonna set up another camera in there, then we'll put one in front of your closet door."

Cynthia nodded. "Thanks."

Shannon had stayed upstairs watching the conversation from above, leaning on the railing. She let out an urgent shush.

Everyone looked up, Reggie stopping on the third stair up.

Shannon was listening intently, her hand hovering out in front of her to keep everyone silent. In sign language, she indicated to Noah she could *feel* the footsteps. She slinked closer to the primary bedroom, barely making a sound.

Meanwhile, Noah checked data on his screens, zeroing in on the sector containing that bedroom. He caught Cynthia's attention and pointed to the screen, making simple hand signs to show that what they heard was not happening in real time. He gave a sheepish grin as he looked back up to Shannon, who was reaching the bedroom door.

Shannon took a deep, quiet breath, then turned the handle, making a small click. The sound of rolling balls erupted, sounding like they were rolling off into the distance, silencing quickly. She opened the door, a silver ray of daylight filling the hall. She sighed.

"Nothing." She said in a normal tone. "But I could feel it in the floorboards, like Reggie said, someone pacing."

Thom looked at his phone to check the time. "Do ghosts usually make their presence known at three o'clock in the afternoon?"

Marcus chimed in from the dining room entryway. "A 'haunting' at odd times is more believable than those *witching hour* stories. Ghosts in the middle of the night are almost always night terrors."

"And the signing?" Cynthia asked.

"Whatever it is that allows us to experience the Echoes," Noah said. "That connection can easily be broken. We do simple signs to keep things silent, allowing our other senses to continue to focus.

Silence is one of our greatest tools. Hence the TRAP is low profile as well."

He looked back up at Shannon. "We got a hit, though. For all this activity we're picking up, when you and Chuck said there was pacing, I had absolutely nothing on the screen, and we're in real time."

"So, what they're hearing isn't there? They're not really *hearing* anything at all?" Cynthia asked.

"Exactly; but now I can take where Shannon was, and where the microphones picking up the footsteps are, and reconstruct the data and plot chronoton courses until we have all the activity happening at once. I can spin this information back to the construction of the house and determine if this event, the pacing in the bedroom that someone can hear from the balcony, has ever happened before. It'll take a little while. I'm gonna break and help Marcus check the sensors."

"I'm not breaking for nothing!" Reggie beamed, then ran up the stairs to set up more surveillance cameras.

11 – ANDREW & JOANNA NEWSTED

Still bitterly cold from being out on the water all day in freezing temperatures, Andrew rubbed his hands together and fought off the shakes almost an hour after getting home. It was only December first, not even winter yet! This much further north, and especially on the lake, it might as well have been. He'd maintained his spirits and seemed to genuinely enjoy his job. Joanna usually had a meal prepared or was cooking when he got home. Thankfully, with winter fast approaching, the days were significantly shorter, and he felt like he got some real rest at night.

Joanna didn't have any more anxiety about the house and hadn't seen anything else unusual. Life in Grand Marais was turning out to be all they had hoped for. She and Loretta had really hit it off and even picked up more clients, like Loretta predicted. Joanna was easily bringing home close to two hundred dollars a week. She and Andrew even bought a decent dining set.

Tonight, though, Andrew felt like sitting in front of the fireplace and watching TV. They'd moved the TV set on a little cart into each of the rooms, trying to find the best place to catch the signals. The sitting room seemed to work best. This evening they managed to get a decent picture on CBS, so they left it there and picked at some fish and potatoes Andrew had brought home the day before.

Mayberry R.F.D. was supposed to come on but was preempted by the news. "Good evening," said Roger Mudd, CBS's Washington correspondent. He continued in a low tone, "Tonight, for the first time in twenty-seven years, the United States has again started a draft lottery."

"What the hell?" Andrew said, shifting in his seat.

The lottery process was explained, and they watched as people milled about an unceremonious set of tables and office furniture until Congressman Alexander Pirnie from New York stepped up to the glass vase holding the plastic pills full of birthdates. He reached in, grabbed one, pulled it out, and handed the capsule to an official sitting at a table.

They opened the capsule, unfurled a slip of paper, and read aloud, "September 14. September 14 is 001."

"Oh my God," Joanna whispered.

Maybe she whispered it. She could have screamed it. For all the sudden rushing sound in his ears, Andrew could barely hear anything else being said by her or on the TV.

As it had been explained, this lottery was for individuals born 1944-1950, and Andrew's birthday happened to be September 14th, 1949. He'd turned 20 shortly after they moved. They were too young to be this far from home, too young to be in such a nice house, maybe even too young to be married, but he was certainly too young for war. At least it *felt* that way; it was hard to imagine being a grown-up, especially with how the world was these days.

The second part of the lottery was based on letters; last name first, and some formula for determining who from the birthdates would be drafted.

N was number 5, and that didn't sound too reassuring.

"What are we going to do?" Joanna asked.

Andrew looked at her as if she was far away. "Go to bed. Go to work tomorrow," he said. "We'll be okay. There's nothing to be scared of."

"But what if you do get drafted?" she pleaded.

"We live in a free country. They feel the need to call on my services, then I'll be compelled to oblige. My father did."

"Your father died in something like this," she hissed, almost immediately regretting saying it.

"You're right." He shrugged.

"We could drive up to Canada!" she pleaded. "I bet we could make it in a couple of hours."

He shook his head, solemnly. "No. I don't like it. I don't like this war, but we're part of it. Like I said, Uncle Sam comes calling, I've got no choice but to answer."

He stood up, walked through the washroom, set his plate in the sink, rounded through the dining room and headed directly upstairs, leaving Joanna sitting there, watching the telecast drone on.

Tears welled in her eyes. Nothing but numbers had been announced. This wasn't a sure thing, but it was still a blow to the gut. She also put her dishes away after turning off the television, smothered the fire, and put up the screen to keep embers from popping out onto the floor and followed Andrew's lead.

Topping the stairs and turning into their room, she saw him lying on the bed, still fully clothed with his shoes on. She didn't say a word but came around the other side of the bed and sidled up to him. He didn't react as she wrapped her arm around him, and she began to weep softly into the back of his neck.

~

Joanna sat bolt upright. She could smell the smoke filling the hallway. Terrified, she jumped out of bed and ran into the hall, expecting to rush down the stairs and discover a fire in the sitting room. What she found, though, was the entire staircase on fire; confusion and doubt screamed in her brain as she hadn't seen the light of flames in the hall, nor did her eyes burn from smoke. But there it was, roaring away up the banister and wall. She had let out a scream.

Andrew was up and in the hallway with her. He looked down the steps and then back at her. "What? Another shadow?" he asked.

She looked at him as if he was crazy. "The fucking stairs are on fire!"

He looked again, then back at her. He was completely baffled and shook his head and shrugged.

She backed up until she hit the wall behind her, clearly looking at something horrifying. He walked down the stairs to reassure her.

Standing in the middle of the stairs, and from her point of view completely engulfed in flame, he raised his hands, "See, nothing."

He continued down the stairs and looked in on the fireplace, walked back up, completely oblivious and unresponsive to the flames all around him. He stopped directly in front of her and put his hands on her shoulders.

"You must be having a nightmare. Come on, come back to bed."

"But… look!" she said, pointing over his shoulder.

When she leaned over to look at the stairs again, it was dark and quiet. The absence of the flames was more jarring than seeing them in the first place.

"There's no fire, Jo," he said. "If anything, it's a bit *too* cold down there, especially on the stairs. Come on."

He urged her back to bed. Realizing he was still dressed in the middle of the night, he kicked off his shoes and shucked his pants and shirt and crawled under the blankets, urging her in with him.

"It's okay," he said, "it was only a nightmare; probably the news."

She looked around the room. A sliver of moonlight splayed out across the bed was the only light, and despite the raging inferno she had seen, she realized she could see normally. Her eyes were perfectly adjusted to the dark. It wasn't as though she had been looking at bright flames. She shook her head, then nodded and crawled under the sheets with him.

"What are we going to do, Andrew?"

"Nothing's really happened; not yet. Maybe it won't. If it comes, we'll deal with it."

He kissed her on the shoulder and hugged her tight. Even though she was trembling, she dozed off quickly.

12 - NOAH BENJAMIN

The group left the house to have dinner in town and opted to visit a bar & grill called Lucy's Dynamo Bay in the harbor. Marcus could still monitor the TRAP's readings through a heads-up display in his glasses and Chuck and Cynthia could pull up video feeds through their tablets. Between them, they could monitor the house in their absence. If anything happened while no one was there, enough video was rolling if they missed something live, it would still be recorded.

The owner and bartender, a handsome, blonde man, came over to the big corner table they occupied. "The film crew! I hoped I'd get to see you guys. My name is Lucas and let me welcome you to Grand Marais by buying you dinner."

The group gave a happy cheer.

"'Lucy'. Is that a nickname for Lucas, or your mother?" Cynthia asked.

"Oh, no," Lucas shook his head. A waiter took their orders as he continued. "No, Lucy's Dynamo Bay has been here since the early 1900s, during the logging boom. Uh, let's see… My Great, Great," he counted on his fingers, "*Great* Grandfather Lucian started the place, and *his* nickname was Lucy. Ever since, each boy is named something with an L-U-C. One day my son Luce will get the place, and everyone will think it's named after him with some tongue-in-cheek lure with the Y in the spelling."

"Wow," Thom said. "Your family's been here all this time. I bet you know a lot about this place."

Lucas bobbed his head from one side to the other. "A fair bit. But I'm sure you mean the Backlund House."

Everyone leaned in as he said it. Lucas could offer some interesting insight if he and his family had lived here for so long. Surely the stories told over a few beers would be worth spinning over and over.

"Starting most recently," Lucas began and leaned against the tall table they sat at. "The last occupants moved out several years back. From what I understand, they were decent folks. Decent enough not to come here, anyway."

The group politely chuckled. Chuck opted to check on his video feeds.

"They had a daughter—I think she was in the Army—she served in Afghanistan before the pullout. When she got home," he paused and thought about his words. "There's no easy, politically correct way to put it: she attempted suicide. That's real. You'll hear stories that she had been fine, but coming home to *that* house broke her. Or that she didn't hurt herself, but something attacked her. Something awful happened there, that's a fact, but *after* that happened, a lot of people became re-interested in the house. The more people that paid attention to it, the more stories popped up.

"The owners wanted their privacy, they left. But, for whatever reason, they kept the house, and it's stood empty ever since. You get people who try to break in, or those who hang out around the house, or even the random utility inspector, and they all come away with stories. Have you already been up there?"

He was looking down at the tablet that Chuck was staring at.

Cynthia chimed in. "We got everything set up and decided to come into town for a bite to eat. We really don't mean to keep you from your bar…".

Lucas looked over his shoulder. A particularly ratty looking man in a black suit nursed something dark in his glass. A pair of buxom girls showing off entirely too much skin laughed at each other. A biker was playing a game of pool by himself. Meanwhile, a bartender cleaned a glass, staring off into space.

"I don't think they miss me." He chuckled.

Lucas eyed everyone at the table again. He seemed to be cataloging details about them, *reading* them. And he was eerily accurate.

"When do you ship out?" he asked Marcus.

"I… uh, in a couple weeks," Marcus said, taken aback. "From San Diego. Wrapping up our documentary and Noah's book tour…".

Lucas continued to eye him, ignoring the deflection. "Keep your head down, kid." He rubbed his neck as he said it.

Then, looking at Noah, he said, "*Violent Echo*, right? I remember—"

Cynthia's attention darted between Noah and Lucas. The smallest twinge of apprehension showed on Noah's brow. Noah was hiding something. Shannon and Marcus exchanged a quick glance.

Lucas smiled and shook his head. "I remember when I heard you'd be coming through. I was kind of excited, really. My Granddad Lucius was pretty close with a couple that lived there in the early seventies. In fact, we—ah, the *bar,* that is—had a pretty good relationship with the B&B from the nineties. Especially when they opted to sell themselves as haunted. People like to have a drink around Halloween and tell ghost stories. The house went quiet though, for a while. Maybe a door creak here and there, footsteps on the landing, the smell of smoke sometimes. They went out of business and the house went back to being a house for a while."

A waiter brought out food. The group commented on how quick the service was. "You're my only patrons. These bums," he said, pointing a thumb over his shoulder, "order well-whiskey and hold the stools down."

The man in the suit lifted a middle finger into the air.

"Ah, Backlund House." Lucas pulled up a chair and sat at the end of the table. "An old man and woman always wanted kids, but they couldn't have their own. They had a good relationship with their siblings and had nieces and nephews stay over as much as possible. As the family aged, the old man said they should build a house right on the lake, big enough to have family over any time. He was a manager of a logging company, his office right in this area. He made a decent buck, and they were saving. Then he died, slipped between the logs of a raft he was trying to re-shore-up. It was the early days of life insurance policies, but he knew the dangers of his job. His widow was compensated, and as a last romantic gesture, she built their dream home.

"They say the spot she picked was destined for that house. The soil had never been turned by man; it was waiting for that house. Construction workers complained of sorrowful moans coming from the woods. When the walls went up, they could hear men chasing each other upstairs, when there weren't any floors. The fire brigade was called out three times during construction because workers swore the stairs were ablaze.

"It was the day she was handed the keys by the foreman, though, only too happy to be done with his job—as far as Madam Backlund knew. A scream erupted from within. From that day on, to this very day in fact, anyone who hears the scream will know what lies on the *other side*. To rush in to help some stranger in distress is to submit yourself to the *house of in between*."

No one was eating. Lucas smiled.

"Lucian had to run Madam Backlund off from his bar. She was giving people the creeps. But she was looking for help. The town thought she'd brought it on herself. If it was a haunted house, it must be her husband seeking retribution for spending all his money on a house too lavish for an old widow. But of course, they couldn't know her plight. They were too scared by the thought of it. Even if they were skeptical, a house to make a woman go mad was no house they wanted to visit. With time, though, she accepted her fate. She had used all the money to build a house. To make ends meet, she invited skeptics in to prove her wrong. She held séances, tried to contact the spirits that tormented her, but no answers came. When the day came, age took her. They say she stayed behind anyway and protected the one room in the house she could. Not the boarded-up séance room. Not her own bedroom. The room with the antique hutch. Yes, it's been there since the day it was built. She whimpers from within, sad to be alone and trapped in that house. But in there, her soft cries are all that can be heard. No other events disrupt that room.

"When you're there tonight, and you find yourself facing the worst frights of your lives," he paused, eyeing each one of them again, then settled on Cynthia. "You can hide there, and Madam Backlund will keep you safe."

Noah gave a polite clap. "You've told that story more than once, I think."

Lucas smiled. "You all stay safe. If you find what you're looking for, I hope it's worth the effort."

He bade them farewell and left them to finish their meals.

13 – ANDREW NEWSTED

No activity on the boat for at least a week. That's what the doctor had instructed. The cold made his break ache something awful. The dull, lingering pain was almost worse than getting his wrist caught, and *snapped,* between riggings. Still yet, Andrew hated sitting in the house all day. Soap Operas were for old ladies, and there was only so much a person could do in February under a foot of snow. Joanna had taken the truck out to clean a couple of houses with Loretta, and Andrew was starting to feel the unease she was always talking about.

The house made awful sounds that defied explanation. It wasn't settling; it wasn't expanding, and the noises always seemed to come from above. The few times it sounded like actual footsteps really set Andrew on edge, and he wondered if there was something to Joanna and Loretta's stories of the house being haunted.

One particular slam, or pop, or whatever the thud sound could be described as, drove Andrew to sit on the porch, bundled up. He sat out there and smoked a few cigarettes. It wasn't his habit, they were Joanna's, but the stress of being alone in a mysteriously noisy house drove him to whatever might take the edge off. When the scream came, he nearly launched himself off the veranda.

He backed down the front steps and looked up at the house. It couldn't have come from inside. He looked around through the trees. No movement.

When something buffeted against the front door, from *inside*, Andrew felt sick, terrified, and weak.

"Hello?" he called out, his voice muted against the snow.

Only a light breeze rustled through the tops of the trees.

"Goddammit…"

He had an overwhelming urge to hoof it to the interstate and hitchhike back into town and spend the day in a restaurant. But with silence came a renewed sense of calm and a modicum of bravery. He stepped up to the front door, listened a moment, then dared to pop it open.

"Hello?"

He shook his head and cursed himself. "What am I thinking… had to have been a hawk or something outside. It… It sounded weird with all the snow on the ground."

He scratched his head with the edge of his cast. "And now I'm talking and reasoning with myself."

He decided to go in and upstairs to check the room, to procure a stronger sense of security for himself. Maybe it *was* a hawk or an owl, and it somehow had found its way in.

He started with the master bedroom, making the right-hand turn off the top of the stairs without even thinking. What he saw chilled him worse than the cold outside.

Like Joanna had described seeing that first day, there was the figure of a man standing in the doorway of the restroom in their bedroom. He was about to yell and confront the figure, but he could hear a whispering, as though the man was talking to, or listening to someone in the bathroom.

That there were two intruders wasn't what shook him. It was that he had heard that whispering before. Before he thought it was leaves, heard through the open door; he leaned back to make sure he had shut the front door. Everything was shut tight. He looked back into the room; the shadow had moved closer to the bed.

It had no discernible features; it was the figure of a man, but as for everything else, it was a shadow. Where a jawline might be looked like it was working, as if the thing was trying to speak to him. But before he could fathom what this was or what it was trying to say, another shadow leapt up from the floor. It didn't make contact, but the fright of it sent Andrew sprawling to the floor.

He jammed his broken wrist on the way down and screamed out in pain. Terrified of his shadow attackers, he tried to back up and ready himself either to fight or run. When he opened his eyes, though, and managed to see through the tears, there was nothing. The sense of dread dissipated, like his body knew he was no longer in danger, but his mind hadn't quite caught up.

"No fucking way."

He let himself finally breathe and spared a disbelieving laugh or two. He sat there for about five minutes anticipating further sounds, maybe another vision, but nothing came. He *felt* like what Joanna had looked like the night of her fire nightmare. He knew what he had seen had really been there, in front of his eyes, but now there was no evidence of it other than the throbbing in his wrist and the cold shakes of adrenaline wearing off.

He slid across the floor and sat on the top step, looking down over the foyer.

What was this place?

Feeling guilty for having doubted Joanna, he prepared dinner for her, despite the newfound pain in his wrist. He found he turned it inward a lot more than he thought he had. The potatoes baking in the oven were still about ten minutes out when Joanna came walking in the front door. She started to call out to him, but then rushed into the kitchen, afraid something was burning.

"What the heck are you doing?" she asked, looking scared.

"Making you dinner. Does it smell that bad?"

She sighed and leaned against the doorframe. "Doctor said no activity."

"I can freaking *cook*," he jeered.

The fear in Joanna's eyes made him rethink telling her what he had seen. She had finally started feeling comfortable again after the lottery call and he didn't feel right throwing that out the window.

They sat across the table from each other, and he listened to her talk about her day. He responded warmly on cue, but something about his own event started to bug him. He was back on that first day when

Joanna saw the shadow in the doorway looking in on them. He had gotten up and crept along the wall to the door, had felt compelled to kneel, and when he reached the edge of the door, he jumped out. His own actions from that first night felt exactly like what the shadow looked like jumping out at him.

Had he felt that ghost's actions?

"Andrew?" she said, looking at him, concerned.

He focused and looked at her and realized he was hovering an empty fork in front of his mouth as though he were about to bite. Embarrassment rushed through him. How long had he sat there like that? Hell, even a second was embarrassing.

"I'm sorry," he said. "I'm really sorry. Being cooped up in the house has me kind of loopy. I'm tired of doing nothing!" he lied.

"Okay," she said. "I wasn't boring you?"

"No, no! Not at all," he said. "You were saying Loretta left a tub running to drain out some cleaner but didn't realize she'd stopped the drain. You walked in as it was about to overflow and saved the day."

She smiled softly. "You'll get out of the house soon, probably injuring other body parts, but at least you'll be out there doing something. I know how boring it can get in here. Especially when there's no sound with all of this snow!"

He smiled back and dug into his baked potato. She hadn't heard or seen anything since the fire, then, or she was hiding from him the same type of thing he was hiding from her. He didn't want to test it, though. She seemed happy. Short of some stress from the news, they had been doing good.

14

He was startled by banging and the sound of wood creaking. He nearly dropped his emulsion bottle at the sound. Equal parts terrified and irritated, he set the jug down and approached the door. Unable to fling the door open with photo paper and chemicals about, he had to calm his nerves.

"What is going on out there?"

Banging again. It sounded angry and forceful, and the intensity startled him again.

He had heard a few disembodied sounds in the house over the last few nights. Could this be part of the old haunting stories? Looking around at his nature photos hanging all around to dry in the red light, he shook his head. He was letting ghost stories get under his skin.

When the bang came again, he banged on his own door as loudly. "Stop it! I'm trying to work in here!"

The sound of a startled shout was followed by, "Dad! I'm sorry, I didn't know you were in there. I'm trying to get into the linen closet and the damn door is stuck."

Banging again.

"Are you trying to tear the house down?" he hollered over the sound.

"What do you mean?" she asked, sounding confused. "I'm pulling, not beating on it."

He lowered his head in tired frustration. "Do you have to have something *right now* or can you wait fifteen minutes so I can clean up?"

An annoyed exhalation preceded plodding footsteps down the hall. "Fine."

"Thank you!" he called out.

He was at a point he could wrap up, anyway. As he carefully drained solutions back into bottles and wrapped up all the light-sensitive materials, he caught glimpses of his photos. These were mostly from around the property. The house looked tired in the photos. Granted, he was doing black and white with an older camera, but it didn't seem like the house was content.

He placed his hand on each item he needed to have in its proper place and finally turned off the red light. As he did, he could hear the closet door in the hall open.

He opened his own door. "You finally get it open?"

No one was in the hall, though. It appeared as though the closet had popped open and the light inside was on. Stepping into the hallway and shutting the darkroom door behind him, he looked down the hallway out to the landing. No one there and no sound. He reached for the closet door and started to pull it open, the light expanding into the hallway.

"Sweetheart?" he called out, confused.

A wave of confusion and disorientation washed over him. He turned back to look in the closet to make sure his daughter wasn't hoaxing him.

"Yeah, Dad?" his daughter called as she bounded up the stairs.

He was dumbfounded. He knew the light had been on. He had seen it against the wall, and the hall had brightened when he looked down that way. But now the closet was dark.

Her footsteps made quick progress towards him. "Oh, good, you got it open."

She slipped past him and grabbed a spare set of sheets. "Thanks," she said, and slipped back past and went down to her room.

"Wait," he said. There were the beginnings of a desperate laugh in his voice. "Are you screwing with me?"

She turned on her heel. "Huh?"

"This door was open, and the light was on. Then I turn around and the light is off…"

She started waving a pointed finger at him. "I think you've been in the darkroom too long, Dad."

He blinked a few times. Could that be it?

He shut the door, then opened it back up a few times with little effort. It wasn't stuck anymore and made no sound. He gave the inside of the closet one more look before giving up.

He headed downstairs and heard the radio on in the library.

"Hey," he said to his wife, who was sitting next to a window and reading. "Did you hear all that upstairs?"

She looked up. "I heard the two of you talking."

"No banging?" he asked as he sat down across from her.

She pursed her lips and shook her head. "No."

"It's got to be something in the wall; maybe a loose stud or something." He said it mostly to himself. "I was developing, and then it sounded like she was trying to tear the door down. When I finally came out, the closet was hanging open and I thought I saw the light on—but it wasn't on."

"Maybe you were in the darkroom too long," she said. "Weird red light, all those chemicals…".

He looked out the window and nodded slowly in agreement. "That's what she said."

"Don't be gross," she said.

He looked back at her, confused, and saw her grinning. He thought for a moment and realized what he had said. He kicked at her, but she dodged him.

"*You* don't be gross." He stood up to walk away. "I think I'll walk down to the water and get some fresh air in case it was the fumes."

"Okay," she said with a soft smile.

He walked out of the kitchen and down through the woods to the beach. It was late September and close to evening; the air coming off Lake Superior was quite cool. He thought about turning back for a jacket, but the breeze and cold would sufficiently shock him and clear out the fumes.

The beach was more like a field of boulders descending into gravel. Some of the rocks close to the tree line were big enough to stretch out on.

"I don't think you're crazy, Dad."

He looked up and saw his daughter coming down the wooden stairs along the rocks. She stepped onto the rocks and balanced by waving her arms as she moved from boulder to boulder to sit next to him.

"It might be stress, it might be chemicals," she said between steps, "but you're not crazy."

He laughed and shook his head. "What makes you think I was worried about being *crazy*? It might *be* the chemicals—that's why I'm out here."

"I've had that happen before." She said, looking out over the water.

He looked at her and saw there was certainly something on her mind. "What?"

"The door." She answered. "The closet door—it sticks, it doesn't stick. The light is on, the light is off. I hear shit all over the house, but the closet bothers me. Like it's calling me, but I don't know what for."

He knew the stare he was giving could be misconstrued for incredulity. He rubbed his face to relax the muscles and spoke through his hands. "I think we're all stressed. I'm sure it was a mix of being in there with the chemicals and it had been quiet, probably coupled with something banging between the walls. It's an old house, but it isn't *haunted*, it's not beckoning you. You probably just want to stay *home*."

"I guess you were right," she said with a nod. "I guess it does feel like home. Right before I'm leaving."

He wrapped his arm around her shoulder and squeezed her tight. "Then you'll have a *home* to come home to; not an unfamiliar house."

"But what if—"

"No." He cut her off.

Neither said anything more as they stared out over the water together. Both struggled with the terrible scenarios of going off to war. Each considered their personal losses and the losses of the other.

He squeezed her tighter. Despite her twenty years, she felt no different in his arms than when she was only five years old.

15 – PHOEBE BACKLUND

Harry's interest in discovering the house's secrets burgeoned on excitement. Behind his straight, stony gaze simmered a fervent passion to unravel this new mystery. It even managed to excite Phoebe. She had lived with these pantomime ghosts for so long, she felt disgusted with herself that she had grown accustomed and learned to avoid them. As far as she could tell, they never *tried* to contact her, but she often found herself in contact with them. The emotions and machinations of these things could override one's own reason, and to that extent, Phoebe felt like Harry had overridden the house. It was exceptionally quiet. Peace had settled about the place, the likes of which she hadn't experienced in some time. If *knowing* what the thing was would end this supernatural torment, then she was glad to let Harry peel back whatever veil hid the truth.

She *had* been this excited about the house once, before her husband Handel passed away. They both had sisters with families who liked to meet up in Grand Marais and take in the lake and forests. Handel was quickly rising in the logging company he worked with and was making excellent money. The plan was to build a house large enough for children, adult siblings, and parents alike to stay any time of the year.

Five bedrooms, four living areas, and a kitchen and dining room large enough to feed the entirety of their family. It was obviously too much for the two of them, but it was always intended to house their families. Handel drew up the plans, making an expansion of the growing trend of four-square homes, adding in the foyer, dining room, and upstairs living room to the middle of the house and splitting one of the bedrooms into two for children to bunk in. The master bedroom was privatized for them, a little smaller than the two bedrooms across the hallway. Instead it gained a large closet and its own private bathroom.

They sat on the plans after drawing them up in their late thirties. They had planned to build it in the next ten years. As business went up and down, it was hard to set a concrete date to build the house. Forty came and went.

In 1908 Handel died, not even reaching fifty. *Knowing* that threat, Handel had purchased his own life insurance policy, naming Phoebe as his benefactor. After much investigation by the insurance company, she finally received a settlement. Combined with what they had saved and selling their old house, she had enough to build their dream home.

Those close to her, such as family, or the workers in the mill who knew Handel well, understood what she was doing. Others in the community saw a widow gone mad, building a house far too big and lavish to live in alone. The contractors, however, saw a job and built the house perfectly. The stories of them hearing or seeing anything akin to a haunting were fabricated years later. The truth of the matter was, they wanted their house in a quiet place, private and secluded; a hiding place from the rest of the world.

As far as recent records indicated, the land had never been used and was cleared specifically to build the house. No known trading posts from the fur trade, no Indian villages, not even a settler campsite could be linked to the area. This house was man's first interaction with the land.

She had visited the construction site multiple times and saw or heard nothing other than men working. The only thing of note during the construction of the house at all was that a hutch, an heirloom of Handel's, was hoisted into the southeast bedroom since it was too large to fit through the bedroom door. That was to be Handel's sister's room, having it in there seemed appropriate; a piece of their childhood in the room she would use on visits.

Once the house was completed and the construction crew was cleared, the foreman and Phoebe walked the house and grounds. It was quiet and beautiful. It was a dream made real. If she couldn't grow old with Handel, at least she could see this dream come true and still entertain their families as they had wanted. The foreman gave her the keys, thanked her for her business, and drove away.

She had stood there, smiling at the house, maybe the first time she had felt good in nearly two years since Handel's death. The smile and happiness was shattered by that fateful scream, though. It was a scream of shock, someone having been startled, and badly, and it sounded like it was coming from inside the house. She had been in every room, looked behind every door and through every window. Fearing a vagrant had perhaps snuck in the back while she spoke with the foreman in the front yard, she carefully went inside and called after the stranger. But there was nothing.

The house had a foul feeling to it, now. She was frightened to be standing even in the front door and called again. Still nothing.

The thought occurred to her it might be a bird, a hawk above the trees. Holding the keys in such a way she could scratch or stab a possible attacker, she examined every room again. Even though everything was new and the furniture had been recently moved in and dusted, there was an old look to the place. It didn't feel like a brand-new happy home. Something screamed of a hundred years of woe. She couldn't place her finger on the culprit, but she felt it in her heart. The house was not the happy place it had looked before she heard the scream from outside.

She took a deep breath to calm her nerves, the first of many. Especially when Harry was excited to invite handpicked guests to attend the next séance. This house did not demand patience or understanding, but solitude. This was her house, though, built to her and her late husband's specifications. Still, somehow it was not her own.

That first night wore on. She heard creaks, steps, and far away, elongated moans. It was her first night in a brand-new house on newly leveled ground; it had to be settling. The house was relaxing into its foundation. At least, that's how she reasoned with the sounds.

A week later her sister Patricia and her sons, as well as her sister-in-law Maddy and her son and daughter came to spend the weekend. The siblings were in the split room, Maddy in the room with the hutch, and Patricia across from Phoebe's bedroom. They had planned to stay until Sunday afternoon. They barely made it to Saturday morning.

The children cried in the middle of the night. In the partitioned bedrooms, Phoebe's nephews claimed they saw what looked like three men fighting, followed by blood running down the wall. There was no such evidence and no signs of a fight. It must have been a nightmare, the adults claimed: nerves in a new house. Maddy, however, found herself frightened as well when it sounded like someone had entered her room, crawled into the hutch, and was weeping. Phoebe thought she had seen shadows in the bathroom and outside her own door. Patricia, in the southwest room, was the only one not plagued with visions and nightmares. But seeing her boys terrified like she had never seen before, convinced her that Phoebe's house was unsafe.

They feared Handel was tormenting them, but Phoebe never once believed it. She considered it, worried about it, but nothing that she saw, nothing that was described to her, sounded like Handel. Something else was at work, and it was then she considered the house might be some kind of gateway to another world.

She prayed for peace and strength. She pleaded with the spirits that haunted her to leave. With her faith tested and no respite to be found, she tried to interact with them, to help them find solace, and she desperately hid from them, thankful when they were quiet. She read up on spiritualists and the occult, against her better judgment, and familiarized herself with every bit of information concerning ghosts and hauntings. Everything was lacking, but she persisted, trying to appease the apparitions anyway.

In the early days, she would be as wild in her moods as the demons were in their actions. She found herself accustomed to the sounds, disturbed by doors swinging on their hinges, and outright terrified of seeing phantoms. She could no longer stay in the master bedroom and opted to use the southwest room as a sanctuary since Patricia claimed she had experienced nothing in there.

On occasion, sounds would still emanate from the house, even while she was in her new room. For the most part she could ignore those, and with time, ignoring them became routine to the point she no longer heard anything while in that room. But it was late one night when she heard a nasty bang on the outside wall below her windows. She looked out, disturbed to see the ghosts milling about below.

She turned the room into a proper sanctuary, boarding up the windows with the curtains still in them so that from the outside the house still looked normal. Inside, she was blocked off from the rest of the world. Short of a few sounds every once in a while, indistinguishable from nature or otherwise, she felt safe. But safe in one room of her own house was no way to live.

As the Great War waged on in Europe, Phoebe waged a war of her own with her house. She traced and retraced her steps, mimicking every aspect of everything she could remember. She kept a journal of all that she did or did not do that caused events to occur. The worst events had come when the house was full. Seven people. The number of people was certainly a key, and one she followed intently, but their placement mostly eluded her.

At first, the séances she held were an actual effort to contact the spirits. It turned out there was no contacting them, no interaction—only observance, and only through the periphery. As people heard of her consistent contact with some other plane of existence, more and more people wanted to attend. People offered great sums of money to interact with a gateway between worlds, though mostly they found themselves terrified. Each subsequent séance revealed a little more as she managed to tease more out of the house. Eventually, she reached a point where she felt she couldn't glean any more information. These were shadows, and they played out the same scenario every time; it was an echo of an event that happened in the house, but not *this* house. This house was between worlds. In another world, this *thing* had happened and would continue to happen over and over.

The séances were a show these days; she had grown bored and tired. Having to conjure the emotions necessary was draining, but perhaps someone with a different perspective could shed light on the mystery.

Harry's determination reignited that old desire to understand.

16 – JARON & SAMANTHA AND HELEN

"What is that?" Samantha cried, bolting upright in her seat and pressing against the passenger window.

Jaron lowered his head close to the steering wheel, trying to see what she saw. A fire in the woods. As he processed the scene before them, he came upon a private driveway off MN-61. Slamming on his brakes, he quickly turned onto the drive. The fire was rising from a house.

"Call 9-1-1," he calmly instructed. "We'll see if anyone needs help."

Samantha nodded and dug through her purse for her cellphone as she stared ahead.

The private driveway stopped with a circular car-park where two cars sat in front of the house. The fire appeared to be burning most fiercely in the center with flames shooting through the roof where it had buckled under the heat.

"I don't see anyone standing outside," Jaron said.

"It says 'no service,'" Samantha said.

Jaron looked down. "What? We passed through a town."

When they had come to a stop and looked back up, the fire was gone. The house was perfectly intact, lit only by the car's headlights and a single porch light.

Samantha yelped. "What the hell was that?"

Jaron stared on, his mouth hanging open, his gaze shifting between ire and confusion. "What the hell kind of prank is this?" he finally asked.

"You think it was fake?"

He turned to her. "Do you see a fire?"

They got out of the car and looked around at the woods surrounding them. It was a new moon this evening, there was little light beyond the porch light and their headlights. Then a light came on in one of the upstairs windows, followed shortly by a light behind the front door. Then the door opened.

"Hello there!" An older woman, maybe in her sixties, called out.

Jaron and Samantha exchanged looks of disbelief.

The old woman stepped out onto the veranda, stopping at the top of the stairs. "It's a bit late and you look a little confused. I assume you saw something from the highway?"

Jaron stepped forward, nodding. "Yes, ma'am. We thought we saw a fire, both of us. In fact, we were *certain* we saw a fire and tried to call 9-1-1."

The woman smiled, then shook her head. "Oh no, if you saw something, you most certainly wouldn't have been able to call for help. It likes a private audience."

Samantha came forward. "I'm sorry… *it*?"

"The house." The old woman said. "It teases, even *coaxes*, people in."

Jaron and Samantha stared.

The old woman gave a grim smile. "You're not from around here, I take it? Passing through?"

Samantha nodded, but neither of them offered anything further.

"My name is Helen Jacobs and this is my little B&B. This is a *haunted* house. What you saw is one of a series of events that repeats itself here. If you're interested to learn more, I can go on, or if you're tired, I have rooms open. I won't charge you much for tonight since it's halfway through already."

Jaron and Samantha exchanged disbelieving glances again.

"Hey," Helen shrugged. "It's cheaper than a shitty motel, and I'll make you breakfast in the morning. If you *stay* until morning, that is." Her grin indicated a challenge.

"That's it? That's your pitch?" Jaron sneered. "You turn on some pyrotechnics when you see some headlights and try to lure people into your lakeside tourist-trap?"

Samantha nudged his elbow, trying to pull him back from being rude.

Helen shook her head. "Not at all. Most people come here looking for an adventure for themselves; to find out they can stay is a bonus to the thrill seekers. Sometimes the house puts on a show, sometimes not. You get a nice night's sleep in a house on your way to wherever you're going, or you get a nightmare of an evening you won't stop talking about. Breakfast is on the house, regardless."

Samantha nudged Jaron again. "We can head up into Canada in the morning. We're probably missing a lot of scenery in the dark, anyway."

Jaron sighed and let his shoulders slump. "All right, sure, *whatever*."

He walked back to the still-running car, parked at the edge of the circle-drive, and grabbed a bag from the backseat. When he got out, Samantha was already stepping up to the veranda. He took in the house again. He *knew* he had seen flames, but he couldn't make out any blemishes on the roof in the darkness. It had to have been a trick. He girded his skepticism and marched toward the door. Inside, the house appeared to be quiet and intact.

"This must have been an old folk's home at some point," Jaron remarked. "There's a lot of *sitting* room in here."

"Well," Helen started, "it was indeed built by an elderly lady, intended to house her family."

She pointed to the room with the fireplace, then went clockwise. "Library, sitting room, sunroom, dining, the kitchen is back there, behind the stairs. Between the kitchen and library is a washroom and lavatory. Upstairs, starting above the library, is the master bedroom. Across the landing here are two small rooms. Opposite them is a medium-sized bedroom. We call that our antique room; there's an heirloom hutch in there from Germany, I think. After Madam Back-lund passed, her remaining family refused to claim the house or its contents. The hutch has been here ever since—it would take disman-tling to remove it. Through the years, no one has had the heart to do so.

"Directly next to the antique room is the upstairs bathroom; it is communal, do please be considerate. You can see the double doors up there; that's the upstairs living room. I did have it set up as an extra bedroom, but I've never had a guest stay an entire night in there, we use it as a gaming parlor. Opposite the master bedroom is the séance room—it is a bedroom as well—though, that's where my husband and I stay. So you know—it will only be the four of us this evening. My husband has already gone to bed and you're my only guests."

Jaron took in a sharp breath. "I'm not sure we should stay. It's a lovely house, Ms. Helen, and I mean no offense, but you're setting up a horror movie scenario and I don't aim to be murdered this evening."

Helen chuckled. "I am a fully accredited hospitality service pro-vider. My credentials are framed and hanging behind you."

Looking over his shoulder, sure enough, there were framed legal documents displayed between the front door and the windows on ei-ther side. The house had been inspected. A fire marshal's safety certi-fication was prominently displayed; nearby, he also noted a food handler's permit.

Heaving a sigh, he looked at Samantha. "It's up to you. I've got a bad—"

He stopped and looked around wearily.

Samantha straightened up. "What? What is it?"

"Is that coffee?" he asked Helen.

She smiled softly. "Indeed. I sleep poorly. I had put the pot on a while before you showed up. I had only been upstairs to see my hus-band to bed. Can I offer you some and tell you more about the house?"

Jaron shook his head in long, slow swings. "All right, I'm at least intrigued. Terrified for my safety, but intrigued."

Samantha nudged him again, but with a smile.

Helen showed them upstairs. "You might like either the antique room or the master bedroom, your choice. I'll note, the master does cost more on account of having its own private bath. Usual rate is $65 a night, but being late, I'll charge you $50 for the master or $45 for the antique room."

"Sure. Master bedroom, why not?" Jaron said.

"I do have to ask for the money up front," Helen said with a sheepish smile.

"Of course you do." Jaron sighed.

Because they were on vacation, he had cash on him and happened to have a fifty-dollar bill on hand. He stuffed it in her hand and rolled his eyes. She chuckled and turned on the light as she let them into their room. As they passed through the threshold, Jaron thought he heard voices but in the moment paid it no mind. Perhaps a television was on somewhere.

17 – ANDREW & JOANNA NEWSTED

When the summer of 1970 came, it was as unusual as winter had been. Not only did February see the coldest low temperature recorded, September was in the middle of a heatwave with temperatures well above normal. The boats still went out, though, and it felt a little cooler on the lake. His wrist had healed up nicely, but when it was cold or if rain came, he felt a dull throb. It had been dry, though, and he was able to keep up with the nets.

Joanna and Loretta had taken on a few more houses and were gaining a reputation in town. They were admired throughout the community for their work ethic and good humor. Today, however, Joanna had the day off.

Personally, she liked the heat and had been walking through the woods and around the lake to take in the fresh air and views. On days off without Andrew she would actively avoid being in the house alone, going into town to shop or visiting with Loretta despite there being no work to do. Even though she hadn't seen anything in the house for a while, it still seemed to exhibit a mood. Today it was nice, though, and the sunshine was all she needed.

It was peaceful and quiet walking back into the house, and she even felt genuinely at home. Maybe whatever occupied the house with them was finally accepting them. She opted to relax and went into the sunroom, where a big couch looked out on the trees and lake.

It was dark when she heard the front door shut. It wasn't loud. If anything, it was shut delicately; it was a wonder she heard it at all. She sat up, stretched, then walked into the foyer through the dining room, ready to greet Andrew and offer him a quick dinner since she had slept late. In the low light of the darkened house, his silhouette displayed a heavy burden.

She came around and flipped the lights on with the switch behind him. When she turned around, she saw a single envelope clutched in his hand. Nausea raced through her, her knees felt weak, and she had no idea how to react properly.

"Is that…?"

He opened it and read the first line with saccharine enthusiasm, "Greetings: You are hereby ordered for induction into the Armed Forces of the United States…"

"No. No, no, no."

She grabbed Andrew, sobbing. He could barely wrap his arms around her, already weak himself. They crumpled to the ground and sat on the foyer floor for what felt like hours.

"I know this is probably inappropriate," he said, finally, in a hoarse whisper.

"Anything you want."

"I was thinking *dinner*."

She laughed and buried her face in his chest. They both laughed for a minute, then helped each other up.

Nothing looked good as they milled around in the kitchen. "How can you be *so* hungry yet have *no* appetite?" Andrew asked.

"I feel like I'm living on instinct: eat, sleep, survive." Joanna said.

Firmly shutting the cabinet he was looking in, Andrew said, "Lucy's is still open. Bar food and a few beers sounds nice."

"Okay." Joanna nodded.

They locked up and headed out. The ride into town was quiet. They held each other's hands as they walked into the bar.

Being the middle of the week, only a few people were even in. Lucius saw them and came from behind the bar, approaching them as if he knew exactly what was wrong.

A whole head taller than Andrew, slender though muscular and usually bright-spirited, Lucius—or Lucy—looked like he felt their pain. "I'm terrified to ask. If you don't want to talk about it, that's okay, but I hope you'll let me cover a round for you."

Andrew held up the envelope, which he barely let leave his hand since pulling it from the mailbox at home.

Lucy straightened up and ran his fingers through his usually coiffed golden hair. "That won't do at all." He shoved his hands in his pockets and cocked his head toward the bar, beckoning them to follow him.

They sat down and he poured them each a draft of their favorite beer. They'd only been in a few times, but Lucy had a penchant for remembering people's poisons. He eyeballed them for a moment, tapping his chin as he did.

He pointed to Joanna. "Fried chicken basket with fries."

"That sounds wonderful," she said, smiling.

"That does sound good," Andrew said.

"Nope," Lucy said, wagging his finger. "No, for you… *Hmm*. A cheeseburger might *sound* good…"

Andrew started to nod, but Lucy shook his head. "But a steak is much better suited for a man condemned to war."

"You don't serve steak, Lucy," Andrew said.

"No, I don't. But for you, there will be a nice hot steak delivered shortly. On me."

Andrew wavered on his seat, "No, Lucy, I might take you up on a beer, but at least let me pay for dinner."

"No, sir." Lucy stopped him. "You all have had a rough night already, and that's on top of almost a year of living in fear. I've got this."

"Thank you," Joanna said, placing her hand on Andrew's to stem further argument.

Lucy smiled and left them alone.

Joanna and Andrew sat at the bar tentatively sipping at their beers. Lucy was right. Ever since December, this had been in the back of their minds.

"I'll of course send money home to keep you in the house." Andrew said, then squeezed her hand in his. "I'll come home, I promise."

Tears were streaming down her face, but she nodded.

Lucy was back in front of them, both his hands on the bar, leaning forward with his head hanging low between his shoulders. "Have you considered your options?"

"Options?" Joanna asked.

"Deferment," Lucy suggested. "College courses. Or conscientious objector."

Andrew shook his head. "My Dad went to Korea, he served his country. I'll serve it, too. It may not be a popular war, but we're involved."

Lucy nodded his head. "You are a brave man, Andrew Newsted. I admire that. But avoiding a war you know your nation doesn't belong in is not cowardice. It is taking a stand for personal beliefs and what you know is *right*."

Lucy's chin trembled as he spoke; he was quite impassioned. The subject seemed to affect him.

He leaned in close. "I can easily get you up into Canada. I mean, it's up the *fucking* road! I can send you on a delivery run. If you don't come back, no one would think any worse of you. Start a new life up there; it's a pretty country!"

Joanna squeezed Andrew's hand firmly.

"You said it would be taking a stand," Andrew said. "That's freedom of speech. And I'm not going to use my freedom as an excuse; I will fight for it, and defend it."

Lucy took in a long, deep breath. "A brave man, indeed. I'm sure many friends will come out of the woodwork to help support Joanna, but you have my word, Andrew; Joanna will be perfectly safe while you are gone. She has a safe place here."

As if on cue, one of Lucy's barmen came from the back and delivered steaming hot plates of freshly prepared fried chicken and a beautiful cut of steak. It looked like an elaborate American gourmet. Lucy reached across the bar and placed his hands on theirs, still holding each other's. He gave them a warm, affectionate smile and left them to their dinner.

18 - PHOEBE BACKLUND

Inviting the same local police chief, Errol Mignola, and reporter from the previous séance, Donald Carter, was a difficult task at first. They had seen plenty to convince them that whatever was happening in the house was something they didn't understand, and frankly, didn't care to. Harry was persuasive, though. Phoebe's doctor, Herbert Lawrence, was invited to ensure medical attention, should the need arise, and the local priest, Father Claude Eugene Francis, was counted among the group.

Phoebe had established that the spirits could not be contacted and reacted to nothing but their own stimuli. Harry was satisfied in that conviction. However, Father Francis was selected as he had served in the Great War as a chaplain. The combination of physical and metaphysical horror they were attempting to tease out might best be handled by someone familiar with the borders of life and death.

The last person for their group, Mildred "Millie" Cotter, was a flapper girl that worked at Lucy's Dynamo Bay. It was once a bar the fisherman and loggers visited but had been converted into a restaurant by day and speakeasy by night with the enactment of Prohibition earlier in the year. It was a poorly kept secret that Errol was willing to overlook as long as things stayed quiet. Phoebe had met Millie on occasion visiting Lucian—the eponymous "Lucy"—about spirits of a different kind. Millie was the sort of person who, no matter the circumstances, could fake a smile so brilliantly it put everyone at ease.

With this endeavor, Phoebe wanted someone who could keep things in perspective.

"Now, Phoebe," Harry said, "the first time the spirits really revealed themselves—to your nephew—there were seven people in the house, but that's not how it starts…"

She shook her head. "The best I can tell is that six people need to be outside, one person inside. That person must be alone and in the master bedroom. That person needs to be positioned, it seems, sitting on the corner of the bed nearest the door. Everyone standing outside should then hear a pop, like a light bulb bursting, and then a startled scream."

Harry examined everyone standing in Phoebe's foyer. Their faces were marked with angst, tension, excitement, and disbelief.

"Since Phoebe of course knows her own house," he said, "we'll let her guide us. She'll remain in the house until we hear the scream—"

"Wait," Phoebe said. "This isn't a show anymore. If you want to see what happens, if you want to know everything that occurs, then we need to take our time."

"I think I saw enough last time, do I really want to see *more*?" moaned Chief Mignola.

"C'mon, Chief," Millie said, "like you ain't seen worse than specters. Surely a car crash or fire makes for worse nightmares than a few shadows."

"Shadows and dead bodies I can take," he responded. "They're real. I can see them. I know what they are, where they come from, and how they got there. This house, though? It's not natural."

"Everything has its place and explanation, Chief," Harry said. "That's why we're here. These ghosts can't be spoken to, they're not storybook apparitions. Perhaps *shadows* is right. We're here to find which way the light is shining."

Errol sighed and folded his arms.

Father Francis cleared his throat. "If I might say a word before we start, then? Whether these spirits are natural phenomena, demons, or the restless dead, all of us could do well with the Lord on our side.

Perhaps a blessing upon the house might provide some solace to whatever otherworldly denizens occupy it?"

Millie rolled her eyes and folded her arms, mirroring the Chief's discontent, but didn't protest much more than that.

As he began to say a prayer aloud, they all heard a distinct *click*. Everyone looked around, nerves and excitement plain on their faces, but Phoebe casually nodded, as if she expected this.

"Follow me," she said, and headed up the stairs.

Harry's face was intent. He tried to examine everything as it happened. What was Phoebe doing, what had she been doing, the groups' actions and reactions, and how did his own senses affect his perception?

They followed her as a group, though the Chief lagged, already showing signs of fright while the rest of the group was nervous or confused.

They reached the end of the hall past the master bedroom where a linen closet capped the hallway. A light was on inside and without a word, Phoebe opened the door wide and let everyone look in.

There, on the back wall written in charcoal was a child's scrawl, was a stanza reaching from the ceiling to the floor:

In the House of in between
Life & Death are but a dream
All & Nothing what it seems
Never mind where you are
'Cause this is where you've always been

"Yeah, okay, I'm done," said the Chief.

He started to walk away and Phoebe watched him intently. As he came even with the door to the master bedroom, he glanced in and froze. Phoebe approached him and they exchanged a heated whisper. The Chief looked back and forth, down the stairs and into the bedroom, he clutched at his chest, shook his head and still left.

Phoebe rejoined the group as they continued to examine the writing. "Chief Mignola will wait outside until such a time as he feels it is necessary to rejoin us," she announced. "This is conducive to our efforts, there is no need to attempt to coax him back inside."

Harry approached Phoebe and spoke in a hushed tone. "This could easily be a trick. You could have rigged this before anyone arrived. Writing on the wall? We never saw the wall to begin with, I've never seen this wall. How do I know the writing hasn't been there all the time and you're running a funhouse?"

The skeptic in Harry was burning through and Phoebe was thankful for it. "I need you like *this*, Harry."

He searched her face. She could tell his periphery was searching his surroundings, wondering what else he could have missed, what she hadn't told him.

"I have become complacent and resigned myself to this house; I expect things. You are correct, though. The writing *could* have been there, and it is there as long as anyone looks at it. Once that observation has ended, once you look away, it goes away."

"Sleight of hand is my specialty, Madam Backlund," Harry said, growing impatient. "I have been impressed up until now."

Phoebe cleared her throat loudly to gain everyone's attention and then she looked at the floor. Everyone looked down where she looked, saw nothing, and then looked at each other, confused, while Harry grew more irritated.

"Please look back into the closet," she said.

They were tentative at first, unsure how to respond to the odd exchange. But as they turned back around, they saw that the light was off and the writing was gone.

"Feel free to explain to me how I turned off the light and erased the writing without so much as moving or making a sound, Mr. *Cardo*," she said, using his incognito name. "Or, explain how the light went off without anyone noticing the sudden absence of its glow."

The look of irritation was replaced again with cautious skepticism. Harry entered the closet and reached to pull the chain on the light, but Phoebe beckoned him to hold still.

"Touch the light bulb, if you will," she said. "It was on this entire time, no? It should be hot."

He stood on his toes to reach his fingertips to the bulb and found it to be room temperature. He looked back at her. "A secondary light could explain this."

"Indeed," she nodded. "Examine the walls to your heart's content. You'll even find that I have torn at the wallpaper at the back, seeking to find where the lettering has gone. There is nothing but solid walls and no room within them to fit a secondary light source anyway. As your powers of observation will no doubt attest, you will recall having seen *that* light on. You may also recall that the wallpaper, where I have scratched and marred it, was in pristine condition under the writing."

He ran his hands along shelves, under and over linens, clicking the light on and off, looking for some telltale clue. He spoke as he examined, "Many spiritualists will use false walls, sliding panels, and mirrors. The fact that you boarded up the room next to us provides a sufficient negative space to slide such a false wall."

"Did you hear the sliding of panels?" she asked.

"I did not."

"You could be wrong? You don't have an explanation then?" asked Millie, but her query wasn't mocking. She sounded as though she hoped for some sort of explanation for what she had seen.

Harry touched Millie's shoulders. "If there is a trick here, I do not see how it was pulled off. Not *yet*."

He approached Phoebe. "But a trick it still *could be*. If this is how things start, Madam, I am yet to be sufficiently frightened."

"I would expect nothing less," she said, "but what do I have to gain? I have charged no one for these events."

"You stand to profit, Madam, and you know it," Harry said.

The excitement he'd displayed at the inexplicable apparition in the bedroom was gone. His suspension of disbelief at the manner of the séance the night before was gone and now spun into doubt.

Phoebe knew he sought to debunk spiritualists, catching them in their own tricks. She also knew that in the event he found irrefutable proof of the existence of a connection to the spirit world, there would be a cash prize. Until he alluded to it now, nothing had been said of that matter. She had no interest in his money, anyway; she wanted someone to understand, to validate what she knew, or to explain it sufficiently away.

"The night is young, Sir," she said, with no apology. "I may call it the house of in between, but it gave itself that name, and it does not care if you believe."

19

She shook him hard and hissed a whisper. *"Vinz, wake up!"*

He came to and started to utter a protest, but she clapped her hand to his mouth and made a *shush* sign with her free hand.

"I think someone is in the house," she quavered.

His eyes widened and he listened. It sounded like voices were coming from the foyer—several—and talking rapidly. He nodded, and she pulled her hand away from his mouth.

He slid out of bed while trying to make as little noise as possible and tiptoed across the room and slid open a drawer. Reaching under his folded jeans, he pulled out a sheathed bowie knife.

Meanwhile, she grabbed her cellphone from her nightstand and prepared to dial 9-1-1. The knife glinted in the low light. She didn't say anything, but he saw the terror cross her face.

"I've got no signal!" she whispered.

His head and shoulders slumped. Persevering, he squared himself and snuck up to the door and flung it open, yelling, "I'm armed and not alone. We're calling the police! Leave now, we haven't seen you!"

The whispering was incessant. He gritted his teeth and burst onto the landing, expecting to see people in the foyer or the sweeps of flashlights. However, there was nothing; the sound died down and suddenly it was a quiet house. Taking slow, steady breaths, he listened for any sound, then the whispering started again. But now he noticed movement. The big circular window above the front door revealed leaves battering the glass in a whirlwind.

He straightened up and let out a sigh of relief. He turned and leaned against the wall between the stairs and the bedroom door. "It's leaves against the window. I'll get up on the roof of the veranda tomorrow and sweep them down."

"Oh, *now* it has a signal." She shook her head in the light of her cellphone.

Looking back up, she saw he was grinning at her. "What? It wasn't funny! It was *scary*, and you were scared, *too*."

"Not that." He shook his head. "You called me *Vinz*, even though it was a potentially dangerous situation. I would think if there was ever a time to call me by name, it would be something serious. Potential home invasion? Still get called a pet-name."

"What?" she grumbled. "Sometimes I have to think about what your name is; it's weird calling you that. You're my *Vinz*… you're my *key master—*"

Suddenly he whipped his head over his shoulder to look behind him, then bolted for the extra rooms across the landing. She yelped in surprise and cried out his name. He didn't hear it, though. All he was concerned with was getting whoever was hiding in the bedrooms.

He could sense them, hear their footsteps and breathing. He went through one door and heard another in the hall open and close. Bounding into the hall again, he could *see* them standing, confused, at the opening of the landing. He rushed and lashed out; he could feel the knife connect with flesh. The weight of their body hit the floor. As he turned, though, there was nothing.

"What the hell are you doing?" she cried out from the bedroom doorway. "You're scaring me. Stop it!"

"You didn't see anyone?"

"What are you talking about?" she demanded. "You took off and I look out to find you waving your knife around in the air."

"No one at all?"

He reached for the light switch across from their bedroom. Nobody, nothing on the landing at all. Rushing through the rooms and turning on all the lights, he continued to find emptiness. Beginning to realize the only thing out of the ordinary was him, he put the knife down on the kitchen counter and went back upstairs.

She was still standing in the bedroom doorway, terrified.

"I'm sorry," he said. "I really thought I heard someone. I swear I *saw* them, but… well, there's nothing." Embarrassed, he shook his head.

She hugged him and petted the back of his head. "I miss her, too. We're stressed. It's too quiet and we know she's not down the hall. A serial killer on the loose certainly doesn't help a good night's rest, either."

Trying to lighten the mood, she continued, "I called you by name…"

He hugged her tightly. "I didn't even hear it. I really thought I was chasing someone." Letting go, he looked her in the eyes. "I'm really sorry. I didn't mean to scare you."

"Be my key master *after* you turn off all the lights."

"Yes, *Zuul*, we shall call Gozer in one of his pre-chosen forms." He huffed off with a laugh.

He went back downstairs to turn out the lights. By himself again and hearing the shuffling of feet and creak of wood as she crawled back into bed, he felt incredibly alone. With the lights off save the one over the sink, which they left on as a nightlight, he leaned against the counter and stared at the knife. It was clean and shiny— no blood, not a smear of any kind.

What had he seen? Was it stress of missing his daughter or scary stories on the news? It had been there, right out in front of him. He knew he had chased it, knew he heard all those sounds. But he hadn't heard her call his name. He closed his eyes and shook his head. Twelve months was a long time to be jumping at shadows.

20 - CYNTHIA MORRISON

Chuck was another redhead like Cynthia, and to see the two of them together, one might think they were related. Cynthia and Chuck both had a penchant to mess with their hair; Cynthia pulled at curls along the right side of her head, and Chuck pet the edges of his goatee. They usually worked with each other in the field and had developed a quiet trust and friendship. With that friendship was a mutually amused frustration with the camera-happy Reggie and Thom.

Cynthia had wanted to see what Chuck was talking about with the footsteps. She also wanted to check out the nearly countless video feeds Reggie and Thom had set up. The van was equipped with six widescreen monitors. Each was split into six screens apiece. And even some of those were alternating between cameras.

"How many cameras are also recording to memory cards?" Cynthia asked.

Chuck leaned forward to check the inventory checklist. "All of them."

They chuckled, but it was Cynthia that noticed a small change in one of the monitors.

"What the hell is that?" she asked.

Chuck leaned forward again and called the screen in question to full screen. It was one of the more recently set up, pointing at the jammed closet. The door was hanging open. They looked at each other.

"You want to come see?" she said, with a wild gleam in her eye. "Fuck no."

Laughing, she bolted out of the van, leaving Chuck to stare at the mysteriously open closet door on the monitor. He tracked the video back slowly. She had noticed it right as it popped open. The handle didn't move, the door just opened.

He adjusted his earpiece and microphone. "Be careful, Cynthia."

"Cynthia? What about the rest of us?" Thom cried back.

"You and Reggie put up so many cameras I'll be able to tell you something's happening before you even see it," Chuck said.

"That's the idea," answered Reggie.

He watched as Cynthia walked through the front door, passing Marcus, Shannon, and Noah talking next to the TRAP. But Shannon quickly followed, hearing Cynthia say the closet was open. Noah and Marcus checked the monitors.

Reggie and Thom were sitting along the window benches in the front living room and got up to follow the ladies. Chuck tracked the group, alternating screens as they made it to the top of the stairs. Cynthia now appeared on two screens: the main hallway shot, and the camera right in front of the closet. She looked back to the others. Nerves and excitement filled her face as she turned and reached for the closet handle.

The closet cast unusual shadows when the door came open. Thom shined a little flashlight into the back of the closet and knew at once they had a killer shot. There was writing on the back wall.

"Are you seeing this, Chuck?" Cynthia asked.

"Yes, ma'am," he confirmed.

"What is it?" Noah yelled from downstairs.

Reggie ran back down the hall. "You'll want to come up and see this for yourself. I don't know if your device is going to pick this up. Not without knowing what you're looking for."

Marcus and Noah followed them upstairs, where they all crowded the small doorway at the end of the hall.

"I know you're all excited, but you're killing my view. Can I get someone to take the camera in there?" Chuck asked.

No one responded, but Reggie turned back and detached the camera from the low standing tripod. He carried in the camera as they found a light switch in the closet. Four feet deep with shelves on either side, it was bare, save for the writing on the back wall. It appeared to be written in charcoal smudges in children's handwriting, but it stretched from the edge of the ceiling to the baseboards.

In the House of in between
Life & Death are but a dream
All & Nothing what it seems
Never mind where you are
'Cause this is where you've always been

"I don't care what your chronotons say about this, Mr. Benjamin. This is fucking creepy," Thom said.

"I will not argue with you," Noah said, gaping at the image.

"Get a shot of the entire interior, Reggie," Cynthia asked. "Try to find out why the door was stuck; make sure there're no cracks on the doorframe."

The camera panned around dusty shelves and bare walls. The doorframe was in perfect shape.

Then a loud thud, like the one they had heard before, came from the primary bedroom.

Everyone jumped, including Chuck in the van. He pulled up the shot of the bedroom and chills ran over his body and a lump formed in his throat. He tried to speak, croaking instead.

"Check the master bedroom," he finally managed to spit out.

"Why, what's in there?" Thom asked.

"In where?" Marcus asked.

"Main bedroom," Cynthia said.

Marcus, Shannon, and Noah wasted no time. They walked back down the hall without question and opened the bedroom door, only to find nothing. They checked the closet and bathroom and saw nothing.

"What did he see?" Noah asked.

"Get everyone out here," Chuck replied. "You're gonna have to see it for yourselves. And get them earpieces."

They all piled out of the house in the dwindling daylight and headed to the TV van. With hearts still pounding, they chattered in fear and excitement.

Chuck already had what he wanted to show them cued up. One full screen for the primary bedroom, and the hallway shot on another to show them side by side. They all crammed around Chuck in the van and stared at the paused screens.

"I reeled everything back to when Cynthia noticed the closet door open," Chuck said, "but I don't see anything on any of the screens until after you all were in the closet. Then there's this."

The video started. They stood around the closet door with Reggie inside filming. In the primary bedroom, however, the darkness from the bathroom seemed to extend outward and distorted the light from the window. As the thud sounded, a figure formed out of the shadow. It was featureless but resembled a male shape. It shrank out of view and the light returned to normal as Noah, Marcus, and Shannon made their way to the bedroom.

"Holy shit," Reggie said quietly.

"Wow," Marcus said in a long breath.

"Welcome to the *House of In Between*, folks," Chuck said.

Noah slapped him on the back. "Good find."

"Are we sure we're not alone?" Cynthia asked. "I mean, that was an audible sound, plus video evidence, right after a previously jammed door mysteriously opening?"

"No, you're right," Noah agreed. "It's good to remain skeptical, rule out all possibilities. Let's sweep the house again, lots of light, handheld cameras…"

"And everyone needs to stay in touch," Chuck said, offering Marcus, Noah, and Shannon earpieces and battery packs. "These should last all night long. Keep it on and up the entire time."

The group of six left Chuck in the van and headed back to the now quiet house, where they went about turning on every light they could. They checked closets, floorboards, walls—everything they could put their hands on. Chuck watched them intently from the van, feeling both safer by himself in the van, but also terrified, like he was watching a horror film unfolding in real time right before him.

21 – CHASE, ADRIANNE, BRENDA, AND HELEN

Adrianne and Chase sat on the veranda of the Grand Marais Haunted Bed and Breakfast. Taking a long drag from his cigarette, Chase scratched at several days' worth of growth on his face. Adrianne stared out over the front yard at the gravel drive and the cars parked there. Her sister Brenda stepped quietly through the front door and looked at them both.

"Where did you find this place again?" she asked her sister.

Adrianne swallowed to clear her throat, the sound audible in the still autumn air. "USA Online. Some urban legends chatroom. These people were talking about haunted houses and what they'd experienced, where they'd been. I looked a few of them up. When I saw this one was on the lake, and we were going to be close by anyway…"

"You don't get to pick where we stay ever again," Brenda said as she motioned to Chase to give her a cigarette.

They didn't look like sisters. Brenda was a redhead, short, and skinny; Adrianne had dark brown hair, was tall and imposing with wide, intense eyes. They also had opposite dispositions: Brenda was the aggressive smack-talker; Adrianne was content to sit back and people-watch. When they bickered, though, it was obvious they were siblings.

Chase had a wife at home but had grown up across the street from the sisters, and many of their family vacations had been together. They kept the tradition going into adulthood. They were the sisters he never had.

"It wasn't that bad," he said.

"Are you kidding me?" Brenda asked. "You had it the worst."

Chase shrugged. "I don't know; I would think seeing someone stabbed to death against my bedroom wall has to be worse."

"Huh-uh," Brenda argued. "I told you I couldn't tell if that happened or if I was still half asleep and freaked out from the noises earlier. You got *hit*."

Adrianne craned her neck to look at them both. "You got hit?"

Brenda huffed, "You were *there*!"

"I saw him fall down—I thought he tripped."

Chase nodded, responding through a stifled yawn and exhaled smoke. "I probably tripped."

"How do you trip from a standstill, Chase?" Brenda puffed on her cigarette and leaned against the house. "Even you aren't that much of a klutz."

Chase yawned again, this time standing to stretch his tall, once-athletic frame. He leaned forward and grabbed the railing. All three of them stared out into the trees that lined the drive and masked the interstate, reflecting on their night in the infamous haunted house.

"There was a story of this couple who saw the house on fire from the highway, but when they pulled up it was fine," Adrianne explained. "After their story got around, business here picked up."

"I went through a few name changes before settling for the rather generic *Haunted Bed and Breakfast*," a woman's voice said from in the middle of them.

They all jumped, startled, and turned to see Helen the innkeeper. "Every iteration where I tried to involve Madam Backlund's name sounded like a brothel, at best."

Chase chuckled and shook his head, finishing off his cigarette. He stepped down into the gravel to snuff it out. "I bet business was *really* good, then."

"*Interest* was, indeed," Helen played along. "But something about an old woman and her perennially sleeping husband doesn't seem too appeasing to *that* sort of patron."

"Given enough time, I'm sure *somebody* would have come calling for that," Brenda joked.

"Tacking on the word 'haunted' seemed to do the trick, though," Helen continued. "I really have the internet to thank, though. And a house willing to put on a performance fairly regularly."

"Aren't you terrified to be in there?" Adrianne asked. "Is it true Phoebe Backlund called demons to the house?"

Helen tut-tutted, "Oh, if only it were demons, those could probably be dealt with. This house has been blessed, probably by every new priest that hears about it. Whatever they are, you learn to stay out of their way. I'll admit, when I'm bleary-eyed and my husband has gone early in the morning for work and there's a figure looming at the door, it can be unsettling."

Brenda pointed as if Helen had made a point for her. "See! Half asleep and you only think you saw something is *unsettling* at best."

Helen smiled. "You saw something? That room is usually good for a story. It can be quite active."

"I don't know." Brenda shook her head. "We were watching the news and there was all that crap about Iraq—and there were the noises upstairs. I probably had a nightmare. I don't think I can really say something I saw in the middle of the night was a *ghost*. Chase, though, before we all went to bed, he got *hit* and went to the floor at the top of the stairs. Right in front of your room. I'm surprised you didn't check it out."

"As you say, bumps in the middle of the night are hard to judge." Helen shrugged. She looked at Chase, though with a hint of concern. "Are you okay?"

Chase nodded. "I'm fine. Better than I was before I got here, I think. It was an experience I think I can safely say I'll cherish."

"You're nuts," Brenda said as she put her cigarette out on the bottom of her shoe and flicked the butt out into the gravel.

She went back inside, presumably to pack.

Chase diligently found and picked up the cigarette butt out of the gravel. "Do you have an outside trash? I don't want to stink up your kitchen."

"It's around the side of the house," Helen said. "Thank you."

Adrianne continued to stare, almost unblinking, out into nothing. "What did you see?" Helen asked her.

Adrianne finally blinked a few times and shook her head. "I didn't see anything. I heard. I mean, I saw Chase fall, but I only heard whispering. We all heard bumps and rattling sounds before we went to bed. But that room I was in—that hutch—something was in it. Something was crying. I didn't sleep at all."

"I've heard it before," Helen confirmed. "Something scared."

"My heart ached, but I was terrified, too."

Chase came back around the front of the house. "I really want to thank you for letting us stay in your home. I think after the shock wears off, we'll definitely look back on this fondly."

Helen smiled brightly and stepped back inside as she said. "No, thank *you*; after all, you paid for it."

Chase sat down next to Adrianne again and packed his cigarettes before lighting another one.

"What do you mean you'll cherish this?" she asked. "That was horrifying. I really did not expect that at all."

Chase leaned back. "Dacia and I are getting a divorce."

Adrianne snapped out of her shock. "What?"

Chase nodded. "I've been staying in an apartment the last few weeks. Probably where I'll end up staying for a while. I've been drinking a lot, too."

"I had no idea. I mean, I didn't notice anything…" Adrianne said, lost for how to respond.

"We drank a lot last night, but I didn't feel it. Drinking's just what I do now."

He continued to answer her original question. "So, we're going up the stairs, being entirely too noisy while trying to be quiet, but I could already hear them: the voices at the top of the stairs."

He leaned forward and started to gesture with his hands. "You two were in front of me, heading to your rooms. That's when I heard something behind me, so I turned around and felt like I was hit. Weird, though. It wasn't like I was hit by some*thing*, but a force shoved me down. So, I'm there staring at the floor, and I hear you and Brenda turn around and react. And on the floor in front of my face I see these drops of water *appear*, like, *plop!* drops of water on the floor. Then this voice, almost inside of my head, but all around, too, says, 'I'm the ghost.' And all this shit going on at home and all the scary nonsense about this house and war and being a grown up when I still feel like a kid—all of it went away."

He inhaled off his cigarette and immediately sighed, the smoke rolling out through his nostrils. "I realized I'm gonna end up dead if I don't get my act together. Maybe a ghost hit me, maybe I tripped, maybe I really was drunk and could have fallen down the stairs and died last night. But here I am now and I'm thinking things will get better—but only if I quit screwing around trying to become a ghost myself."

Adrianne was still at a loss for words and only stared at him, looking as lost as she had been before looking out over the drive.

"So, thank you, Adrianne," he said with a toothy smile. "We may have had a scary night, but I think it was what I needed."

"Happy to be of service," she said, unsure.

Brenda came out carrying all their bags. "Can we leave now? All of the doors in the house, every one of them, slammed shut. I'm done here. I need a boat and a beer."

Chase stood up and took a couple of bags from her as they headed over to the car. Adrianne wondered if there was some divine providence to their stay. If what Chase said was true, and he felt like he was on a better path, maybe her and Brenda's frights really would be worth it.

22 – ANDREW NEWSTED

After Basic and Advanced Individual Training, Andrew was allowed to come home on leave. His and Joanna's mothers came up to visit. The day he came home, in addition to family, Andrew's fishing crew was there; Loretta had come, and Lucy sent a keg free of charge. He arrived in his Army greens; the girls cried, and the boys laughed and patted him on the back.

A few families had seen their boys drafted in Grand Marais, this wasn't the only welcome home party going on, and in the evening, several of the families were supposed to gather up in the Cook County Community Center. Right now, though, Andrew wanted nothing more than to be with his wife, at least for a little while. He stole her away from the party and they went upstairs to their bedroom.

"They've made you so skinny," Joanna said, running her hands along his sides.

"I swear, when I'm back, the fishing will be like a vacation." He rolled his eyes. "They work us from sunup to sundown, running, jumping, climbing, crawling over and over. It might be fun if there wasn't all the yelling. *And* knowing what's coming."

Joanna grimaced and her eyes grew moist. "I'm sorry. I'm home *now*, that's all that matters." But he knew it was a line.

They stood in their room and she hugged him tight. "It's been quiet, so quiet in the house without you. I was afraid I would have more nightmares or see stuff, but it's been quiet."

"Good," he said. "I want you to feel safe, especially in our own home."

"I'll feel safe when you're home for good."

"I know. But I'm here for a week and then it's only a year. Can you believe we've really been here *longer* than a year?"

"Yes," she said, "I can because it has felt like it."

He smiled and hugged her tight. "Come on—let's get back down there before they start getting the wrong idea."

"What's wrong with the *wrong idea*, hmm?" She tugged at the edges of his shirt. "My fit-man, all dressed up."

He laughed. "I'm going to hold you to that once we clear everyone out."

He opened the bedroom door and stepped into the hallway. Before Joanna followed him out he thought he saw the door between the two smaller rooms across the balcony swinging back and forth. His steps stuttered. Joanna ran into him and asked what he was doing. When he looked back, the door was shut tight. Two people in a house full of rooms. They didn't use the rooms but hoped to fill them up with a family; a plan that kept getting postponed.

"What—what is it?" she asked him.

He shook his head. "Déjà vu or something. Let's get downstairs."

He couldn't bring himself to share what he saw. Not anything from before, not now; even this may have been his imagination. He couldn't compromise her sense of security. He was near to being a world away and—as much as he was afraid of it himself—potentially never coming home again.

~

Joanna got the week off and hosted her and Andrew's mothers. The house gave them no problems. Andrew worried all week that something would happen after seeing the door inexplicably swinging. It was brief; it could have been a trick of the light. But coupled with Joanna's experiences and his own, he felt unwelcome in his own home.

Something nagged him, urging him to escape. He sat in his recliner in the sitting room with a small fire going and the ladies watched something on TV, he didn't even know what.

Escape.

He shook his head. Escape from *what*—his own house? No, he wasn't afraid of his house. He was afraid of the war and the war came to him in this house. It wasn't fair that all of this was making him anxious in his own home. How could he leave Joanna here?

She had said she hadn't seen anything, that she felt okay. There were their friends, too. Loretta, of course, would see her most often and he trusted his fishing crew to look in on her and keep her company. They all had wives or girlfriends, she wouldn't be lacking for companionship. He looked over to her and she happened to catch his glance and smiled back.

He stood up, straighter than felt comfortable. He had to force himself to relax. It was okay, this was *home*. "Ladies, I'm beat. It's been a long day and I think I shall retire; I'll probably wake up early, anyway."

Joanna got up with him, "Mom," she said to her mother, then looking to Mrs. Newsted, "*Mom*, good night. Feel free with the TV and anything in the kitchen."

Both moms stood up, his own mother hugging him tightly, "I'm so glad you're home, even if for a little while."

He looked at her in the low orange glow and knew she was happy to see him, but terrified of every passing minute as well. He could see her looking at him as she probably had the first time he rode a bicycle with no training wheels, or when he went to school on his own. This, though, he might not come back from and the fear of it all was plain across her face. He hadn't seen her or Joanna's mother since last Christmas. Both looked as if they'd aged years in days: more gray hairs, a few more wrinkles, and a frailty to their frames he didn't recognize.

"I'll be back before you know it," he said. "I'm here now, but I'm tired. Maybe I can take you all out on the lake tomorrow."

"It's freezing, Andrew!" Joanna said.

He thought about it a moment. It was January 1971. He hadn't seen their mothers in *over* a year. It was Christmas '69 when they'd gone back to Nebraska to visit for a weekend. That had been a tearful, somber experience, too.

He shook his head. "Some warm coats, a couple of fishing poles, we'll have a great time!"

Joanna smothered the fire leaving glowing coals to warm their mothers who were going to stay up a bit later. Looping her arm through his, she led Andrew up the stairs and to bed, shutting the door softly behind them.

Thinking nothing of the lights being off, Andrew began to undress on his side of the bed. It would feel great to sleep in his own bed again, instead of the flattened-out cushion of a mattress he had at basic. And after his leave was up, he may not sleep in a proper bed for an entire year! The thoughts kept him from noticing Joanna stripping down to nothing at all.

Joanna approached him silently and pressed her naked body against his back, rubbing his chest and shoulders with her hands. He reached back and touched her thighs, then turned on the spot and embraced her, kissing her and lifting her up onto the bed. She put her finger to his lips to keep him quiet, reminding him that tonight they really *weren't* alone.

They made love, trying to make it last as long as they could stand without making a sound. When they finished, Joanna didn't roll off him but stayed on top, laying her head on his shoulder. He wrapped his arms around her, and they laid there holding each other until they fell asleep.

A clicking sound, like a door popping open, woke Andrew. Looking around the room, nothing was out of order, but the noise sounded purposeful. He and Joanna had changed positions in their sleep, and he had been curled up with her back to his chest. He slowly slid out from under the covers and grabbed his boxer shorts.

Looking left down the hallway, where their mothers were staying in the small bedrooms, Andrew saw nothing. Every door was closed: their mothers' doors, the door to the room across from them—even the upstairs restroom door was closed. To his right, though, a sliver of light beamed through the jam of the closet at the end of the hall. With a furrowed brow, he stared at it for a long time. He hadn't heard footsteps going by, and he hadn't heard the pull chain for the light in the closet clicking. It was the closet door popping open. Unusual, since that door usually stuck and was hard to pull open, forcing them to use it for things they didn't need too often.

He forced himself to walk down the hallway, passing the door of the room with no windows, which made him think for a moment that when he got back, he would cut those windows back out. He reached the closet and pulled it open, readying his body to spring, either into attack or away. No one stood on the other side of the door, though. But against the back wall was crude, childish writing, smudged in what looked like charcoal from the ceiling to the floor:

In the House of in between
Life & Death are but a dream
All & Nothing what it seems
Never mind where you are
'Cause this is where you've always been

"Holy shit," he said, drawing out each syllable.

23 - NOAH BENJAMIN

With the temperature dropping, the group had invited—*insisted*—that Chuck come in.

He refused, even though hours had passed without incident. Though they adjusted the thermostat, Reggie and Thom gathered loose sticks from around the house and made a small fire in the fireplace. Everyone was starting to relax; even the TRAP finally calmed down and showed normal readings.

Thom looked at his phone to check the time again. "Hey, I don't have any service."

Reggie laughed. "Excuse him, he doesn't read the technical briefings. If it says 'FCC,' he checks out."

"The TRAP purposefully mutes radio signals unless we know the frequency," Shannon explained. "After the Bluetooth incident in Boston, we had to make sure we were reading only our signals. We have our equipment flagged, but cellular is too 'loud,' so we make a bubble around the machine."

"The blocking field isn't large," Noah said. "If you need to make a call, service should kick back in about ten feet away from the house."

"No, I just noticed," Thom said. "I'd only call Reggie if I was this scared any other time—and he's here."

Reggie scoffed. "You want to check us in together to make your ex jealous."

"Oh?" Noah asked. "Are you all…"

"No!" Thom said with a laugh. "Well, we dated a few times but nothing serious came of it."

"I wasn't trying to pry," Noah said.

"It's all right," Reggie said. "He likes prying, that's why we make better friends.; easier to gossip with a friend than to have a nag in your ear all the time."

Thom flipped Reggie off, and everyone chuckled.

"Okay," Reggie said, changing the subject. "We've looked all over the house for vagrants or kids and… nothing. Not a broken window or busted-in door. What's with the writing in the closet and what the hell did Chuck see on the monitor?"

Chuck chimed in through all their earpieces, "No ghost stories, please!"

They all laughed again, but Noah answered anyway. "I have no idea about the rhyme upstairs; that might be some recent graffiti. The door sticking may be foundation problems. The temperature changing outside, us in here, and having the electricity on; maybe it popped itself open. But the apparition—that may be part of the history of this house. It's said no one can stay too long in the primary bedroom. Apparently, Phoebe Backlund didn't even stay in there despite living here for years."

"Locals know the stories of Phoebe as *Madam* Backlund," Cynthia said, "the crazy old spiritualist conducting her séances. But other stories about the house never mention people by name. Are there any other firmly documented hauntings here?"

"Oh yes," Noah said, excited to share some history. "The last family here, like Dennis and Lucas explained, dropped off the face of the Earth after moving out. I can't say for certain if they were affected by the house. Holding onto it like they are, and Dennis's explanation that they don't want anyone else moving in… I don't know; *maybe*? They could have been haunted; they could want to come back someday.

"Before them, the owner ran a bed-and-breakfast out of the house. They didn't advertise it as haunted, but word spread through chatrooms on the early internet that made it a tourist destination of its own for a few years. It was a couple that thought they saw the house on fire from the interstate that started that."

Reggie piped up. "I read about that when we were researching the house. They stopped to check out the fire and make sure no one was hurt or inside. But the lady who owned the place coaxed them into staying. I don't think she had any other guests that evening and the couple was a little leery. She convinced them everything was on the up-and-up, but as the night wore on, they thought they were being harassed by the owners. They didn't have any cellular service either, but I think they were on old bricks, anyway. By the time they got out, they threatened to sue because they thought everything was faked or the work of the owners. Word got around and the house thrived on the haunting stories for several years. She passed away still owning the house."

Noah nodded. "It stood empty for a few years after that, much like today, and again in the eighties when several attempts to demolish it were made. Issues ranging from proper permits and licenses to freak equipment failure make it seem like the house refused to go down. I think between Phoebe's passing up until the sixties, it passed between a few owners with minor documented events. It was a young couple in the late sixties that had some of the worst experiences in the house, if only because they simply could not escape."

Cynthia stopped him. "You know, we had a hard time pulling up a comprehensive story, Noah, and we're basically right next door in Duluth. This house exists in forum posts and amateur websites. How is it you know so much? And what was Lucas on about when he stopped short with you?"

Marcus and Shannon smiled.

"And why do those two seem to get giddy when this mystery topic comes up?" she asked, folding her arms.

Noah looked around nervously, then let out a heavy sigh. "When I was a kid," he started, "when my group of friends was frightened out of the woods? I thought I was going to die."

He quickly caught Reggie, Thom, and Chuck up on his experience before going on.

"When I studied the woods as an average paranormal investigator…" he trailed off and laughed to himself. "As average as something like that can be. When I was out there looking for EVPs and orbs, I kept thinking to myself, *why can't I remember it*? The evening was gone to me. I was thirteen when it happened. I remember things from earlier clearly. But that night, all I remember is *fear*. When I finally got my hands on the TRAP, the woods were the first place I went. I set it up. I knew exactly what I was doing. When I saw the results, I knew what had happened—and why I couldn't remember. Two people died that night: Sophie and Prairie Dinklage."

Cynthia let out a gasp. "The last victims of the *Corpse*."

He confirmed. "Grand Marais's very own serial killer from the early 2000s. Sophie was the adult with us that night. She often chaperoned the neighborhood kids when we'd go on our adventures, thanks to her daughter. She was a single mother; her daughter Prairie was never more than two feet away from our group. A major nuisance, but the group loved her like a sister and defended her justly. But a group of boys was no match for—"

"That happened *here*," Cynthia interrupted.

Noah pointed up and out randomly. "About six miles from here." His throat hitched as he continued. "Sophie and Prairie didn't leave *anything* behind. I knew, later in life, *what* had happened. But I didn't realize—*understand*—what had happened so close and at what time. The machine showed him come upon our camp—easy targets for a killer whose M.O. was to shoot people dead in a location they might not be found for a while. The Echo didn't even show them move. He opened their tent and shot them. That's when the rest of us got up, scared, and ran. Chronotons move over everything and leave marks everywhere, but for some reason these *traumatic* events leave deeper marks. Us kids running was bright and clear in the readings, but Sophie and Prairie were barely distinguishable from their surroundings."

The group hung on every word. The room was silent for a moment.

"Yeah," Noah started back up. "I grew up around here. I know the stories. Backlund House, haunted graveyard, serial killer infamy. And Lucas? I mean, he owns the best kept secret around here. He knows everything and everyone, that's sort of his draw. His family's been here forever. He grew up with the stories, too. But it's seeing that ghosts are more related to actions or to how people act. If we can solve this mystery, maybe we can discover our lasting mark on the universe."

"As tickled pink as I am to hear your scary ass shit, Mr. Benjamin," Chuck said into their ears, "you've got some activity upstairs again. The kids' rooms. They're… *Christ*, it's like they're *breathing*. I can hear breathing and the door between the two rooms is moving back and forth. Please, please, *please* check this out carefully."

Shannon and Marcus wasted no time. They made their way upstairs stealthily while Noah and the others checked on the TRAP. Marcus activated his glasses, which were synced to the TRAP. The two devices could share data and visuals. It also acted as a video recorder and still photography camera. They shared the feed from the headmount with the television crew. At the top of the stairs, Marcus looked back down at Noah for confirmation. Noah looked at the screen with some confusion, then without looking at his team, signed that the readings had gone back to static and patched the TRAP to Marcus' display. Marcus and Shannon exchanged nervous glances but continued forward.

Cynthia knelt close to Noah, stabilizing herself by holding his shoulder. He turned his head and met her eyes. They were scared.

She asked, "What if there's someone up there, for real?"

He pointed to some blobs in the quivering wireframe of the house. "That's Marcus and Shannon," he whispered. "Chronotons affect us, react with us—but by being such mobile and active objects, it's harder for the sensors to penetrate and track the chronotons on us, making for nearly blank spots. Here's us. We're all accounted for and no one else is here."

Looking back up, Marcus was staring wide-eyed and intently into the nearer kids' room. Shannon signed they could see the door moving.

Noah called up Marcus's visual on one of the screens so they could see what he saw. "With this we can confirm what we're looking at," Noah whispered. "Shannon and I usually wear them as well; they allow us to analyze our own points of view later and determine the veracity of our own observations."

Marcus took another furtive step forward, then froze. The door slammed between the kids' rooms loudly. Then the door to the further room opened and slammed; the room across the hall slammed; Marcus fell and Shannon yelped. The upstairs living room door slammed, and coming from somewhere was a distant sound of shattering glass.

"That should be it." Noah said knowingly.

Things got quiet, and the "static" on the TRAP also seemed to settle down.

"That was the *chase*!" Shannon said, perhaps too loud.

"I felt like I lost my footing," Marcus said. "I had a hell of an urge to get up and run, like I was slamming the doors myself to slow down a pursuer."

"What's 'the chase?'" asked Cynthia.

"I know this one," Thom said. "Supposedly inhabitants would catch someone lurking in the kids' rooms, and when they were found out spying, the 'intruder' would give chase. There would be the urge to run and hide, slamming random doors but running into that living room, the intruder would chase the victim right out of the window. It's always been a bullshit story because there's never been an emergency call to the house for an injury."

Shannon opened the living room door where the windows were intact on the opposite wall. "You all heard the glass shattering, right?"

"It sounded distant—but yeah." Thom confirmed.

Marcus leaned against the railing and took a few calming breaths. "Anything on the earlier readings or this?"

"No correlations." Noah said with confidence. "Nothing has ever happened in this house up to now that would explain these events."

"So?" Marcus said.

Noah stood up from his chair and puffed his chest. "We have a bona fide inexplicable paranormal event. This is entirely out of the confines of explanation. The more evidence we can gather, through the TRAP, video, audio, our own accounts and testimony, we can try to put together a picture to explain the mystery of this house."

"How many more stories do we have to go through?" Thom asked with a huff.

"I'll go through as many as it takes," Reggie said. "We're the only ones here and we're recording it all. This is going to be huger than huge! Let's get some reaction shots."

Cynthia patted Noah on the shoulder and followed Reggie and Thom back into the sitting room.

24 – HARRY HOUDINI

Harry remained upstairs and slowly examined everything he could see and touch. He entered the closet, the séance room, the master bedroom. He tried to find some evidence of trickery. The more he looked, the more he debunked his own ideas. Phoebe sat downstairs in the reading room and stared out into the front yard where Chief Mignola sat in his car, staring back at the house. Doctor Lawrence and Father Francis discussed the War in the sunroom. Millie and Donald flirted in the kitchen.

The soft chatter of the four speaking with each other stopped in coincidental sync, causing an awkward silence. The void of sound perked both Phoebe and Harry's ears. Phoebe knew what to listen to, but the light-footed sprint from the end of the hall to before the doors of the upstairs living room signaled that Harry had heard it as well.

Donald peeked in on Phoebe with a questioning look. She could hear the doctor and priest quietly enter the foyer. Phoebe stood from her chair and slipped into the foyer as well, followed by Donald and Millie. Standing almost on his toes, Harry had one hand up, finger to his lips. The other hand reached out towards those below, signaling for them to still.

They all listened intently, but Millie heard it first and gasped sharply. "Is that… *breathing?*"

Harry waved his hand, trying to silence her. He slinked forward to look into the small bedroom near the balcony. Only he could see the door between the two small rooms swinging back and forth. He kept his eyes on it intently, but also on those below. The silence had been serendipity; there was no way Phoebe could have orchestrated random conversation to end and trigger this eerie scene. The clockwork appearance of the house's activities was too refined; the house itself seemed to act with intent.

The reality was in the perception, looking away or changing his focus could break the event. He continued to listen, trying to pinpoint exactly where it was. Continuing through the hall, he entered the further of the two small rooms and could still see the door swinging. Oddly, the room on the other side was much darker, as if the windows were blocked with heavy curtains. As he looked deeper into the room, he saw the shadow of a man. Looking through the window to the front yard, it was dark outside. But in his periphery, he could see daylight through the window to his right.

The shadow suddenly moved in a menacing lunge towards him, and he slammed the door in an effort to block whatever it was. It had been purely reactionary; an animalistic urge despite his refined self-control that, even in the moment, confused him. He ran through the door he had come in and slammed it as well. He stumbled against the hallway wall and tripped up, then felt something rush past. The double doors of the upstairs living room burst open with such force that they immediately bounced back and shut, followed by the sounds of a violent scuffle and glass shattering.

Harry quickly picked himself up and threw open the doors, only to find nothing out of place and the windows intact. He looked down at Phoebe, "Those were the sounds we would have heard in the séance room, yes?"

She nodded her affirmation.

Father Francis crossed himself, and Dr. Lawrence rushed up the stairs to check on Harry.

"That was *amazing!*" Donald said. Millie hung on his arm and stared on in confused terror.

Harry cupped the right side of his neck, then checked his hand as though he expected to see something.

"Are you okay?" Dr. Lawrence asked.

"I felt a pinch and pressure at my neck as I fell, like a laceration."

Dr. Lawrence looked but saw nothing. They only exchanged curious, nervous glances.

"These things happen," Phoebe said. "They can be set off by where you stand or what you see or hear at any particular moment. At first there was no discernible order to them. But like this house, there are joints to the events, a structure that holds them all together. You may see only one room at a time, or you may follow the events from beginning to end."

Harry and Doctor Lawrence came down the stairs, and they all gathered around as she continued to explain.

"The stanza in the closet is an opening," she said. "It is both the result of these events and the cause. What you saw, Mr. Houdini, involves at least five people, or whatever these specters are. We will see it again, and it will happen over and over for however long these things happen. Perhaps one day if the house is destroyed, it will then be over. But for now, it is the beginning of a terrible fate for whoever was involved in whatever this is. Three people die, and the other two go through the window. It is not a terribly high drop, but I know I would not want to go through a window falling ten feet to the earth. But it is not over there. If you are prepared and willing, all of you, we may *begin*."

She said nothing more and climbed the stairs.

Harry took control of the group. "Let's step outside then. We'll let the Chief know what's going on."

They walked across the yard to Mignola's car and they could smell cigarettes a good ten feet away. How the smoke lingered in the cabin of the car suggested he had smoked non-stop since coming outside. He stepped out and walked around to greet them.

"You've all had enough, then?" he asked. "Is it over?"

"Only just begun, Chief," Father Francis said.

"Harry got knocked over pretty good," Dr. Lawrence said, "and we were all given a pretty startling preview of things to come."

"Now we're following Madam Backlund's rules again, like the night before," Donald said. "She showed us what made the sounds we heard in her séance room, said we could see it all in order, not visions, but whatever this thing is, from start to finish. Sure you don't want to come in?"

"I don't think I'd even want to sit through a motion picture of this ordeal," Mignola said.

~

Phoebe stood in the doorway of the bedroom. This was only slightly different from any other time for her. It should honestly have been *no* different. But this time she noticed details she had overlooked before: dust gathering on the comforter, for example. She hadn't slept in this room in years. She may have grown accustomed to the fact that her house was haunted, she may even know its tricks, but shadows lingering out of view and indecipherable whispers from another dimension didn't make for good sleeping conditions.

Crossing to the bureau, she pulled out the letter from Minnesota Life Insurance. It was an explanation of benefits, how they would be paid, and what actions she would need to take with her taxes. There were no personal notes from the issuer, no special instructions provided by Handel, a form letter probably typed up hundreds of times. Each "u" was offset by the tiniest amount. This was the letter that made it real, that her husband was truly gone. She had buried him before even receiving it. She knew he was dead. His co-workers, their mutual friends, and family on both sides had gathered and mourned. But one Thursday afternoon when the postman delivered this letter, it suddenly became real. She sat in their old bedroom, before this house had ever been built, and cried.

Tears were rare these days. It had been many years, but she still missed him. Perhaps if they had been able to build the house together, it never would have been like this. If it had been built with love instead of sorrow and longing, it wouldn't be filled with so much alien pain. Here they were, though, and here she was again, drawing up the anguish and longing, all to put it on display for others to scrutinize.

Now she knew that whatever these events were, they had little to do with ghosts or demons, but everything to do with anger and sorrow. She had walked the steps of each of the apparitions and she would guide this group with the intent of pinpointing their actions. And, should everyone cooperate and see through to the conclusion, perhaps they would have touched the other side and grown as a result. Perhaps seeing and feeling the entire event would reveal its truth. If there was no truth to it, though, then there could be no point, and with no point, they were floating along aimlessly.

25 - ANDREW NEWSTED

Day broke on the last day of leave. Andrew had stressed over the words in the closet, the words he had read clearly in the middle of the night, only to find no evidence of them the next morning. Joanna caught him standing there, staring blankly with his mouth hanging open. Fortunately, he recovered quickly and grabbed a blanket, lying that she had been shivering in her sleep. Being a cold-natured person, she inadvertently corroborated his fib.

Even now, slowly packing, stalling to stay home, he mused about what he had seen. Was it real? Had it been a nightmare? Even when he was pensive, Joanna was happy to have him home. He couldn't shatter that illusion of security; it really *might* be all in his head.

Sliding quietly into the room, Joanna dared to defy the war one last time. "We can hop in the truck, cross the border, and forget all of this. Lucy has contacts in Canada. He could probably get you a job real quick."

"They'd have a warrant out for my arrest tomorrow," he said hoarsely, not having spoken all morning. "And Canadian officials are delivering draft dodgers to serve their time."

She sighed. "I think I'd almost feel safer with you in jail than going over there."

"As much as everyone dislikes this war, some of us are going over there to protect innocent people from communists. I'll try and stay on that side of our involvement. I'm going to protect a free world."

"Spoken like a true hero."

"Then how come I feel like shitting my pants and hightailing it like you say?" he asked, slumping his shoulders.

"Being a hero doesn't mean *not being scared*," she said, crossing the room to hug him. "It's what you do when you're scared that shows how *brave* you are."

He inhaled sharply, then let it out in a slow, measured sigh. "We need to get going."

He closed his small, blue suitcase and looked at her squarely in the eyes. "I love you, Joanna. I will come home to you and I hope you'll have the patience to wait for me."

"We took vows, Andrew. For better or for worse; this is definitely leaning into worse territory, and I know I'll be lonely, but I'll keep busy with work. Maybe I can surprise you when you get home with some additions to the house."

His eyes light up and he touched her belly. "You think?"

"I don't know," she chuckled. "But for how many times we did it this week, I'd be surprised if I *wasn't* pregnant."

"You're pregnant?" asked Joanna's mother from the hallway, her eyes ready to pop right out of her skull.

"Mom! No! I don't know—quit eavesdropping!"

Joanna's mother smiled deviously at the both of them and went down the stairs.

Joanna closed her eyes and shook her head as Andrew smiled and laughed. "Frankly, I'll be glad to see them gone," Joanna said. "I've forgotten how bad a mother can be."

They stood there staring at each other for a long while and tears started to well up in Joanna's eyes as the reality started to sink in. Andrew wrapped his arms around her neck and hugged her to him. They had no words; there weren't any sufficient to carry the weight of their emotions.

"What are you all doing up there?" cried Andrew's mother.

Joanna and Andrew both simultaneously heaved sighs. Joanna broke loose, wiped her eyes, and whipped around the corner to look down the stairs.

"We were having a moment. Thank you for asking!"

"Haven't you two had enough moments all week long?" asked Joanna's mother. "Sounds like bowling balls rolling all over the place up there."

Joanna squinted her eyes at them. "What? We're standing here. We were hugging."

"Sounds like you're racing on roller-skates," Andrew's mother agreed. "If it's not you, you might need to have some pipes checked out. Come on, let's go someplace else and cry."

Andrew stepped out with his suitcase. "Thanks a lot, mom, you sound real heartbroken."

"Cry here," she said, shrugging. "Cry at the airport, cry all the way home, cry myself to sleep every night until you get back."

He waved his fist in-between their faces while giving her an angry look. "I'll give you something to cry about!" he said in a low, mocking tone. "How's that? Not nice hearing it back, eh?"

Her joking demeanor immediately crumpled into a quivering frown. "I'd gladly take back every spanking if I could keep you out of this."

He set his suitcase down and hugged his mother, who completely broke down, almost giving out at the knees if he hadn't held her up. Joanna and her mother held each other's hands as they could only stand and watch, their own terrified tears running down their faces.

Andrew made sure his mother was stable and wiped at his nose and eyes, looked at all three of them, and beckoned them. "Come on," he said, "let's get going."

As he pulled the front door shut, he took one last, long look at his own house. Would he see it again? Would Joanna really be safe all by herself for a year?

They piled into Joanna's mother's station wagon, Andrew taking the wheel to head to the Cook County Airport, about a half-hour's drive.

If they spoke, it was in such small single word responses that it could hardly be considered conversation. The closer to their destination they got, the more somber they all seemed to grow.

The other families had already gathered. The small plane that would take them down to Duluth was warming up on the runway.

Soon they'd be switching planes to begin their trip to their ultimate destination, the Republic of South Vietnam. They would end up in large groups, no one knowing anyone else, everyone really wanting to go home. That's how it was in Basic; that's how it was now; that's how it would be for a year.

He hugged his mother first, then Joanna's mother, and then he held Joanna for a long time. There weren't a lot of words to say. They all said, "I love you," "be careful," and "write," over and over. When they were told it was time to board, an urgent panic spread throughout the gathered families. It was real now; their sons were leaving and might never come back.

Joanna felt small in his arms as she huddled into him. He hugged her tight as she began to cry. "I feel like this is the last time I'll ever see you," she said.

He pushed her away to arm's length. "You can't think like that. I'm coming home. I promise."

He pulled her back in and gave her a passionate kiss. "I love you, Jo, very much. I'll be home soon."

He hugged their mothers again, walked towards the plane, turned and waved, then boarded the plane to Vietnam.

26

"Got a letter," she said.

When he came in through the door, she realized she had been sitting at the dining room table for nearly half an hour, her head resting in one hand, holding a letter in the other. When he asked if everything was okay, she knew he could tell it wasn't. She looked up at him. Fear came over him.

"She's okay," she reassured. "That's really all she says."

Holding the letter out for him to read, he came through the foyer to the dining room.

Even though he grabbed it, she went on. "There was an attack; Taliban, Al-Qaeda, some shit, I don't know. She can't ever say anything with detail. They lost a few."

She stopped and could feel the tears and the inevitable sobs working their way into her throat. She couldn't help but consider those people's families.

She tried to yawn it off. "God, I think I'm going to be sick."

She turned to look at him again as he read the short letter. He was thinking the same thing she had surmised; she could see it on his face as his eyes scanned the page.

Even though the letter was supposed to be positive, letting her parents know that she was okay despite a horrendous day, she was crying out for help to bring her home. She was scared.

"Am I a horrible mother?"

He dropped the letter down. "Why would you say such a thing? We raised a *soldier*! I think you did a damn good job!"

She shook her head. "That's not what I mean." She exhaled heavily. "I read the letter and wished she would have been injured so she could come home. I feel terrible for even thinking that. There are families out there that have lost their babies to all of this, and I'm being selfish."

He came closer, set the letter on the table face down, and wrapped his arm around her.

She leaned into him and felt tears burst from her eyes. She wept quietly for a moment before burying her face in her hands and trying to rub the feelings out.

"I don't know," she mumbled through her hands. "Maybe she's better off over there. The *Corpse* attacked again last night, killed a mother and daughter among a group of campers. A few miles from here!"

"I hate that name," he said, letting her go and sitting down at the table. "This is like some Son of Sam or Zodiac Killer nonsense. It's disgusting; it sensationalizes his spree."

She didn't respond and he didn't say anything more. It was a diversion, a change of topic. They were thankful their daughter was okay, though obviously shaken up. But they both harbored desires to get her back home. Discussing the nightly news let them rationalize some reason they were glad she *wasn't* home, but there was no rationale in her being gone, in the war, or in a serial killer. Their world was falling apart.

They made dinner together with little more than chitchat. They watched a few shows in silence. The nightly routine went along as it did, probably helping them keep it together.

When he finally noticed that she was silently weeping again in bed, he rolled over and held her. There were no consoling words to offer; nothing could be said that would make any of this any easier. He could not deny feeling any less scared or depressed.

She gripped his arm around her and whispered, "I love you."

He squeezed her. "I love you, too."

Holding onto each other, they both let tears flow until it was too difficult to even keep their eyes open. It wasn't the only time they had fallen asleep this way. Fearing it wasn't the last only made it harder to sleep.

27 - NOAH BENJAMIN

As the night wore on, every little creak and bump grated on their nerves. Noah sat steadfast in front of the TRAP. Why had the haunting always been attached to the house, but not to an event? In Dorchester, the flux had been a random mistake; in other places, they seemed to be tied to the people involved.

One school of thought suggested that hormones interact with the chronotons, adding unknown weight. The particles' passage always creates grooves and paths in space. However, in these emotionally charged instances, the imperceptible becomes observable in the right circumstances. Perhaps hauntings are like pheromones, attracting or warding attention—a natural process.

Electronic devices seemed to pick up the evidence easiest; the static of an old untuned television, audio recorders, still cameras and video recorders. But even that was a product of observation—electronics acting like an amplifier. The TRAP used a Doppler effect to detect the movement of chronotons. This was a more advanced ghost hunting tool. Yet here, there was no causal "ghost." Nothing was causing the events, and the chronotons looked like they were about to stop altogether.

"What's bugging you, Noah?" Shannon asked quietly.

Beckoning them into the dining room, Noah made hand signals for Marcus to disable his eyepiece and everyone to disconnect their earpieces. Shannon and Marcus exchanged concerned glances.

"We have a problem," Noah said, followed by a sharp inward breath. "The static is constant. I can spin chronoton activity backwards, to the present, and I've even run forecast models, and I get nothing that indicates anything has ever happened to match the events."

Marcus and Shannon waited for him to go on.

Noah reached up and scratched his eyebrow with his pinky, flicking away imaginary debris. "Think of it like Schrödinger's cat," he sighed. "Superposition. You put a cat in a box with a vial of poison, a bit of radioactive material. If an atom decays, the vile breaks and the cat dies. Or, nothing happens and the cat lives. The idea is that at some point between sealing the box and opening it later, the cat will be in a superposition of being both dead *and* alive, and the reality isn't revealed until someone actively observes the cat—I think we're in *that* box."

Shannon began to nod. "But Schrödinger also said that was absurd."

Noah rolled his eyes. "The chronotons are behaving the same no matter when or how we look at them. It's like these events have happened in the past, present, *and* future. It's like that *because* we've looked at it."

"Is this *it*, then?" Shannon asked. "Is this the birth of a haunting?"

Noah shook his head. "I don't know. I don't know if by our observing it we're making it happen. We could be the cat for all I know."

"Or the poison," Shannon countered, but then she shook her head, too. "You think what we're seeing is legit and not a malfunction?"

"Noah," Marcus started, "it's your call. We can stop, we can call it a bust."

Noah considered it a moment, then looked to Shannon. "I mean, this could be it. This could be documenting the shaping of time and space."

"Look," she said, "I trust you. I trust Marcus. Cynthia and her team don't seem so bad. For all the surveillance between Marcus' equipment and theirs, no one is gonna get away with *murder* by any means. When's the last time you could tell someone you knew how Schrödinger's cat felt inside the box?"

"Boston," Noah said.

She pushed his shoulder. "I'm willing to stick it out if you are."

"That's not all," he sighed again.

"I knew it," Shannon chided. "What is it? Spit it out."

"These events don't happen after tomorrow," Noah said, rubbing his eyes.

"But the future-cast is only a possibility," Marcus said.

"I've run it three times. It's like this *place* doesn't even exist after tomorrow."

"The poem in the closet," Shannon said. "*Never mind where you are / 'Cause this is where you've always been*. Whatever's going on here is only ever happening in the *now*. Somebody already figured it out."

"We can leave," Marcus said again.

"No," Noah said firmly. "Shannon's right. If we trust each other, we can remain observers and objective. We have an amazing opportunity to redefine the concepts of our place in the universe. We can leave our mark, even if as ghosts."

He turned back toward the machine, his hand covering his mouth as he scratched his cheeks. What had Phoebe thought that first night in the house alone, her dream home now a den of unseen horrors?

"That's it!" Noah shouted.

Everyone had settled back down around the fireplace, but craned their necks to see what Noah was on about.

"I need a volunteer," he said, walking into the sitting room. "Shannon or Cynthia. You've got to stay in the primary bedroom alone. The rest of us need to leave the house."

"Oh, hell no," Chuck said into their ears. "This isn't reality TV where you dare someone to do stupid shit."

"No, it's not a dare," Noah said. "It's the missing criteria. We keep stumbling into random events, but the most notorious hauntings had one thing in common: women, alone in the house."

"Phoebe would ask her participants to let themselves in the front door," Reggie said, "but to wait in the foyer for her to come down. She sat in her bedroom until the appointed hour, often at random times."

"Phoebe must have figured it out," Noah smiled. "And that's how she seemed to always hold such astonishing séances."

"Let's do it," Cynthia said with a devilish grin.

"Really, Cynthia?" Chuck groaned.

"Hey, what better reporting than a firsthand account, right?"

"She's got you, Chuck," Reggie said.

Noah clapped. "Fantastic!"

Cynthia stepped closer to Noah. "No ghost ever hurt a person, right?"

"It's okay, Cynthia," he smiled. "It's *not* ghosts, it's natural phenomena. Think of it like watching a movie, only you're sitting in the middle of it. The event isn't happening to you, it's going on all around you."

"Marcus fell down, remember?" she pointed out.

"It's okay," Marcus said, stepping in close, too. "You get caught up in it. Have you ever been walking along and you expect your foot to hit the ground, but you end up stumbling because the next step was an inch or two lower than the last? And that weird falling sensation rushes over you, but it was only an inch?"

Cynthia nodded.

"It's nothing like that," Marcus said with a toothy grin. "But you'll be okay. There's a bed in there; sit on the corner for a few minutes. We'll come in, and it'll be like a roller coaster ride."

"Roller coasters have seat belts," she reminded him.

Noah clasped his hands around her shoulders at arm's length. "You don't have to. I bet Shannon would jump at the chance. Hell, she'll probably demand a go at it if this works."

"You're damn right," Shannon said. "But I'd be nervous, too, Cynthia. The apprehension is worse than anything I've ever seen or heard; but I know what I'm hearing and seeing."

"Okay," Cynthia said with a nod. "Okay, okay, okay—let's do it." She turned on her heel and headed to the staircase. Looking up, the stairs suddenly seemed much steeper and much higher than they had before. All the lights were on, but the house began to take on a dark atmosphere, like it knew what they had chosen to do and it was setting the stage appropriately.

"Okay, all of you get out," she said firmly, trying to shore up her own bravery. "I've got a hundred and fifty thousand cameras on me, more lights on at once than this house has probably ever seen, and Chuck in my ear."

Noah grabbed her wrist. "Thank you," he said sincerely. "And good luck."

They all went back out into the front yard and started towards the TV van.

Cynthia managed to make it up the stairs and turned immediately to the right. It was the first time she'd stepped up here since they had opened the closet. It was still hanging open and the cryptic poem was staring her down. She shook her head and turned into the bedroom. She half expected to see the apparition next to the restroom again, but the electric light killed the shadows that had been present earlier in the daylight.

At first, she sat on the corner of the bed like they had suggested, but having her back to the bathroom door made her nervous. She slid back and leaned against the headboard so she could see both doors.

Outside, before they got to the van, it seemed like the lights flickered and they stopped to look back. The lights flickered again and they heard a scream: a quick, startled scream from a woman. They all made to run back in, but Chuck stopped them.

"That wasn't her," he called out to them, "and I don't think she even heard it."

Reggie and Thom hopped up into the van and looked at the monitors. Cynthia was sitting on the bed, leaning against the headboard and staring out into the hallway.

"Then what the fuck was that?" Thom asked.

As if in answer to his question, the lights flickered again, only inside the house. Cynthia sat bolt upright, and when they flickered again, all the lights went out. With the darkness came Cynthia's own shocked shout.

Marcus and Shannon looked at each other, then at Noah. "That was almost exactly the same as what we heard out here," Shannon said.

"It's like the Echo is catching up to *us*," Marcus said.

Noah suddenly looked apprehensive. "God, I hope I was wrong."

"Wrong about *what*, Noah?" Chuck asked aggressively.

Noah didn't respond.

"Guys?" Cynthia's voice chimed in. "Sorry about the yell. I'm fine; scared shitless right now, but I'm okay. I heard a pop when the lights went out."

"I'll check the breakers," Reggie said, and he took off for the back of the house.

"Come on," Noah said. "Let's get back inside and make sure everything's okay."

"And me, too, right?" Cynthia said, chiding.

"Of course," Noah gulped. "You were part of that statement."

Shannon shook her head and walked back toward the house.

Noah ducked into the van before heading back. "Everything seem okay? Cynthia's okay?"

Chuck nodded without looking at him, but spoke anyway. "I understand the need for privacy, Mr. Benjamin, I won't accuse you of anything. But there were at least three cameras on you when you and your team unplugged your earpieces."

"We were discussing the observer effect," Noah conceded. "Our being here could be the reason any of this is happening. But that's all we're doing—observing. No one is in any danger."

Chuck said nothing else.

"Okay," Noah said. He patted the edge of the van door and walked away. Before he made it three steps, he heard the door slide shut. Noah grimaced, then made his way back to the house.

28 – NICOLE & TONY AND HELEN

Most booked only one night; a dare to attempt staying the night in a haunted house. Nicole and Tony had reserved the weekend. The Haunted Bed and Breakfast had the best rates in town despite being a tourist attraction. Either they got enough business they could afford to avoid inflation, or they weren't getting enough.

Tony sat in the reading room with a small fire crackling. It was Saturday night and so far there had been nothing unusual. It wasn't a total bust, though. The property was beautiful and peaceful, even if it was advertised as being terrifying. The sun was down but the light outside was still bright enough to see through the trees. Even though he had a book open in his lap, he hadn't read a word in several minutes, instead staring outside. This was a place he could move to.

His girlfriend Nicole sat in the kitchen with the innkeeper Helen. They made idle chitchat over a cup of tea. The both of them were relieved their stay had been uneventful. It was their fourth anniversary, and they wanted a pretty place to go while also having something memorable to look back on. Instead of ghosts, they got heavenly relaxation.

Nicole walked in and broke Tony's daydreaming.

He smiled softly. "Let's move here."

Nicole eased into a chair opposite him. "I think Helen might take issue with that."

"No, seriously." He closed his book and leaned forward. "To Grand Marais. I'm sure we could find jobs; heck, maybe we could open up a shop or something. It's… *nice* here."

Nicole queried, with an upward inflection, "I think you're stealing *my* lines?"

He shrugged. "Why not? I don't think I can recall a time I felt so at ease. This whole place is calm. Even their haunted houses are tranquil!"

Nicole chuckled.

Behind them they heard a creak, but neither recalled hearing footsteps. They shot nervous glances at each other before looking back into the foyer. They caught a figure ascending the stairs on the other side of the wall.

Nicole chuckled again, this time with relief. "Helen must be going to bed."

Tony nodded in agreement, but couldn't help looking over his shoulder again. The woman might know her own house, but he still couldn't hear footfalls. When he returned his gaze to meet Nicole's, he also saw Helen standing in the doorway that connected to the washroom and kitchen. He jumped at the sight of her.

Nicole looked over and shared in the shock. "I thought you went upstairs?"

Helen was stone-faced. If there was fear or excitement, she wasn't showing it. She only shook her head *no*.

Tony and Nicole simultaneously took deep, audible breaths.

Helen began to laugh. "I'm sorry. I had to mess with you!"

They both glared at her, slack jawed.

"My husband came down to get a bottle of water from the kitchen," Helen explained. "He's very sneaky and many a guest has thought him a ghost, too."

Her guests settled into their chairs.

"The house has been quiet, though. I hope that hasn't detracted from your stay. You've been so pleasant to have around, I'd hate it if you were disappointed."

"No, not at all," Tony defended. "I was just saying I really like the place; this town."

"It is cozy," Helen agreed. "But I think I'll head to bed as well. Good night!"

She walked through the room and turned up the stairs behind the wall. Despite stepping lightly, Tony could distinctly tell she was on the staircase, then walking down the hall. A door clicked shut, followed by soft movements in the ceiling above the kitchen.

"I didn't hear him at all; nothing like that," Tony said, indicating the stairs and ceiling beyond the walls.

"So what? He's quiet." Nicole shrugged.

It was now completely dark outside, the only light from a few lamps and the small fire. He set his book on the small table next to his chair and stood up to cross over to the fire.

"Maybe." He conceded. "But maybe the ghost stuff is all a hoax anyway and they play tricks. Put on a show."

He grabbed the poker and stirred the wood to spread it thin, letting the fire die down. He accidentally knocked a red-hot chunk down and it skittered across the floor. "Shit!"

As he turned, the first thing to strike him was the utter darkness around him. It was pitch black. He was blind, save for the solitary red and orange glowing chunk on the floor before him. He defensively raised the poker out in front of him.

"Nicole?" he called out.

The darkness began to feel threatening. There was someone in it, someone preparing to attack.

"*Nicole!*" he nearly shrieked.

Suddenly there was a violent commotion in front of him and he was unable to resist the urge to run past it into the darkness. As he reached where the foyer should be, the blackness subsided, giving way to the soft yellow lights and an unaffected flame. He was still holding the poker, which he looked at with a surprised disgust as though he were holding something foul.

Nicole was still in her chair staring at him, clearly disturbed and frightened. "Tony? What the hell was that?"

"The lights didn't go out?"

"No," she stated. "And if this is your idea of a joke, it *isn't* funny. I don't even know how you made those sounds."

"Sounds?" he stammered. "I called your *name*."

"You croaked out a death rattle as best I could tell. I thought you were going to vomit."

He shook his head, feeling so confused he *might* vomit. He crossed the room again and replaced the poker. Turning around, he noticed there was no coal on the floor.

"I didn't knock anything on the floor?"

She shook her head. "You barely stirred the fire when you whirled around on the spot like a madman."

He rubbed his temples.

"Come on," she said, standing up. "Why don't we get you to bed? Maybe Helen spooked you."

He nodded and followed. As they went upstairs, they heard a distinct click and saw light fill the hallway.

Nicole prepared to apologize to Helen for the commotion, but it was only the closet at the end of the hall. They stared a moment, expecting to see Helen come out with some bed dressing. There was no sound or sign of motion, though.

Tony went ahead and approached the closet and threw open the door. Before Nicole could come up behind him or ask any questions, he had forced the door firmly shut.

He turned around and caught her surprised expression. "Nope," was all he said.

He repeated the word a few times as he pulled out his wallet and pulled out a couple of hundred-dollar bills and lay them at Helen's door. He marched down toward their room at the opposite end of the second story, dragging Nicole along by the arm.

"*What* did you see?" she finally got out.

"Enough." And that was his final word.

He single-handedly packed up their loose belongings and lead her out of the house to their car. She never did get an answer out of him about what he saw.

29 - JOANNA NEWSTED

Both the mothers offered to stay a little while longer, but Joanna declined. They had lives they needed to attend to back home, as much as she needed to continue with hers. She helped them load their bags, hugged them both, and exchanged teary goodbyes. The sooner all of them could get on with life, work, and routine, the faster the days would pass.

As they drove down the long driveway through the woods around the house, she waved after the car from the front porch. It was overcast as snow was falling, dusting the trees, yard, and house. Everything was turning gray as if on schedule. She rubbed her arms and turned back into the house. Trying to think of something to occupy her time, she looked into the sitting room; the empty recliner reminded her of him.

Shaking her head, she climbed the stairs. She was worn out from all the day's emotions. It was later in the afternoon; maybe she could fall asleep and not wake up until morning. If she was asleep, she wouldn't have to think about him being gone or worry about him. The longer she slept, the more time would pass.

All the light coming into the house had taken on a cold, blue tone. It made everything look frozen and uncomfortable. She walked into their bedroom and pulled the comforter and sheet to his side of the bed. Staring at it for a moment before climbing in, she kicked off her shoes, forgoing undressing, and curled up. Sleep came, but not before there were more tears. She could smell him on his pillow.

~

Her eyes snapped open. It was dark, almost pitch black. The disorientation that came with the seemingly sudden change in light made it hard to process; it didn't feel like she had been asleep for long. She couldn't focus. Something had startled her awake. Was it a sound, or had she felt it? Her heart was racing, though. Something had certainly jarred her awake. Moving only her eyes, she tried to find anything to focus on; even the edge of the bed in front of her seemed lost in darkness.

Then it came again, the sound of breathing. The heavy breathing of someone who has put in some great physical effort was sounding from everywhere. She tried to still herself. Was it her own breathing? Holding her breath and trying to remain completely silent, she heard it again, now coming from one of the small connected rooms on the other end of the balcony. She sat up slowly, trying to keep the blankets from making any shifting or rustling sounds.

As she sat there trying to determine if she was hearing something, her eyes focused more and she could see the door to the hallway. Next to her was Andrew's tall dresser, and she could now make out the edge of her vanity and the closet door. A small pistol was in the bottom drawer of Andrew's dresser. She had only ever shot it once, but if she could threaten and frighten away an intruder, her lack of experience wouldn't matter.

Moving as slowly as she could to avoid making sound, she got her feet to the floor, knelt, and turned toward the dresser. Sliding the drawer out seemed to take greater effort in still being silent than navigating the sheets! She got it open enough and slid her hand under a few pairs of jeans to grab the pistol from between the folds of some oilcloth. Standing and turning on her heels, she kept herself low and the gun pointed out, even with her midsection.

As she entered the hall, her vision in the darkness had vastly improved. She could see the grays and cobalt blues that made up every surface in the midnight light. As she came even with the stairs, the door between the two small rooms swung slightly on its hinges, like someone passing it back and forth between outstretched hands. She stared in disbelief. No one was there.

The breathing stopped as though it recognized it had been caught. The door slammed shut, making Joanna jump and almost fire the gun straight into the floor. Then the other doors on that side of the hall all opened and slammed shut. The urge to run away, although in no specific direction, screamed in her legs. Panic-stricken, she could only watch with chills running up and down her body as the double doors of the upstairs living room flew open so forcefully that they bounced back shut. Half a beat later, the sound of glass breaking rang through the house.

Confusion and disbelief kept her rooted to the spot. Adrenaline tingled and burned as her flight response continued to erupt. Other than seeing the doors open and slam under no obvious influence, she didn't know what to run from, or that running would do any good. Tentatively raising the gun toward the end of the hall, she crossed the balcony to check the living room doors.

Opening with little effort, as they should, she expected to see the windows shattered, but there was nothing. The windows were still intact and firmly in their frames.

They had used this room, especially in the summer, to relax, playing cards on the floor. Andrew had wanted to turn it into a parlor, maybe one day bring in a pool table. For the moment, it had a folding card table and a couple of folding chairs sitting right in the middle of the room, not even askew. Whatever had made the sound, it wasn't here now. It was like the night she had seen the fire on the stairs. The lack of explanation was as scary—if not *scarier*—than the event itself.

She backed out onto the balcony, turning to her left to look at the three doors that opened and shut on their own. Then back to the right, where the windowless room and the master bedroom were. There was nothing. As the panic died down, crawling back into bed sounded good, but she couldn't let her guard down. Not yet. She leaned against the wall in front of the stairs and slowly slid down into a sitting position. Her knees up and heels cocked out, she held the gun between her thighs, pointing at the floor in front of her.

Knowing she should be scared made her feel more secure. She was aware; she was paying attention, and Andrew's reasonable explanations rang in her memory. It was the middle of the night; this could have been a waking nightmare.

Trying to keep her eyes glued to the front door, she found her gaze either drifting in random directions, going unfocused, or even her eyes closing of their own accord. She could try to stay awake or concentrate as intensely as she wanted to, but her body demanded sleep, and eventually, her eyes didn't open again.

When daylight finally woke her up, she found her legs spread out before her, the gun lying on the floor between them. Her arms were cradled on her stomach, and her neck ached incredibly from hanging her head down on her chest all night. She must have slept there for hours.

She had to force herself to stand. Bones and cartilage snapped and cracked at almost every joint, and working out the ache in her neck proved difficult for her hands alone. Barely able to bend forward to pick the gun back up, she rubbed and squeezed at her neck with her free hand. Perhaps a hot shower would do the trick and loosen her up. She put the gun away without a second thought about the night's events.

Leaning against the shower wall and letting the hot water run down her body, she realized she didn't care, even if what had happened was real. A few slamming doors were hardly anything to fear. Not after having to say goodbye to her husband.

30 - PHOEBE BACKLUND

Approaching dusk, only a few lights had been on when the bulk of the group walked out of the house to await their signal. When the small lamp on the bureau flickered and buzzed, Phoebe knew it was about to start, and it would be strong. There was an electrical *pop!* and the light went out—no doubt all the power to the house was out. She could not hear it, but knew that outside at that moment, a startled woman's scream rang out. She always wondered why she couldn't hear the scream from inside; was it because she was sitting in the middle of it?

Even though they expected it, and three of them had heard it before knowing *exactly* what to expect, there was an urgent rushing in through the front door.

"Phoebe?" Dr. Lawrence called out. "Is everything all right?"

She stood and carefully replaced the letter and cleared her throat, suddenly aware that her chest felt quite heavy with emotion. She'd felt that before, but it had been a while. She took a long, deep breath and then stepped back out into the hall, looking down at all of them from the top of the stairs.

"Yes, quite all right," she said, but then cocked her head in a question of her own. "Where's Father Francis?"

"We saw the power go out," Millie said. "He went around back to check your breakers."

Phoebe's eyes widened, visibly disturbed. "No, this won't do. We'll have to end this now."

"Did we throw something off?" Harry asked.

"No," she said, coming down the stairs. "Quite the contrary—we're following it too closely."

Harry stepped in front of her at the bottom of the stairs. "What do you mean?"

"Not now, Harry—" she said, but he placed his arms on the banister and the wall blocking her path.

"What is this?" Harry demanded.

Phoebe didn't answer but leaned to her right and looked out the window in the reading room. There she saw Chief Mignola striding intently toward the back of the house. Phoebe shoved Harry aside and rounded the bottom of the stairs, passing through the dining room into the kitchen.

The others followed her, but not too closely, afraid of the look in her eyes as she passed them by. She burst through the door in the kitchen that let out to the side of the house; they heard her hiss something to someone outside. Harry approached the door. Phoebe had grabbed Father Francis, and the Chief was taking a wild swing at where the priest had been standing.

Phoebe dragged Father Francis back into the house, the look on her face suggesting she expected terrible things to occur, but the priest was confused and about ready to demand answers. Harry had an idea, but he let the scene play out.

"What is going on here, Ma'am?" Francis asked.

Phoebe hissed again. "We must remain quiet! Everyone back into the dining room, away from the foyer."

Urging the group forward, she continued to guide him. Father Francis began to repeat his question but was interrupted by the door opening again and Chief Mignola lurching through it as if he carried some heavy weight in his arms.

"What the hell is going on?" Francis asked, dropping all pretenses of character.

The gaze she shot him was possibly more terrifying than the odd circumstances surrounding them. It reminded him of the look of medics who knew their patient was going to die. They continued into the dining room, out of the Chief's way.

"I think you would call it possession, Father," Harry whispered, watching with intense interest. "I would, under normal circumstances, accuse the Chief of playing a part given to him, and you, Madam Backlund, of casting him. However, the way he moves…"

In the darkened house, it was unclear whether Mignola had anything in his arms or not, but he struggled. He desperately wrestled *something* through the kitchen, to the dining room, and into the foyer while heading for the stairs.

"He's not possessed," Phoebe said, reassuring the priest. "Not by any sort of malicious spirit or demon, anyway."

"Can we free him?" Francis asked.

"It would be like trying to wake a sleepwalker." Phoebe said. "The shock could be far more detrimental than letting it run its course."

Seeing how he moved, adjusted, and reacted to whatever it was that he was holding wasn't making sense. Their minds told them he shouldn't be able to do it, yet his body leaned far back without falling and shifted as though countered by some other weight.

"Is he in any sort of danger?" Dr. Lawrence asked.

"Fuck that, Doc," Millie said, shocking the men. "Are *we* in any sort of danger? The Chief's got a gun, for crying out loud!"

Phoebe shook her head. "The best we can do is wait. That or disrupt his actions without confronting him."

"How do we do that?" Donald asked.

"Shutting a door that should be open or moving a piece of furniture," Harry guessed aloud.

"That would do it," Phoebe nodded. "Once he bumps into something that shouldn't be in the way, he'll come out of it—and be terribly confused for it as well."

They went around the stairs and saw that Mignola was halfway across the balcony, dragging his charge to one of the small bedrooms.

"Come with me, Doctor," Harry said. "We can move one of the small beds in the way of the door that separates the rooms."

"Will that work?"

"I believe we are seeing what I saw happen earlier, and he will try to pass through the door, if there happens to be a bed there that wasn't there before, surely he will be blocked or trip and fall out of whatever rut he seems to be stuck in."

"A rut?" the Doctor asked. His eyes lit up with understanding. "Like, his actions are like a carnival ride. He's on a track, and if we can change the setup, he'll simply fall off without us disrupting him too jarringly."

"Well, we can hope," Harry said. His excitement had been renewed. Now he was chasing the unknown again.

They followed the Chief upstairs where Harry motioned Dr. Lawrence to enter the second room and move the bed in front of the door. Harry would enter the room with the Chief to ensure everything went according to plan, or break the course of events, anyway. The Chief was in no sort of control over himself. He stood awkwardly inside the door of the bedroom, holding up whatever it was that he was holding.

In the other room, Doctor Lawrence quietly shut the door between the rooms and slid the bed in front of the door. The sound didn't seem to disrupt Mignola in the slightest. Harry could hear voices downstairs, but they were not those of his companions. As he tried to listen and pick out what was being said, Mignola let out a pained moan. There may have been a word or name in it, but it was unearthly, Harry was shaken by the sound that had escaped the Chief's throat.

He could hear a distant cry in response and steps running up the stairs. He leaned back to see who could be coming up but saw no one. He then found himself inclined to rush the Chief, but the sensation felt like he had forgotten where he was—or that anyone was even in the room. He lurched forward, feeling control of his body slipping from him, but still his body moved. He could feel himself encounter something, and with the encounter was a sense of relief, but when the Chief suddenly looked into his eyes, dread washed over him.

Harry struggled to stay in control of his body, but he was indeed on a ride. He could see things that weren't there. His sensation of movement was like someone else controlling him.

The Chief lashed out and Harry could feel a sharp pain in his neck. He was forced and pinned to the wall. There was a distinctive thud in the wall behind him. The warmth of blood spilled from his neck, down his back, and across his chest. He tried to pull away, screaming in his own mind to break free while his body obeyed these otherworldly commands. When a chill ran through him and weightlessness seized his brain, he finally smashed back into his own reality and broke free, pulling to the side and stumbling out into the hall.

He grabbed at his neck and felt nothing, looked at his shirt and over his shoulder, but there was no blood. He concentrated on controlling his breathing, centering himself in that intense moment. Phoebe had suggested before that she felt life fading, had been an aggressor. She had fallen into all these apparition's routines. He felt like a puppet on strings. Had he seen into another time and place?

31 – JOANNA NEWSTED

Ten butts on the ground and working on an eleventh. Andrew would disapprove, even though he smoked when he was stressed as well. They both nursed on a pack kept in the junk drawer of the kitchen. One of them would replace it on the sly occasionally. Even though he'd been gone some months now, she'd replaced it too many times to count. The intervals between packs were getting shorter.

Eleven butts on the ground and a twelfth getting lit.

The squad car turned onto the long gravel drive from MN-61 as she exhaled a cloud of hot breath and cigarette smoke. She didn't care that it was ice cold and gave up on the excuse of the cigarettes providing warmth to her lungs. After finally reaching the police on the phone, she waited half an hour in front of her house for them to show up. She dropped the freshly lit cigarette and ground it into the gravel. Folding her arms tight to keep her hands warm, she approached the car as it came to a stop a few feet behind her truck.

"Mrs. Newsted." The officer stepping out of the passenger side greeted her. "We're here to check the premises."

"Officer Daniels," she replied. She tried to offer a smile; nerves and the cold had made her sound curt.

David Daniels was one of her and Loretta's customer's neighbors. They would often gossip with each other for a little while before or after cleaning. He was nice and young and had avoided the Draft.

The other policeman, Garrison Pritchett, was an older, over-weight looking man. To see him get up and go at the policemen versus firemen summer picnic, he was clearly a mountain of muscle. His mother had worked for the police department and his grandfather before her had been chief. Officer Pritchett stared at the house like he knew exactly what he was walking into.

Pritchett turned his head toward her while his eyes continued to stare at the second story. When his gaze finally broke free, he said, "Do you mind if we take a look around the house first?"

"Take your time," she said through chattering teeth. Having the company of the policemen allowed her to relax, but in relaxing she suddenly felt the brunt of the cold around her.

They both put their hands on their pistols without drawing and took a side of the house while Joanna waited next to their car. It was early afternoon and overcast. The even, gray light cast little in the way of shadows. The cold air carried every crunch of their feet on the frosty ground.

They left the motor running, which gave Joanna a bit of warmth to lean against. From the cab, she heard the radio crackle to life and the mumbling voice of a dispatch lady; a moment later the voice of a man responded, though still unclear. It reminded her of what had made her call the police in the first place.

Insistent whispering and distant murmuring voices seemed to follow her throughout the house. She tried to ignore them at first, chalking the sounds up to dead leaves outside. As she tried to take a nap, though, they began to take on a malevolent tone. She couldn't shake the dread that someone was either in or around her house.

Apathy was replacing her concern for being taken seriously. This was the third time she'd managed to have the police come and check around the house; she knew if they didn't find anything they would accuse her of crying wolf and wasting police resources. She didn't care.

From around the house, she heard one of them jostle the kitchen door handle. A moment later, the distinct creak of one of the shed doors opening. If she could keep it warm enough, she would gladly stay in there with all the lawn and gardening equipment.

A stray beam of sunlight brightened the trees around the house for a few seconds. Joanna pulled out the pack of cigarettes and prepared to light her thirteenth as she appreciated the serenity of the moment. Then a frightened shout broke the silence.

Frozen in place, the fear adding a chill to her core that rivaled the cold of the air around her, Joanna waited for another sound. Thinking one of the officers might have stumbled onto something, the sound echoed in her head. It wasn't a man's shout, and it hadn't come from behind the house. It was distinctly the cry of a frightened woman, and it had come from *inside*.

Officer Pritchett came around the left side of the house first, followed by Daniels a few paces behind, scratching the back of his head. Had it been *him*?

"We didn't see anything unusual, Mrs. Newsted." Pritchett shrugged. "Doesn't look like the ground has been disturbed around the back of the house, either. We can look inside if you'd like."

Stunned, she stumbled on her words. "You didn't hear *that*?"

She pointed to the second story, almost exactly at where Pritchett had been staring when they pulled up. Looking down the length of her arm as they both looked toward the house, she realized she was pointing at the master bedroom.

"Hear *what*, Mrs. Newsted?" Daniels asked.

"There was a…" her eyes shifted, knowing the next words would be insignificant. They wouldn't believe her because they hadn't heard it themselves. She shook her head before finishing the sentence. "I thought I heard something from inside the house, but you two were closer. If you didn't hear it, maybe it was a bird behind me, echoing through the trees, or something."

Officer Daniels approached but kept a respectable distance. His tone immediately upset her, but she held her tongue. "Now, sweetheart, I can't even guess how lonely you might be in this big house without your husband. Do you have any friends or family that could stay with you—or that you could stay with?"

She knew he meant another man. A big strong man to chase the bogeymen away: her *daddy*. Disgusted, she turned on the spot, folding her arms, cigarette pack and matches still in her hands.

Grimacing, maybe realizing he had spoken poorly or was instead annoyed with her, he tried to be more realistic. "If we keep coming out on false alarms, dispatch might not take you seriously when the time comes you actually need us. Or maybe a responding officer wouldn't have the necessary urgency to get here in time."

Pritchett put his hand on Daniels' shoulder and nudged him aside.

"I've met Andrew, Joanna," he said softly. "I've seen him with the guys at Lucy's on occasion. He had the look of a young man going to war: scared, trying to make it day to day. But I saw something else in his eyes. I see it in yours now, and… I saw it in my *grandfather's* on occasion."

Joanna turned her head to investigate Pritchett's face. There was concern there. Before she could ask, he continued.

"My mother embellished the stories. She told her own version based on her memories of what he told her, which were from his memories from a long time ago, like a game of telephone. I was very young when he passed, but I remember her goading him to tell my brother and me the story, so we could hear it from the old horse's mouth. That look you wear, that I've seen on Andrew, came over him; *haunted*. I was scared before he even said a word. But I was only five. I never thought anything of it, never believed the stories anyway, and frankly, still don't. Still, I see that look in you and your husband's eyes, and I have to respect that something happens here I can't explain. I can't even guess at what, but I *can* tell you that in twenty years on the force, from the entirety of my mother's career, and even my granddad telling me tales from damn near the turn of the century, *nothing* bad has ever happened here. The tenants before you never once called the police."

"They couldn't get out fast enough, from what I understand," she interrupted.

He chuckled. "True enough, but I always figured they were being hounded by the bank; bought more house than they could afford, I reckon. Much to you and Andrew's benefit, way I see it. In the long run, anyway. Look, David doesn't mean to say you can't handle things on your own—"

Joanna saw Daniels shift his weight back and forth. She hoped he was embarrassed; more likely, he was impatient.

"—But this place isn't a prison. You *can* get up and leave if you need to. As of right now, though… we don't see anything, we have to report a false alarm. Now, you've got a lot of open space here. You're more likely to see deer than another human snooping around."

They didn't believe her, and they were ready to mark her as a childish nuisance, regardless of how nice and supportive they tried to sound. Despite their attempts, Joanna would rather have heard what they wanted to say: *We feel for you, but stop it.* She wished she could.

Neither of them said anything else. She could tell they were looking to be released. Even though they offered to inspect the interior, they didn't want to. Either because they truly believed nothing was amiss or they were too cowardly to defy their own admonitions. Joanna was unable to muster anything more than a nod to excuse them. The officers made their awkward and silent exit, leaving her standing alone again with cigarettes in hand and a screaming house.

32

He pulled up to the house and looked at the clock on his radio. It was late. His wife should be home, and half the lights should already be on. Her car was here, why was the house completely unlit in the lowering dusk? Maneuvering next to her car to shine his headlights into the library, he saw her turn the corner and take a seat. She was fine, but no lights. The power must have gone out.

The breaker box was on the outside of the house, next to the kitchen door that led into the backyard. The power could genuinely be out, but he hadn't noticed any other exceptionally dark homes or driveways coming home. Checking the breakers would only take a little time.

Along the back of the house was a grassy rise. Out in the yard, along the path leading down to the beach, was a shed for their tools and yard equipment. He took in the scene for a moment. It was serene. Conversely, he looked up to see the sealed windows of his darkroom. It was strange that those windows had been nailed shut with their vintage curtains between them and the false wall. What had the old lady been up to? Why hadn't anyone ever opened the windows back up? He shook his head and returned his attention to the task at hand.

~

The glare of headlights across the top of the room signaled her husband's arrival. Despite having walked into the room to sit down and read, she hadn't seen his car pull up for the glare of her lamp on the window. Looking over her shoulder, she noticed he wasn't coming for the front door; he was going around the side of the house. She went to the kitchen to spy on him.

She couldn't see anything through the back door. She crossed the kitchen to look out the window over the sink. Still nothing. It was getting darker and he had no flashlight. What was he doing back there?

She yelped as he forced the door open.

"What were you doing back there?" she exclaimed.

She noticed his weird posture, but he quickly righted himself, looking like he had dropped something. He turned toward her, a menacing look on his face.

"Are you trying to scare me?" she asked. "Because it is not funny. I don't care if the Corpse has been caught."

He looked around as though he had no idea where he was. He raised his hands out in front of him. "I have no idea how I got here."

"What do you mean?"

Taking a few deep breaths to collect himself, he continued to take in his surroundings. "I pulled up and all the lights were out, so I went to check on the breakers…"

"The lights are on… they *were* on," she corrected.

Fear and confusion filled his eyes. "They were on?"

She nodded in earnest.

"I walked around the house…" he made gestures tracking his movements outside. "I checked the breaker box. I can still feel the panel in my hands as I lifted it. Then I'm inside and you're talking to me."

"You looked like you were dragging something through the door."

He shook his head. "The lights were on the whole time?"

She nodded again.

He reached up and rubbed his temples. "I'd say I need a drink, but apparently I'm already blacking out."

"A few more weeks," she reassured. "And we'll all be home together again and the nightmares will end. I'm sure of it."

33 - HELEN AND HELEN

The knock was slight, as if it wasn't directly on the door. Then there were slow, soft steps retreating down the hall. Someone on the other side of the door was scared, but perhaps even more scared of causing their own disturbance. Helen knew there were no furtive knocks in this place and decided to investigate.

When she opened the door, the young woman, only a few steps between the end of the hall and the empty master bedroom, quickly turned. She was horrified, eyes wide enough to see whites all around, but seemed thankful. She silently glided the few steps to meet Helen at her door.

Helen looked over her shoulder into the room before closing the door behind her. "Can I help you… um…?"

"Helen, remember?" the girl whispered, her Welsh accent barely perceptible. "We have the same name and had a laugh."

"Yes," Helen the innkeeper said, with a courteous laugh. "Is something the matter?"

Young Helen looked at the closet as the innkeeper realized the hallway was lit by light coming from within.

"I heard the closet door pop open," young Helen explained. "Though, when I got up to investigate, I realized my husband was not in bed. I thought he might be trying to scare me and had gone into the closet. Whatever was in there, it wasn't him. He's nowhere in the house."

The innkeeper raised her head in a slow, deliberate nod. The young woman had nearly white blonde hair. Her face was round and in her frightened state, her eyes and mouth wide and round as well, Helen felt a pang of guilt for thinking her face looked like a bowling ball.

"Don't worry, ma'am," the innkeeper assured. "He's on the grounds and no doubt having an experience few get to claim."

Young Helen tilted her head, her eyes shifting up and down the hall. "How do you mean?"

"Follow me."

The two Helens walked down the hall, passing the unoccupied bedroom. Young Helen glanced inside and jumped as she saw a shadow in the far window.

"The house certainly has its grip on you! Stay close to me, know that I am here. Remember, you are always safe. Think of it like a ride."

"Rides break," Young Helen lamented.

They descended the stairs. Young Helen had investigated the lower floor quickly before gaining the innkeeper's attention, but now they both noticed the front door hanging ajar.

"I must warn you, what you are about to see is not your husband."

Young Helen's eyes looked as though they would roll right out of her head. "Is he *possessed*?"

Helen laughed and had to restrain and quiet herself after the initial outburst. "No; think of it more like *sleepwalking*."

"Should we get *your* husband?" young Helen begged.

"Oh, no. I've dealt with this before; my husband is quite the sound sleeper. To wake him and get him around would take longer than dealing with it ourselves."

Before they could exit the house, the back door in the kitchen banged open. Helen nodded as though she expected the intrusion while young Helen gripped her arm.

"Come on, let's retrieve your husband."

As they came around the stairs, they saw Young Helen's husband. He was in the kitchen and hunkered over something, lumbering through the door.

"Bradley?"

The innkeeper put her finger to her lips to silence her guest. "Remember, *sleepwalking*. You don't want to *wake* him, only point him in a new direction."

Careful not to get directly in his way, the two came alongside Bradley as he fully entered the kitchen. His arms were curled out in front of him as though he carried a heavy weight, though nothing was in his arms. His stance seemed impossible. He leaned far back and dug his heels into the floor as though countered by an invisible charge.

"How can he do that?" young Helen whispered as they followed him.

The innkeeper shrugged. "In the state he's in, he believes he can. We need to apply light pressure to his shoulders; gently push him outside of his intended trajectory. You push him towards the dining room, and I'll nudge him toward the door. Then turn him—no more than an inch."

Young Helen nervously agreed and placed her hand on her husband's shoulder. They were already near the dining room, and he looked as though he was preparing to turn into the foyer. The innkeeper placed her hand on the back of Bradley's shoulder then gave the go ahead.

At the small movement, Bradley dropped his unseen weight and righted himself into a normal standing position. Young Helen drew breath to speak, but the innkeeper stopped her.

"We will direct him back to bed and he will be none the wiser."

Young Helen did as she was directed. Guiding him up the stairs, over the balcony, and back into the first guest room where they shared a simple double bed was easier than she thought it would be. She stepped back into the hall with the innkeeper.

"Can you tell me what that was?"

After heaving a sigh to measure her words, the innkeeper spoke in normal tones. "I've been there. I've seen two other tenants in as many years in the same position. The first was woken up in the foyer where they entered a screaming fit worse than any horror film would have you believe a person could scream. She was an animal then. Fortunately, she didn't recall it. Though her friends and I are stuck with the memory. Myself? I woke up in your room. Fortunately, I had somehow not woken the sleeping couple… not that they ever admitted anyway. It's a disconcerting feeling, waking up from sleepwalking. I don't recommend it. But! You have a fantastic tale to share with your husband in the morning, which he will never believe; not that he'll admit, anyway."

Young Helen looked like a bowling ball again and the innkeeper took that as her cue to bid her good night.

34 - CYNTHIA MORRISON

Countless red eyes stared at them from all angles. The battery-operated cameras continued recording and fortunately the TRAP hadn't lost power with the blackout. It did, however, go into a conservation mode and the monitors had shut off. Stepping in, Thom produced a small flashlight.

"Cynthia?" he called out.

"Yeah, I'm okay!" she called.

Following the shine of light, she stepped out of the primary bedroom and stopped carefully at the top of the stairs. "What happened out there?"

Noah started up the stairs. "Outside we saw the lights flicker briefly, followed by a frightened scream—"

"Yeah," she said. "I'm embarrassed about that; I'm sure that'll be the lead-in for your special."

"—then the lights went out inside the house, and you screamed," Noah finished.

"Wait… what?" She cocked her head to one side.

"We heard what happened—*before* it happened," Noah said with an awkward grin.

"We set it off? We can experience the events in order now?" she asked.

"Everything has fallen into place, like we planned. We can see everything happen in a straight line instead of a jumbled mess and get a proper reading—"

Cynthia stared at him hard from the top of the stairs. Then, raising her head as if something was occurring to her, she said, "Are *we* this event?"

"Uh…" Noah took a step back down the stairs.

"You've been searching for the birth of a haunting," she recalled. "Is that what this is?"

"I don't know… not yet," he stammered.

"What about the rest of it, Noah?" she asked, with a hint of malice. "The violence, the fear?"

He blinked rapidly, surprised.

"Will that *happen before it happens*, too?" she continued.

"Why don't you tell her the rest, Noah?" Chuck croaked in their ears.

Cynthia pointed to her ear. "Chuck can hear us all. What aren't you telling all of us?"

Looking defeated, he shook his head and took another step down.

"He really doesn't know," Shannon interrupted. "But everything we've read on the TRAP indicates that this has always happened. The haunting events are always in real time with no culprit. And there is no culprit, not even possibilities."

"Well, what the hell is going on here, then?" Thom asked.

"Are we the *ghosts*, Noah? Your Echoes?" Cynthia demanded. "Are we creating this event? Because I feel pretty damn tense right now, and I'm sure your chronotons are picking up a fair amount of *pissed right the fuck off*."

"Okay," Noah conceded.

Everyone looked toward him.

"Okay, *what*?" Cynthia asked.

"We've got a ton of data," he said. "I'm sure all the video angles and sound recordings we haven't even pored over yet are full of stuff. The TRAP has compiled information, and we've already seen things move, We've got apparitions on film. If *we're* causing this, then we can stop. Let's pack it up and head home. Everyone's scared, and I'm not about to have blood on my hands to prove a point."

They stood around exchanging glances in the glow of Thom's single flashlight. As the silence stretched out, Thom finally remarked on the darkness still enveloping them, "Where is Reggie? The lights should be back on by now."

"Chuck?" Cynthia called out.

The quiet over their earpieces extended unpleasantly.

A dull thud made them all jump.

"That sounded like it came from outside." Marcus said. "I don't think that was the house."

"It's dark and now we're missing two people," Noah said. "We stick together, head back out, and we pile into the van."

Shannon leaned over the TRAP, popped open a side panel and pulled out the hard drive after a forced shut down. She looked at Thom. "Do you have anything you can grab quickly as evidence?"

"In our van," he said, "there's a computer that backs up everything streaming into the van."

"Okay," Noah said. "Let's be quick."

Thom led the way out and towards the TV van, but the sliding door was already open. Stepping up to the van, Thom pointed his light inside, but quickly turned away. "Oh, shit, oh, shit!"

Cynthia sped up to a run to close the gap. "What is it?"

Thom kept cursing over and over. Cynthia put her hand on his shoulder and reached down his arm to take the flashlight from him. Seeing the beam quiver against the ground, she realized she was shaking. Nerves, adrenaline, and pure fear overpowered her motor functions. She took a deep breath and shined the light into the van.

Smeared across a closed cabinet affixed to the van ceiling was a handprint. At its edges where the smear was thinnest, it was bright red. She said nothing, only stared in disbelief.

Noah, Marcus, and Shannon cautiously approached and looked over her shoulder into the van, seeing the bloody handprint.

"We need to leave," Marcus said. "Right now."

He walked away to the other van, leaving the other four standing in shock.

"Reggie," Thom said. "Reggie!" he cried at the top of his lungs into the night, his breath visible in the starlight and shine of the flashlight.

He started toward the back of the house, but Cynthia grabbed his arm. As she stopped him, the flashlight's beam swept across the second van, stopping Marcus in his tracks.

"Are you fucking kidding me?" he roared.

Everyone looked at him, Cynthia focusing the beam on him.

He turned around, furious. "Look at our van's tires."

Cynthia flashed the light on the tires, seeing they were completely deflated. "Oh my God," she said in a quiver. "What do we do now?"

"Call 9-1-1," Noah said. "Do it now. Don't waste any time."

"What about Chuck and Reggie?" Thom asked. "We can't leave them."

"No," Cynthia said. "He's right. We can't try and be heroes right now. This has gotten serious."

Shannon pulled out her phone. "I've only got one bar; this could be a completely shit call." She dialed 9-1-1 and put the phone to her ear.

As her eyebrows furrowed, Noah could tell it was going to be bad news. She pulled the phone down and looked at the screen.

"It dropped before it even connected," she said. "We may need to get out to the road."

"We're facing a killer, maybe?" Marcus said. "The woods are a death trap; we're exposed where we are."

"Didn't you say it was the TRAP that caused cellular problems?" Cynthia asked. "I thought you shut it down. Shouldn't we have service back?"

"I did," Shannon said. "The sensors may still have power, but all we have to do is unplug them. We're probably safer inside, especially if we stick to the foyer."

Mortified and somber, the group headed back into the house. Once inside, Shannon went straight to work on the TRAP.

Thom checked his phone again, the light blue glow revealing the look of disappointment on his face. "I've gained one whole bar."

"Call," Noah ordered. "Call over and over, get us help."

He sighed, but his frustration was interrupted by a sound from upstairs.

A pained voice called out from the kids' room. "Thom?"

Thom bolted up the stairs before Cynthia could stop him. The others could only watch in stunned silence as he ran straight into the room.

Thom could see next to nothing, save for floating red lights. Barely any light shone in from outside through the windows, but he ran for his friend on memory alone. He immediately slammed into another body, grabbing out and stabilizing himself and the other person.

"Reggie?" he said. "You son of a bitch, how dare you scare us like that? Do you know if Chuck's okay?"

No answer. He realized Reggie hadn't physically reacted to him, either. He took out his phone to use as a flashlight. An arm shot out and Thom felt an awkward pinch in his neck. He dropped his phone as the pain erupted, but the knife in his throat caught his scream. Escaping his mouth were only a wet gurgle and a fair amount of blood.

The knife had stabbed straight through and pinned him to the wall. Before his eyes went dark, Thom saw that one person had been holding a body up. Trying to say something, or maybe even to scream or cry in pain, Thom faded and was gone before his killer dropped the first body to the floor, leaving them both dead.

35 – JOANNA NEWSTED

In the six months since Andrew had been flown to Vietnam, Joanna had only received one letter. His mother had received two, but it had been quiet for months for her, too. The nation fretted over the death toll and anti-war protests turned almost as violent as the war itself. Angry mobs attacked politicians and veterans. As for Joanna, she wanted to know her husband was safe.

The Tomlinson's had been notified of their son's death: killed by the Viet Cong during a skirmish in a swamp. Joanna waited with them and the other families who had been broken apart by the war at the airport, waiting for their son to be returned to them in a casket. Joanna felt sick when she saw the ceremonious delivery of his remains. She hadn't heard from Andrew or been notified of anything. Was he okay? Was he *alive*?

On the days she worked, she did a good job, but Loretta could tell she wasn't herself. There was never a heartfelt smile. Conversation was often limited to single syllable answers, if not grunts. If she wasn't working, she would sleep. Loretta tried to be her companion, tried to give her a place to stay other than a big empty house that held nothing but reminders.

Loretta didn't know, though, that Joanna was in a self-imposed hell. The house kept her company, reminded her of more than her missing husband. It imposed its own horrors upon her. If she napped, there were nightmares. Trying to catch a solid night's sleep, there were

nightmares. And as the days, weeks, and months wore on, they inten-
sified until sleep was only in concentrated bursts.

Doors slammed and the unseen menace breathed, sometimes
loudly and right beside her, sometimes from far corners of the house.
She felt as though she was under constant surveillance. Shadows
seemed to stare her down from corners and doorways. Somehow, in
her longing for her husband, she had become as paranoid as a soldier;
the *enemy* was out there, unseen, but certainly present.

One of the most frustrating aspects for her while she was in the
house was the lack of contact with the outside world. As events grew
more intense, it seemed she was more imprisoned by them. She would
try to call out to her mother, to Andrew's mother, to Loretta—she
dared calling the police department when the front door kept coming
open, but they had written her off as a nuisance.

Despite engaging the deadbolt and even jamming a chair under
the knob, there would come a desperate knocking and battering, then
the door would burst open, knocking aside whatever obstacle may be
in its way. No one would be there, but if she was anywhere near the
door, the sense of dread and panic of an attacker would rush over her.

In particularly desperate moments when she would try the telephone, she would find it wouldn't connect, or only briefly, and then
lose connection. She had repairmen come out, but nothing was wrong
with the lines or her equipment. She was trapped, and she found herself resigned to it.

When guests were over—whether she wanted them or not—the
house was quiet, and no one else saw the events. The fishermen and
their wives, and even Loretta, made sure to avoid the subject of the
house itself; most locals were afraid of it. They knew she lived there;
they knew her husband was off to Vietnam; and by looking at her,
they knew something was wrong.

Arriving at one of their client's homes ahead of Loretta, Joanna
sat in her truck and stared blankly ahead. Exhaustion had become so
prevalent that the act of dozing off had become foreign to her. She felt
her head begin to tilt forward and her eyelids grow heavy. Being nowhere near her own house, she let herself relax. She could hear herself
beginning to breathe heavier. It reminded her of the strange breathing

in the house, but she knew it was her own and tried to shove that notion aside. She wanted some peaceful rest, even if for a few minutes.

What felt like sleep gave way to a curious feeling, like she was standing and holding something up. It was heavy and awkward, and she was holding it up with her forearms. In her right hand was something, a *knife*, and while she held this heavy thing in her arms, she waited. She was in the small bedroom nearest the balcony and the door was hanging open. She said something, but her voice was hoarse and low, she couldn't make out her own words.

From the hall, another voice spoke and the sound of someone running up the stairs followed. None of the words were clear and despite knowing where she stood, she could see no clear definition; it was all a feeling of knowing, not actual perception. The other person who called out rushed into the room and rammed into what she was holding, almost knocking her down, but she kept her balance. This other person acted like they recognized her, but no, not her, what she was holding. She was holding a *body*. She was holding this body up to make it look like it was standing. And as the other person realized what was happening, she lashed out with the knife, stabbing them in the neck. The knife made a distinct clunking sound in the wall behind them.

Mixed in with the sound of the knife hitting the wall, a knocking sounded right next to her ear. She was startled awake and looked toward the source. Loretta was there, knocking on the driver's side window of the truck. Her heart was pounding—from the nightmare, and from Loretta's effort to wake her. She shook her head and opened the truck door, reaching into the passenger seat and grabbing her bucket full of supplies.

"I'm sorry," Loretta said. "I didn't mean to scare you. Maybe I should have let you sleep. Doesn't look like you've been getting much of that."

Joanna shook her head. "No, it's okay. I was having a nightmare anyway."

"I know this sounds weird," Loretta said, "but why don't you stay the night at my house tonight? Maybe a change of scenery and some evening company will let you relax and get a good night's sleep."

Joanna forced a smile. "I appreciate it, Loretta," she said, running her free hand through her hair. "But it's okay. I don't think it matters where I sleep; I miss my husband. Even when I've been out, I feel completely alone."

They walked toward the house as Loretta sorted her keys. "Still no word yet? Nothing at all?"

Joanna shook her head. "I tried to talk to one of the officials when they delivered the Tomlinson boy. They said even if they did know, they couldn't report on where he was due to security issues; word gets out to the wrong set of people, and they could be set up with an ambush. They tried to give me that 'no news is good news' bullshit."

"And his momma?" Loretta asked.

"Same," Joanna nodded as they stepped into the house. "But my phone has been messed up, I can't be completely sure. Thing hasn't even rang in more than a month. If you've tried to call, I'm not ignoring you."

"As a matter of fact," Loretta said, "I tried to call this morning. I was gonna pick you up, take you to breakfast."

Joanna sighed. "I'm sorry. I don't know what's going on."

Setting her own supplies down, Loretta made a point to stand in front of Joanna and catch her full attention. "It's that house. You've got a lot of negative energy going on—from your own emotions and whatever the hell is happening there. You need a break from it all, a *real* break. I'm telling you, stay with me, even if for a few hours tonight; get out, have some company, use my phone to make some calls. I don't mind, I'll pay the long-distance bill."

Joanna was prepared to deny her again but saw the concern etched on Loretta's face. She knew Loretta wanted to help—she cared—and putting her off repeatedly wasn't helping any more than any other option.

Joanna nodded. "Okay," she said. "I don't know that trying to sleep in a strange house would guarantee me any rest, though."

"Strange house?" Loretta asked. "Sister, you got the strange house! Besides, you were asleep in a truck in the middle of daylight in front of a *strange* house."

Joanna chuckled for real.

"That's better," Loretta said. "I ain't gonna piss on you and tell you it's raining, but the Army guy is probably right. If there hasn't been any word, then there isn't any word to tell. Maybe he's got himself holed up in a safe place no one can reach him and he's riding out his tour."

Joanna nodded again. "Maybe."

"Okay," Loretta said, "Let's clean *this* strange house. Always smells like cat pee in the bathroom and these people don't have any pets. *That's* strange!"

Joanna shook her head and chuckled again, walking off to the kitchen to start her duties.

36

Each letter seemed worse than the last; the effects of war were weighing on her daughter and the prospect of coming home soon brought little solace. Ups and downs came sharply. One paragraph was well written and discussed how they had ensured a neighborhood was safe and they played soccer in the street with some kids. The next was written in different ink and scribbled hastily—most likely the next day—about how one of the kids had stepped on an IED and was "lucky" to only be losing a leg.

Today's letter was the worst, though. There could be little else that would break her heart more than reading her daughter's explanation that she wouldn't be coming home on time. A clause called "stop-loss" was being enacted on her unit and they would have to perform back-to-back tours. Her baby wouldn't be home for another year.

She climbed the stairs, letter clutched in her hand; not knowing what else to do with herself, she crawled into bed. Her husband would be home soon enough. There was nothing they could do but wait and pray.

She was shocked awake by the front door bursting open. He was calling her name and the surprise of his urgency made it difficult to respond at once.

His fast, heavy footfalls up the stairs drowned her initial response, but she said again, "I'm fine, what are you yelling for?"

"Fine?" he cried. "I heard a shout from outside! Are you okay?"

She shook her head. "I didn't shout. I was asleep before you came in. I'm fine, though. Thanks… I guess?"

"Are you messing with me?" he seethed.

"I am not messing with you," she said. "But—" she patted the bed next to her, "sit down. We need to talk."

His eyes went wide and he curled his lip. "What?"

"Please sit."

He took a deep breath and sat down on the edge of the bed next to her.

Handing him the letter she placed her hand on his knee. "She's been ordered to stay for another tour."

He looked over the letter, but the spoken words stung him. "That can't be… *possible*. That's not *fair*."

She didn't say anything, letting him read the letter instead. It explained the protocol and what it meant and how it was legal, if not deceitful. His daughter went on to say there were some crying foul and threatening to walk, but she would serve on. Anything else would make life harder later. He felt a swell of pride at her perseverance, but also crushed by this seeming double-cross by his own country.

"Oh my God!" his wife cried.

Looking at her quickly, he followed her gaze through the bedroom door. The shadow of a man darted out of the way. Bounding from the bed and into the hall, he could see no one there, but the front door was hanging open. As he rushed down the stairs, it occurred to him he didn't hear any footsteps at all, but his momentum carried him out onto the veranda. He couldn't see or hear anything out of the ordinary in the front yard.

He rushed back up the stairs and checked all the rooms in succession and found no one. He was reminded of the night he thought there was an intruder.

She was resting her head in her hands when he stepped back into the bedroom.

"Do you ever get the feeling this house is *haunted*?" she asked, looking at him with a mix of frustration and fear.

"Absolutely not," he shook his head. "I won't even entertain that notion. These are our own boogeymen. We're stressed out and scared as it is; anything more is causing us to jump at shadows."

She frowned, not looking confident in his answer, but she nodded in agreement anyway. Finally relaxing from the adrenaline surge, he sat down next to her again and reached out, urging her into his arms. He held onto her on the bed for a long while before they forced themselves to go through their nightly routine yet again.

37 – HARRY HOUDINI

Harry leaned against the frame of the door with his back to Chief Mignola. He could hear the menacing breathing again, but this time it was coming from the Chief. Harry looked over his shoulder and could see Errol staring him down. Which way would he run? Would the bed be enough to shake the Chief loose from whatever held him now?

"Are you in there, Chief?" Harry asked.

The heavy breathing continued. It sounded like someone coming off a startling decision. Whoever the Chief was, they had killed two people now, and Harry himself had felt one of those deaths. If there was an afterlife, a great beyond, this was the closest he could come without visiting the other side himself. There was now no doubt in his mind at all—whatever was happening here fell squarely in the paranormal realm. There was no explanation, but it was happening.

Staring at the Chief, Harry could see that Errol Mignola was standing there, but this person was completely out of place.

"Who are you?" Harry wondered aloud. "Where are you from?"

The Chief didn't answer, but turned toward the connecting door. Upon opening, he swung the door back and forth on its hinges between his outstretched hands. It was an odd sight. His body language and the expression on his face showed the weight of the two murders settling in.

Again, from the foyer and the balcony behind him, he could hear the muttering of voices and shuffling of feet, but not from anyone part of their party. He stepped onto the balcony to try to gain more perspective on everything that was happening, even if invisible. There was a sudden scuffle and a bang against the floor. Harry could feel himself falling in line with the events again.

If a moment ago he'd sensed fear and lack of hope, this was anger and vengeance. He held himself, though, and felt the force pass through him. The door in front of him slammed shut.

Part of him felt concern for the Chief's—and everyone's—well-being; another part of him concentrated on the brief window into the event he had witnessed. Someone fell and someone—this entity—rushed up the stairs to check on the perceived victim. Instead, it was presented with the bodies on the floor. They could see the assailant—whatever it was that possessed Chief Mignola. But it stopped in its place; this individual was planning to attack the assailant.

The door between the rooms and then the door at the end of the hall slammed, but it was followed by a brief silence. The door at the end of the hall opened without a sound, and Dr. Lawrence stepped out. Harry could tell despite the confusion and caution on the Doctor's face, it was not the Doctor.

Harry stood on the balcony outside the course of events, near the upstairs bathroom door. Mignola threw open his door and Harry knew instantly their attempt to break the cycle had failed. If anything, they had fallen further in line with it. The Chief leapt across the hall to the opposite bedroom and pulled the door shut as he lunged back from whence he came. Harry thought it was an odd move, but seeing as Dr. Lawrence bolted to the sound, it became evident it was only a ruse.

The Chief lunged toward the Doctor, sending him careening to the floor, then straight on top of Harry. Now Harry found himself in a struggle for his life as he fought with Chief Mignola—but it wasn't *really* the Chief, and he wasn't really Harry. He could hear the gasps of the people in the foyer below as he struggled to retain control of his own actions, but he could also sense the feelings of this other individual, all confusion and fear. Again, Harry felt split down the middle. Part of him wanted to observe, while the other, stranger part that had inhabited his physical space desperately wanted to fight for survival.

Harry fought, too, for control over his own body. He was able to change the direction of the grapple and found he was in full control of his faculties as he flipped Mignola over and onto the balcony floor. The Chief's eyes went wide as the disorientation set in, but also the realization of what had transpired.

When Dr. Lawrence finally stepped out into the hall, the double doors of the upstairs living room banged open and closed again, followed by the sounds of a fight and then the breaking of glass.

"I think I was possessed," Errol said.

Harry helped the Chief up and the Doctor came to check on them both.

"That was amazing," Herbert said.

"Speak for yourself, Doc," Errol said. "I was in the backseat of my own brain. It felt like a dream. I'm real sorry, Mr. Houdini, I wasn't in control. I didn't mean to hurt you."

Harry shook his head, but before he could say anything, Millie finally realized Harry's identity.

"Houdini?" she said, surprised. "Like, *the* Houdini?"

But the event hadn't come to an end by their breaking out of it. There was the sudden rush of footsteps down the stairs and through the foyer. Father Francis, Donald, and Millie all jumped in surprise as something passed them and opened the front door.

Phoebe watched, more interested in the groups' reactions to the events than the events themselves.

The front door slammed shut. Two sets of feet rushed into the house and off in different directions. The front door came open again and determined footsteps entered the reading room. Harry, Errol, and Herbert rushed down the stairs to try to take in more of what was happening, but they could only hear. It was now dark outside, but the moon was shining brightly and filling the darkened house with silver beams and blue shadows.

The front door opened again, and before anyone could get out of the way, a shadowy figure burst through the foyer and after the sounds in the reading room. A woman screamed and everyone jumped. Sounds of a fight similar to what had been heard upstairs came from near the fireplace. Footsteps ran past everyone and up the stairs, then slammed almost every door. The fight in the reading room continued until a burst of muted fiery light erupted from the fireplace. It was like seeing flames behind smoked glass; they were there, but somehow distant and lacking energy.

One of the fighters broke off and lurched away and up the stairs. Were they seeking to help or harm whoever had run up before?

Everyone in the group was pressed against a wall in the foyer, trying to stay out of the apparitions' way. In the low light, Harry could see that all of them, save Phoebe, were mortified. This wasn't the ghosts of *Hamlet*, or even *A Christmas Carol*, this was something violent and menacing.

Harry tried to concentrate on everything he had experienced, to try and determine where it was going or what it all meant. The pursuing set of feet up the stairs threw open the door of the master bedroom, but then promptly crumpled to the floor, and silence set in.

"Holy shit, Mrs. Backlund!" Millie said, breaking the silence and causing everyone to jump. "How the hell do you sleep at night in a house like this?"

"I heard tales of ghosts in the War," Father Francis said. "Ghosts of the recently dead visiting friends and family in impossible places, ghosts in the trenches, and on the battlefield. But that was a crisis; people see things when they're scared. It's a nice day next to a lake in a beautiful house; why is all of this happening?"

"You don't think it's ghosts, then?" Donald asked.

"The Chief came at me with intent," Francis continued. "But not that of his own. He was possessed by something that was after where I was, not after *me*. Harry tripped up Chief Mignola upstairs, and the fight ended. This thing isn't trying to hurt *us*, it's no demon; I think we're getting in *its* way."

"It's not over, is it, Phoebe?" Harry asked.

She looked at him with a straight face and only shook her head.

38 – HELEN AND DANIEL

Most every room was affected. If one didn't see or feel anything, then things were most certainly heard. Daniel had sat in the sunroom in the morning to enjoy the natural light and view over the newspaper and a cup of coffee. Four hours later, the lunch hour had passed, the cup of coffee sat with a third of cold coffee left, and Daniel sat terrified, knowing he needed to at least get up to go to the restroom.

The downstairs toilet was between the kitchen and the library living room. It might as well have been on the opposite side of the house—or an entire world away.

Daniel held the paper up and made half-hearted turns of pages to look busy, to hide in mundane action. He shivered in his chair, cold sweat filling his armpits and the crack of his ass. If he didn't get up soon, he might wet himself. If he lowered the paper, though, he might be faced with the thing making the sounds.

At first it was upstairs, the faint and distant shuffling of feet: innocuous. Surely someone was moving about. When the sharp bang came, even with the wall separating this room from the one on the front of the house, he jumped, but thought nothing of it. That is, until a moment later, when what sounded like a group of people in the foyer proved to be nothing *but* sound. Looking out through the dining room there was no one there, though sounds came from that room.

The shuffling upstairs turned into hard steps, running, stumbling bodies slamming together and into walls and the floor… Only to stop. Only to start all over again.

When a voice spoke directly to him, said his *name*, Daniel jumped and tore his paper. Every muscle in his lower half clinched in an attempt not to lose his bladder.

The innkeeper, Helen, held a hand to her chest, startled. "I'm so sorry, Mr. Arnold!"

Daniel heaved a few ragged breaths before he let the paper go and waved his dissent. "No, I'm sorry; I think… I uh… I lost track of time."

She bared her teeth in a nervous smile. "That's why I wanted to check on you; hadn't heard a peep from you. I wanted to make sure everything was okay?"

Had she not heard anything at all?

The urgency of his body's current dilemma snapped back to the forefront of his mind. "I'm sorry, again; please excuse me a moment."

She stepped aside as he hastened through the dining room and kitchen.

~

With relief came newfound relaxation. Finding a furtive Helen milling about in the kitchen, Daniel felt a pang of guilt for rushing away so quickly.

"I'm sorry, again," he pleaded. "I think I let the house get to me. I thought I heard some movement upstairs and I let my imagination carry me away. I was glued to my chair in there and you startled me out of my stupor."

Helen sighed, relieved. "There's no need to apologize for that. That room, for the most part, can be quiet. But when something happens, it's like a broken record; I've never quite understood it. I should have guessed you had been gripped and maybe should have approached a bit more delicately."

"No!" Daniel laughed. "We can't keep going in apologetic circles. If anything, I should thank you for getting me up!"

She smiled and motioned, offering him a cup of tea as she pulled down supplies for herself.

"Yes, thanks."

"What did you hear?" she asked.

He grimaced. "You know, I can't believe I came here on my own. I can't tell you if I really heard anything or if I let my imagination run wild. It sounded at first like someone walking upstairs, then maybe some talking, then a fight, and it would start over again."

She nodded as she put a kettle on the stove. "That sounds about right. I can't say it wasn't your imagination, but I can tell you that it's only been us since about eleven. *Well*, us and my husband; but he's a day sleeper and swears he's never heard a thing the years we've lived here. The other couple went into town. It may have been their exit that triggered the sounds you heard."

Daniel sighed. "Maybe. I think I regret coming *on my own*. Honestly, though, it's what I hoped for. I guess it's true—*be careful what you wish for*."

"Indeed." Helen nodded. "I don't mean to pry. I like to leave my guests to experience things in the raw, be it the house or the natural surrounding beauty. But I don't get single visitors; it's couples or groups mostly. What brings you here, *on your own*?"

They sat at a small kitchen table with two chairs. He leaned back, lifting the front legs of the chair about an inch. "I write," he stated. "I wanted to experience something new, different, *weird*. Found this place on the world wide web. Tired of hearing about bullshit in the Middle East, bombings, rockets… The whole world is on edge, and I just wanted to get away for a weekend. Instead, I make myself more scared than I imagined possible. I guess *there's* inspiration."

The kettle began to hiss. Helen got up and crossed the room, ready to prepare both their cups. Daniel took in a breath. He was ready to ask about her—about the business, the house, to learn more if he could—but the back door flung open as if from outside, and something shuffled across the floor. They both jumped, but as Daniel looked at Helen, she merely looked perturbed. Daniel, on the other hand, felt ready to let loose his bladder again.

"You know what?" Daniel said, nearly knocking his chair over as he tried to get up and out of the kitchen. "I think I'll have to take you up on tea another time. Maybe I can catch the couple in town and see what they're up to!"

Helen crossed to the door and closed it lightly, locking the dead-bolt. She knew it had been locked before, but that event didn't seem to care about locks. Shaking her head as she resumed preparing her own tea, she spoke to herself… maybe a little to the house, too.

"This is why I get their mailing address."

She sat back down at the table after readjusting Daniel's askew chair. She drank her tea in peaceful quiet.

39 - CYNTHIA MORRISON

Thom's mumbling voice ceased when something hit a wall with a dull *thunk*. What followed sounded like a body falling to the floor. Silence seemed to pour down from the balcony. Cynthia, Noah, Marcus, and Shannon exchanged worried glances.

Cynthia, standing at the base of the stairs, called in a forced whisper, "Thom?"

Nothing.

Noah noticed a red glow emanating from his right. As his eyes finally adjusted to the darkness, he saw embers in the fireplace. Waves of fear gripped him as things started to fit together; Cynthia's scream and now the odd sounds from upstairs as they stood in the foyer. He stared at the embers and wondered how the fire would start.

"Can you call out?" Noah asked in a whisper.

Shannon was standing with her arms caught in awkward positions, her phone having gone dark before she could try to dial out again. She checked, lighting up her face, but shook her head. "It's fluctuating. I've got nothing right now."

Noah pulled out his own phone, Cynthia and Marcus followed suit, but no one had a reliable signal.

"Thom?" Cynthia called upstairs, still in a quiet voice, but louder than before.

"We need to leave," Noah said. "We need to stick together, get out to the road, and find help."

"But Thom…" Cynthia said, taking a step up the stairs.

"Cynthia," Noah hissed. "He's not responding and he's not coming out. Someone *else* must be up there because we all heard someone call his name."

"How do we know it was *someone*?" Cynthia countered. "Maybe we've set off the event like you planned and Thom saw something to make him faint? He could need our help and you want to run away?"

Noah grimaced, looking to Shannon and Marcus to back him up, but there was only frightened confusion in their faces.

Cynthia was already halfway up the stairs and on her way to the top when Noah turned back to look at her again. "Cynthia!" he begged.

"Thom!" she called out in a full voice, echoing in the relative silence.

Realizing she still had the flashlight in hand as she made the top of the stairs, she clicked it on to light her path. Before she could cross the balcony, she stopped and gasped as she saw Thom inside the door of the first kids' room. He had slumped to the floor in a stiff sitting position.

"Thom?" she whimpered.

Taking a few more steps forward, the light revealed blood had poured out across his front from a gash in his neck. She bent forward and covered her mouth, but the beam fell on another body. Reggie lay dead on the floor in front of Thom. She opened her mouth, but if it was to scream, sob, or be sick, her body couldn't seem to choose.

Something caught her attention despite the sight before her. The sound, *that* sound of heavy breathing, but this wasn't ethereal, this was real and in front of her. In the shaking beam of light, she could make out the partition door swinging back and forth, sending a cold rush through her that shocked her back to her senses.

She took a step back and recalled what had happened before. To her right, through her periphery, she saw that she was about even with the double doors of the upstairs living room. She spun to retreat down the stairs. Fear raced through her and she stumbled and fell face first to the floor.

Noah and Marcus both bolted up to her. Noah stopped to check on Cynthia, but Marcus charged into the kids' rooms. He slammed the door shut as he went through, and the connecting door slammed, but Noah couldn't see anything. He helped Cynthia up and walked towards the stairs. The door Marcus had gone through opened, then the door on the opposite side of the hall slammed. The first door, the kid's room, opened and closed again. At the end of the hall to the second kid's room, Marcus leapt out. But there was only him.

Noah and Marcus approached each other, and Cynthia yelped as she saw a figure come up behind Marcus. Something flashed towards Marcus as the attacker swung their arm. Marcus grunted, stumbled, and fell to the floor, almost tripping up Noah. Noah caught his footing, but not before grappling with the attacker. They bashed through the upstairs living room doors, the force of their entry sending the doors bouncing on their hinges and closing again. There was the sound of a scuffle followed by shattering glass. Cynthia could hear Noah's voice make a frightened gasp, but then nothing.

Cynthia looked down at Shannon, who was standing there in shock. Trying to shake off the fear, she rushed down the stairs and grabbed Shannon.

"We have to get out to the road, like Noah said…" she said into Shannon's blank face.

Shannon slowly nodded.

Cynthia led Shannon by the arm out the front door, but their attacker had already managed to come around the house and was already at the steps of the veranda. Cynthia yanked Shannon back into the house and slammed the door, fumbling to lock the door. The assailant kicked the door in with incredible force.

The blow knocked Cynthia to her left, toward the sitting room, and spun Shannon off toward the living room to the right. Cynthia scrambled toward the fireplace to grab something to defend herself with. Fumbling in the darkness to grab the fire-poker, she dragged it through the coals, spreading several bright red chunks across the floor. Exposed to fresh air, the flames danced. She waved the poker back and forth in the darkness but could see nothing.

40 - JOANNA NEWSTED

Heavy breathing everywhere, shadows at every corner, and doors slamming. Footsteps, shouts, screams, and the sound of glass breaking. Everything all happened at once but never happened at all. Sometimes Joanna felt like she was being chased—or was under attack. Other times she felt like she was the one chasing, that her invisible assailant was right around the corner and she could pounce on them, but nothing was ever there.

Tonight, the sounds were too intense. It always started when she tried to go to bed, which made her question her own sanity. Was it sleep or the lack thereof that set off these events? Were they all waking nightmares? She didn't trust herself to seek out help and any time someone else was in the house, nothing happened.

Tonight, it was too much. Launching herself out of bed, she pulled the mattress through the door and dragged it to the room with the hutch. Nothing ever seemed to happen in there, not that she could hear, anyway.

As soon as she slammed the door, the breathing stopped. The house had gone quiet. The little bit of light coming in from the moon revealed how dusty the room was. She tried to think: When was the last time she had come in here? Two months ago? It had started getting chilly, she grabbed one of the big comforters they kept in the antique hutch, the only piece of furniture in this room.

She dropped the mattress on the floor. With the silence, she could think more clearly, even relaxing the slightest bit. Maybe she would move the bed and her clothes into this room.

As she spread out the sheets to crawl into bed, she thought about the other rooms in the house. The two small ones across the hall had stood empty, save cheap thrift store furniture they had thrown in there for their visiting mothers almost a year ago; she hadn't even stepped inside since their mothers had left.

She hadn't gone into the upstairs living room since the first time she heard the windows shatter. She had heard that event several times since but knew she wouldn't find anything. She avoided the room with no windows, though for no real reason; something didn't feel right about it. Andrew mused on making it into an entertainment room, maybe one day setting up a film projector for their own private theater. For now, at least, she avoided it.

Sitting on the edge of the mattress, she realized she had no pillows. She sighed and decided if they had fallen in the hall or along the balcony, she would grab them. Otherwise, she would bunch up some comforter and wait until morning.

Looking through the barely opened door, she saw a pillow was indeed on the floor on the balcony. Only about three steps out. She closed her eyes and leaned her head on the door frame. This was childish; she felt six years old, ready to dart through the darkness to avoid whatever unseen monsters may lie in wait.

This house was her monster, though; she had come to expect certain sounds and visions, one following or preceding the other. She was trapped in a cycle.

Right now, it was different, though. Deciding she would sleep in another room, it had already grown quiet. She opened the door enough to slide through and stepped quickly and quietly to grab the pillow. Leaning down, before her hand touched the pillow, the closet at the opposite end of the hall popped open. She shut her eyes and gritted her teeth. Grabbing the pillow, she stood up, noticing a change in the light through her shut eyelids.

She opened them and saw that the light in the closet had come on and the door was hanging open about an inch.

"Fuck you," she said, tired and frustrated.

She turned around and ignored the new event and went back into her new bedroom. The decision to disregard gave her a sense of power and bravery. She could beat this house. She didn't need anyone's help, and she didn't need to run away or be scared.

"This is my house now," she said out loud. "You live with me. I make the rules in my own house."

With the last forceful statement, she slammed the door, fluffed her pillow, and threw herself down on the mattress. Pulling the covers up all around her, she curled up and dared to feel comfortable. She yawned and her muscles tightened for a second, then she nestled her head into the pillow and shut her eyes.

The door opened.

Her eyes snapped open. The door swung open enough that a body could pass through; not much wider than she had opened it herself. In the dust, new footprints formed among her own and the smears from the mattress being pulled into the room. Despite seeing their formation, she heard nothing. Come to think of it, the door had a slight creak after opening about an inch, yet it hadn't made a sound now. Delicately, as if someone was trying to sneak along, the footprints stopped at the hutch and one of the big twin doors opened. Finally, the sound of someone carefully crawling into the hutch, as though they were trying to hide.

The door slowly closed with a soft click. Joanna stared, terrified, yet curious. This was something she hadn't seen before. Somehow, this didn't feel threatening. She lay there wondering if she was dreaming. She watched the hutch and listened intently. There was no sound, not in here, not from the hall, not even from outside in the trees. Sitting up and trying to put her full attention on the antique, she heard it: soft sobbing.

At first, she was mortified. This frightened thing in the room with her seemed to mock her. Like the house saying that she was indeed afraid and didn't hold the control she thought she had. She forced herself to consider the events, though. Almost everything else—from violent slamming doors, to menacing shadows, her nightmares of murder, even visions of flames along the staircase—all of it had been terrifying. *This* was sad and lonely. At her wit's end, trying to hide, and whatever *it* was out there was still following her. Tears began to well up in her eyes.

Was this Andrew?

Had he been lost out there in the jungles and… killed? Had his spirit found its way home, and even now, was stuck in the hell of war, but trying to come home to her? Frustration and fear washed over her as her tears began to flow. She hadn't cried in some time. Living under stress and fear all this time, there was never an opportunity to let her emotions come forward. *Was* this Andrew?

She lay back down, crying, letting go of months' worth of emotion. Andrew's absence and the house's relentless torment were colliding in this, the quietest room in the house. Her husband must be truly gone. She didn't need a telegram or two uniformed men showing up; she could feel it—all of this—was the war's toll.

~

The telegram had been misplaced at the post office, sitting under a box for almost three weeks before it was found. Joanna read it over and over again, sitting on the box springs of their bed, still in the master bedroom. She had come in to try to move some necessities to her new bedroom when she saw the yellow car pull up outside. At first her heart leapt, thinking Andrew was home, somehow unannounced. Instead, the driver had delivered the telegram, explained why it was late arriving, apologized, and promptly left.

She looked at it again.

> REGRET TO INFORM YOU YOUR HUSBAND PRIVATE ANDREW NEWSTED WAS ON TWELFTH DECEMBER WOUNDED IN ACTION IN VIETNAM…

Details would follow. Not how he was wounded, not the severity, no prognosis, *and* it was late being delivered. Surely his mother would have received a notification as well. Did she know more, being his direct next of kin? She read it again. Nodding, she realized her increasingly intense experiences in the house *must* have correlated with his being wounded. With no contact, no letters, no phone calls from anyone—somehow, she must have been notified in this bizarre way. The house had been warning her all this time.

"Joanna?" came a call from downstairs.

She looked around the room, her brow and nose scrunching her eyes into slits. The voice was loud, but hoarse; it sounded real.

"Joanna?" the voice called again. It was followed by heavy footsteps and a strange clatter of wood and metal.

She stood up and stepped into the hallway. At the bottom of the stairs, Andrew stood in an Army uniform, leaning on crutches. He had a cast on his left ankle. She stared at him in complete disbelief. It must be a trick, another apparition. Or was it the ghost of her husband come home?

"There you are, Jo," he said with a tired smile. "I tried to call you a few times on my way home—even when I got here—but there wasn't any answer."

She ran down the stairs, terrified he would disappear if she took her eyes off him. When she was close, she could see he was tanned, had lost even more weight than the last time she saw him, and he carried a lot of stress of his own. But he was standing there. She could smell him and feel him as she reached out and tentatively touched him.

Finding he was real, she grabbed him and began to sob.

He held her to him and they shared a long moment of being together.

"Didn't you know I was coming?" he finally asked, choking back a hitch in his throat.

She held up the telegram she had received only hours before. "I got this only this morning."

He looked at it and saw the date. "I wrote you and mom both two letters since this happened. I was wondering why I wasn't getting anything back. I was beginning to think bad thoughts… well, I was thinking a lot of bad thoughts, really; I hadn't been in contact with anyone for almost a year!"

She shook her head. "We never got them."

She tried to formulate words to explain the situation, but immense relief consumed her instead. "You're home." It was all she could get out before grabbing him again and sobbing into his chest.

Still leaning on the crutches, he wrapped his arms around her shoulders and held her. Explanations could wait.

41 – NOAH BENJAMIN

Cold earth and wet grass.
Taste of blood.
Try to rise; no, that hurts. Better lie here a while.
But, why outside?

Noah stood up so fast he wasn't sure how he'd exactly done it. Despite the adrenaline waking him and propelling him to his feet, the incredible pain in his chest and spine made it hard to even take a breath. Recalling how he ended up out here, though, drove him forward.

A sliver of moon had finally crested the treetops. He could see hundreds of tiny reflections on the ground in the shards of glass from the window he and the assailant had fallen through. He remembered getting in close, realizing it was a man, and fighting hard to avoid a knife. They stumbled through the upstairs living room and—either because it was too dark to see, or from subconscious motivation—they went through the window, falling ten feet to the ground. How long had he been out?

No time to think. Where was the other guy?

He tried to take off into a run, but his entire body screamed in pain, making him stumble. He cradled his own ribs, trying to take deep breaths, though he only found short, shallow ones. Looking up, he noticed the mainline from the breaker box had been cut, but the box was open. Reggie had gone to check when the lights had gone out. Was he the culprit?

He forced himself forward—he had to get inside, had to find Cynthia and the others. The kitchen door was jammed and offered him no entrance. As he rounded the house, he could hear the door being kicked in. He had to hurry. He had to push through the pain.

As he made it to the front of the house, the door was hanging open, but he could see no one. Climbing the stairs was the worst experience of his life, worse than falling to the ground. *Worse than having to ride his bike uphill into the wind when he was 13.* "I hate hills," he used to say.

No, he shook his head, he needed to focus.

Stepping through the door, he could see hot coals strewn across the sitting room. Light, weak flames danced about in the fireplace. Cynthia was standing in front of the fireplace brandishing a poker, but she couldn't see. The figure of a man stalked forward. Noah charged him and the two of them went smashing to the floor. Cynthia screamed.

They struggled with each other again and Cynthia ran away, charging up the stairs. Multiple doors slammed. Noah thought Cynthia must be trying to hide.

Good, Noah thought as an elbow crossed his chin.

His body was in incredible pain, even panting from exertion was setting his lungs on fire.

Fire? *Yes*! If he could get this guy toward the fireplace, Noah might get the upper hand.

As they continued to wrestle, one of them kicked a glowing coal under the busted chair and another went careening into the foyer. They reached the hearth and Noah violently banged his attacker against the brick. Feeling a momentary lack of resistance, Noah shoved the man's head into the fireplace. Immediately, the assailant howled in pain and threw Noah off him, sending him sprawling across the floor. As the attacker thrashed, he threw more coals and embers across the room.

Noah dragged himself up and struggled up the stairs. He had to find Cynthia and get out. He had a hunch she might be upstairs in the primary bedroom, but he only made it as far as the top of the stairs before he felt a blow across the back of his head. It was dull and set a ringing in his ears, the outside world suddenly muted as if by cotton balls. He fell to his knees and looked at the floor. His eyes began to water and when he blinked, a single tear fell to the floor.

"*I'm* the ghost," he said to himself in an astonished whisper.

Before darkness overtook him, he recalled Phoebe Backlund's séances and catching the tears of a ghost outside the primary bedroom. Not that hokey ectoplasm, this was something real and out of thin air. Now he knew it was of his own making; all of this was his fault.

"*Huh,*" he said, before passing out.

42 – ANDREW NEWSTED

They had been incredibly lucky. Andrew was the only one wounded, and he hadn't even noticed until after they got to safety. They had been ambushed while on patrol between villages, but their troop was able to hold their position until air support arrived. Andrew thought he had tripped, but he scrambled into action and did his job. When standing started to hurt, he thought he had twisted his ankle, but a hole in his boot was oozing blood. They made it to the next village on their patrol, where the residents were gracious enough to tend to him as they waited for a helicopter.

The bullet barely missed his Achilles tendon and lodged between his tibia and fibula. He stayed in the field hospital for a few days before he was moved to Quang Tri and eventually made his way home. Despite his physical injuries, he was clearly haunted by the war, especially being under fire and seeing the effects of the war on the locals. They were still coming to terms with the utter failure of the mail system, which was an injury all its own. But Andrew was home for good.

He scratched his temple, though it didn't itch. As he did, he even wondered about that and thought too long, realizing his gaze had probably glazed over. She was waiting for a response. Thankfully, she was patient.

Inhaling deeply, he shook his head, blinked rapidly, and put his arms to his sides. The words formed in his head, then an alternate response, and then another. He frowned, exhaled, and reached for the glass of wine.

He swirled the drink and reminisced about the week he'd been without beer and drank Joanna's merlot with dinner. He'd been hooked. A small smile graced his lips before he took a drink. Over the rim of the glass, he saw she was still waiting for a response.

Sighing heavily again, Andrew tried to explain, even if only to himself. "I want to, I do. The guys ask to have a beer; Lucy's is right there as we dock. And I want to, but I feel… *tired*? I don't even know. I know they're tired, too. That's *why* they want to stop at the bar, to relax."

He looked around the room as if it might offer a better explanation or answers to his own questions. The sunroom was mostly relaxing. They'd put a second-hand couch Joanna purchased off one of her customers against the wall to stare out the windows, with nothing more than a couple of small tables on either side. The room felt barren, but the simplicity was nice on a sunny day when the chop on Superior sparkled through the trees.

He started to nod. "I feel like this room."

She cocked her head and gave a confused smile.

"It's comfortable in here, with you," he said. "But it's also empty, with the beautiful world outside the windows. I'm comfortable here in my own little space, but any more people in this room and there wouldn't be any place to sit, and I would get anxious. Would they mind? Would they think less of me because we don't have but a couch in this room?"

"Of course not…" Joanna said, reaching across the couch to touch his knee.

"No, not that," he shook his head. "That's how my head feels… like I have a lot of space, but putting anything more in it is too much."

He shifted his position, crossing his legs a different way. "A party?"

"You've been home for over a month," she said. "You're back to work now; shouldn't we celebrate?"

He picked up the glass again and downed the rest. Gritting his teeth against the bite of alcohol in the back of his jaw, he relented. "Okay."

She smiled wide, but seeing he was still uncomfortable, she kept her excitement tempered.

They watched the dusk turn to night before they even got up to eat anything.

~

Andrew's crewmates with their girlfriends, and Loretta coming over made the house feel lively. Andrew was glad they were there once they had arrived. Earlier, he had been a ball of nerves. He felt both nauseous and faint. He had been in a firefight in Vietnam—shot, even—yet his nerves over hosting a party seemed to make him feel the worst.

Joanna soothed him, though, in a number of ways, and he was thankful. Once Loretta arrived with a bottle of Joanna's favorite wine and he poured the three of them a glass and casual conversation took hold, his nerves finally began to relax. Laughter felt good. He could tell as he felt better that Joanna and even Loretta, had begun to loosen up as well.

A pang of guilt erupted at that notion. Was he making everyone else around him nervous? He drowned the thought with another drink. Fortunately, he was also distracted by a knock at the door.

As his crew showed up over the next hour, he felt his spirit lift. Joanna had been right: a party felt good. He continued to notice that the better he felt, the more joyous those around him became. It seemed even the house welcomed the diversion.

Lights seemed brighter, the air felt inviting…

"Have you seen any ghosts?" Garret's girlfriend asked.

Garret had been out on the boat every day. He never called in sick and always put in more time than was expected of him. He was also soft-spoken, sometimes going days without much more than salutations. He elbowed her in the side.

"What?" she chuckled. "Everyone knows about this house; I can't be the only one curious…"

Joanna became slightly nervous and started shaking her head, but Andrew felt particularly light. Even though he knew the question should make him feel self-conscious, he felt compelled to share.

"Yes, we both have," he nodded. "House is full of 'em. We've had to take to naming them."

The group collectively leaned in, excited to hear tales firsthand of the house.

Inhaling sharply, he looked at the empty glass he had raised to try to drink. He thought for a moment and couldn't remember how many he had had. That was probably enough, then.

"When I had broken my wrist before being shipped out, when I was stuck at home, I honestly found myself getting used to them," he boasted. "They'd bang on either side of the doors, run up and down the hall and stairs, slam doors. But any time you went to check… *nothing*."

Joanna felt twinges of horror as he dismissively explained major events with minor details. Would he beckon something? Was he tempting fate?

The house remained quiet for the guests--even as Andrew became more boisterous and their guests became more engrossed in seemingly small events.. There were varying levels of disappointment and gratitude at that. The evening wore on as stories of legends and corroborating firsthand accounts were exchanged. Even Joanna relaxed enough to share a few of her minor events.

The evening turned into early morning and their guests began to depart, each taking a moment to hug Joanna and Andrew both. They gave somber "welcome back" and glad tidings at Andrew's return. They thanked their hosts for the good time and disappeared into the night.

As the last guest left and they shut the door, there was a distinctive click from upstairs.

Joanna's eyes went wide, but Andrew only shook his head.

"Nope," he said. "We're going to just clean up. We can put on a record. Tonight is ours alone…"

He looked up to the landing. "All the guests have gone; you missed your chance!" he shouted. "Now my wife and I are going to enjoy the rest of our evening *by ourselves*."

Joanna gave a nervous huff, but there were no other sounds from upstairs. Save for the Beatles, the house remained quiet.

43

She leaned back in her chair, folded her arms, and loudly sighed… again. They had been waiting for nearly an hour. She could tell her husband was ignoring her; he was re-reading the same magazine he had picked up when they arrived.

"We could have gone down there to pick her up," she huffed.

"This is still faster, even with the delay," he said without looking up. "Like I said, *ten* minutes ago."

"I hate the waiting," she growled. "At least if we were driving we'd be *moving*."

He finally set the magazine in his lap. "Five hours there and back in a car, or an hour and a half here where we can get up and go to the bathroom when we want?"

She scowled at him.

"Read a magazine!" he said, putting his face back into his.

"You have the only one!" she whined. "And when did you develop a fascination with fly fishing?"

He shrugged. "It's interesting. Maybe we should give it a try sometime."

"You haven't read a word of that thing, have you?"

"The pictures are pretty neat."

Snatching the magazine out of his hands, she said, "You be bored for the next hour!"

Now *he* sighed heavily and folded his arms. For the next hour, he watched reruns of *Frasier* playing on a TV across the lobby. The sound was too faint and the captions too small to read, but it was something to focus on while they waited.

When the small single-engine plane landed, taxiing their daughter from Duluth to Grand Marais, boredom and frustration were wiped away. It took all their control not to break for the runway and tear the door off. Instead, they walked out to the edge of the tarmac calmly and waited for the plane to come to a stop. When their daughter—dressed in her fatigues—lumbered her way out of the tiny door with her duffle bag, that was when they lost composure.

When she walked up, her mother grabbed her and cried while her father hugged them both.

"Jeez," she said, "you look like you didn't expect me to come home. Don't you have any faith in me?"

Her father laughed, her mother cried harder, and in that moment, she finally felt safe.

As they piled into the car, her father asked, "It's late. You want to get some dinner? Anywhere you want. I hear Lucy's Dynamo Bay is friendly to military."

"That place is a dump," her mother said.

She laughed. "Honestly, I'd really like to eat at home… even if it's just mac and cheese. I'd really like to have dinner at home."

Her father nodded in agreement. "You got it, sweetheart."

The ride home was filled with light chitchat. No one was ready to discuss war stories yet, but they settled into being a family again right away. Getting back to the house, she was glad to see that it looked more lived in. *Now* she was home.

There was another teary embrace as they entered the house. Everyone could relax after a long two and a half years.

The three of them worked together in the kitchen to prepare dinner. They laughed and played as they set the dining table. Over dinner, it was still more light conversation, but the exhaustion in her face from her flights and long time away from home became increasingly apparent.

Yawning, she asked, "They caught that killer, right?"

Her father nodded. "Yeah, late last year. It was a bit after his last two victims. Turned out his name—the *Corpse*—was pretty apt. He had AIDS *and* cancer. He died in the hospital after charges were officially brought against him."

"I don't suppose you can have any greater justice than that; a trial would have given him more spotlight," she said. "At least I know I can sleep safe tonight!"

Her mother chuckled, though there was an undertone of nerves.

As if in response to the awkward laugh, there was the distinct and sharp bang of a door slamming upstairs. She jumped, looking at both her parents.

"Is there someone else here?" she asked.

Her father sighed. "No, the house pops, especially toward the evening. I've had a couple foundation people out, but they can't pinpoint the problem. I was worried it might be unsettling…"

He sounded like he was lying.

"No… I'll be okay," she said, perhaps lying as well, even if to herself.

She stood from the table. "I am *so* happy to be home. I love you guys. A lot. I missed you so much." Tears welled up in her eyes. She wiped them away and forced out a breath. "But I am *exhausted*!"

Her father stood up and gave her a hug. "You don't have to explain anything at all. You're home now. Take your time; I think we all need to decompress."

Her mother stood and hugged her as well. "We're happy you're home, too. I love you, my sweet."

Even though they were the same height, her mother suddenly felt small in her arms.

She let go and waved her hands in her face. "Okay! I'm probably gonna cry myself to sleep now!"

They exchanged nervous laughs and exchanged goodnights as she grabbed her bag and headed upstairs.

Her room didn't look different from the day she had left. She closed the door and started to strip out of her fatigues. Looking at the antique hutch, she smiled.

"Hello, old friend. I'm back!"

She pet its edge, then plopped backward onto her bed. Looking down, surprised, she had forgotten how soft civilian bedding was. It was probably going to be a long night, but at least it would be a long night at *home*.

44 - ANDREW & JOANNA NEWSTED

It was stormy and Andrew called in sick. His nerves were already fired up from the early morning thunder; now being out on the water was putting him on edge. Joanna could tell something more was going on, so she opted to stay home with him.

"Do you remember why we moved here?" she asked him.

"Because I could fish."

They had crawled back into bed after calling their employers and dozed under the sound of rain and rolling thunder.

"And do you remember when we were kids and every time a storm rolled in you'd run me outside and we would watch the lightning?"

He groaned. "Kids? That was only a *few* years ago. God, where does the time go?"

"A whole lot has happened since then."

His chest heaved as he sighed. "Get to your question. You're obviously going somewhere."

"Don't be rude," she said, patting his chest as she lay against him. "I'm saying a lot has happened, lots of things have changed. Not just for us, either. But these things you loved you're avoiding now. I know you don't want to talk about *over there*, but I wish you'd let me know. I'm here. I'm with you, always, no matter what."

The rain pattered against the windows and roof. Combined with the little bit of wind through the trees, Andrew couldn't tell if he was hearing the voices coming from the bathroom again or if they were in his head. He tried to heave a sigh again, but the breath got caught in his throat and he shuddered instead.

"I'll tell you this once," he said, his voice like ripping paper. "The napalm attacks we lay down to clear out the Viet Cong—napalm is fire in jelly. It sticks to your skin and burns you alive. They tell you to find water if it gets on you. Water will stop the burning, but as soon as it touches the air, it burns again. You've got to scrap it off, with a knife or whatever, while it's under water.

"A few guys laying suppressing fire got hit by the napalm as it came in. Before I knew I was hit, I was trying to help. Get them out of their clothes, drop them in this creek, which was really just puddles of standing water, and scrape the shit off. This guy, we only ever knew him as Markowitz, he gets it on his jaw. I don't even know what to do. He's screaming so loud I don't know how to react or get him to listen. I don't even know who it was that came up, but they told me to dunk him deep in this water and they would get the stuff off as fast as they could. So, I did. It didn't seem like long. The other guy said, 'c'mon,' I raised Markowitz up onto the bank and continued helping out.

"I think about it, and I hold my breath; it doesn't seem like that long. I didn't find out until we were in the village waiting for evac. I asked, and all I heard was a voice say, *He drowned in the creek.*"

Andrew stared at the ceiling a long time before Joanna kissed him on the cheek. There were absolutely no words to be said. His new-found aversion to water was apparent, and she wasn't going to press it. She knew he had done his best, that he was trying to help, and that Markowitz was most likely incapable of holding his breath in that situation. Reassurances weren't going to help him. She hadn't been there, and despite the horror of the story, she could never know what was in his head. She opted to stay quiet and listen to the rain, but she didn't let him go.

When she dozed off and Andrew could hear her light snoring, he slowly crawled out from under her and stepped out into the hall. He passed the stairs and leaned against the railing, looking over the foyer. Straight ahead, the big round window above the door was streaked and blurred, making the dark forms of the trees dance at their trunks. Still, he thought he could hear the whispering.

Taking a step back, he looked into the bedroom. Joanna was sound asleep and the bathroom door was closed. Looking to his right, the closer of the two small bedroom doors was hanging open. The door between the rooms appeared to be swinging slowly back and forth on its hinges.

He rubbed his eyes. Despite the muted daylight coming from the foyer and other rooms, the small rooms looked darker. Even though he was only a few feet away, it also looked like there might be a body slumped against the wall, though it seemed like he was seeing it from far away.

Whoever or *whatever* was affecting the partition door, it seemed to take flight as Andrew stepped closer to investigate. He rushed through the room and flung the partition open, only to have it bounce shut behind him. From the hall he could hear a door slam somewhere on the side opposite him. Stepping out and rounding back to his original starting point, something hit him as it rushed by. He felt it in his neck as he fell to the floor at the end of the railing.

As consciousness fled, he found it hard to collect his thoughts. There was something about being in the war, about being scared of going to the war. But how could that be? He was already home.

~

Andrew was standing before he realized he had stood up. He checked his neck and body. There was nothing, no blood or bruising. Had he imagined it all? Had he been *sleep walking*? Hearing a sound, he became motionless to try to pinpoint its location. The sound of Joanna's snoring relaxed him a little.

He stopped at the top of the stairs and looked in on her. She was sound asleep and completely unaware of the man standing over her on the opposite side of the bed. Andrew was about to yell, to fly through the room and attack this stranger, but a sharp pain struck the back of his head again.

There was nothing between feeling the pain in his head and lying on the floor outside their bedroom; nothing was amiss, nothing out of place, and the voices had stopped. The rain seemed to have come to an end as well. Without making too much more noise, though Joanna had slept through slamming doors and his own body smacking the floor twice now, Andrew pulled his pistol and cleaning kit out of his dresser and went downstairs.

They only had a couple of chairs and a TV tray set up in the sunroom with the high windows. Joanna didn't say a word or even offer a questioning expression as she sat next to him while he took apart and cleaned his gun for the third time that evening.

45 - PHOEBE BACKLUND

After the events unfolded upstairs, Father Francis sat next to Phoebe in the reading room. It was exhausting and far more than he had expected, but nothing near as bad as being overseas. He felt a pang of guilt, though; when Phoebe had first encountered her ghostly problems, she had gone to the church for help, and they had ignored her. Members of the community even *shamed* her—especially when she conducted séances. He hadn't been there at the time, but he felt Phoebe's plight, especially after seeing it firsthand.

"What do *you* think it is, Mrs. Backlund?" he asked. "Honestly. *Your* honest opinion."

"Something we're not meant to understand," she said, looking him in the eyes. "But something from which we can glean a lesson. I think you were on the right track when you said it's no demon. There's a pattern here, and it doesn't care who you are. I fear it, though, from a respectful point of view. Errol could have hurt you."

Francis nodded. "It makes me wonder, though, how much of any of our actions are our own?"

"Shouldn't I ask *you* that?" she teased.

"I'm not going to lie and say I have all the answers or tell anyone how they should live their life," he defended. "We've got a guidebook in the Bible, and we've got an example to follow in Jesus, something greater to aspire to, but even God and Jesus got upset and let anger get the better of them at times. I have to wonder, all these terrible feelings we can feel, is that God or the Devil controlling us? Or are all the question marks we end up with proof that we're on our own?"

Her brow knitted into furrows as she stared at him. "Has the house shaken you, Father?" she asked worriedly.

"In the War I held a number of hands as the life left them and it never got easier. Not a one of them wasn't scared," he said. "I saw terrible things no one should even imagine. I pulled through with a mix of rationale and prayer. When I came home, I realized I needed to keep things simple and realistic. Life is hard and often cruel, and no matter how much you pray, God's not going to intervene until you do something for yourself. It's not handouts for beggars; it's rewards for hard work. I see things in war and know that we've got our work cut out for us. I see what I saw upstairs and I realize the tests are impossible. How much of this is floating along and how much is truly in our hands?"

Leaning back in her chair, she chuckled. "You're not asking for answers," she said. "You're asking for *my* answers."

"I did ask for your honest opinion." He smirked.

"I think once you're done here, you're done," she said. "But sometimes God has a way of telling you to keep your head up, to watch out. For you, it's to see that there are still questions for which no answers can be had. For Harry, there are still surprises in the world. For Errol, the more you try to run from something, the faster you head straight for it. For me… a sense of purpose, perhaps. I'm a caretaker of this house and its secrets, yet everyone I invite walks away with some lesson."

"I think that's all anyone can hope for in life—to have an impact." He nodded.

He watched her as her own words sunk in. These were things she thought—knew for herself—but saying them aloud to someone else made them seem more real.

46 - MARCUS SHEPHERD

Shakespeare indicated sleep and death were similar. As he lay dying, Marcus felt fear. The blood flowed from the wound in his neck; his jugular had been nicked under the right side of his jaw. Severe enough, but also slow. Bleeding to death on the upstairs landing of a haunted house wasn't exactly how he thought he'd go. When he had awoken, too weak to even move from the loss of blood, he wished he had stayed passed out. *To die, to sleep.*

A lot went through his mind. It almost seemed like everything he could possibly think about rose to the surface. An eternity to think. Was *this* the *afterlife*? The brain wondering as the body died? At least he wasn't lying this way on a ship in the Pacific.

Was that a consolation? Was dying in an empty house in a Lake Superior resort town better than as a soldier protecting his country? Was being murdered less scary than dying in battle? Maybe this was a battle…

He had looked in both kids' rooms, but being dark, he knew he could have missed something. The door slammed in the hallway. He and Noah had rushed toward each other. Commotion.

He felt nauseous even recalling it. A pain in his neck, then black. That must be how death was like sleep. Short of waking up, how does one know they've been asleep? How would he know when he was dead?

Sounds came to him like dreams. Were they imagined? Was it something he heard upon passing out? Fighting, scuffling, rushing, doors slamming, and glass shattering. Hell, this *could* be the Pacific for all he knew in that moment. Things were stretching out. Was this Basic? Was it that night in Centralia?

Three months ago, North Korea ramped up its ballistic tests again, firing a test rocket that made it thirty miles off the coast. But that had been a ruse. When everyone was monitoring the missile, the North launched a cyber-attack on the South, crippling traffic lighting. It seemed strange, until it was realized in the confusion that several Northern cargo trucks had slipped past the demilitarized zone. Soldiers poured out into key law enforcement centers, staging an invasion. One country was holding another hostage. When China was implored to do something about their ally, the unthinkable happened: they sent support troops to the North.

Marcus, working closely with Shannon and Noah in Baltimore at the time, decided to join the Navy. His own decision terrified him. Shannon had broken down in an unusual display of emotion. He had to follow his heart, though. Chasing echoes in time had been a blast, and his experience with the TRAP was truly quite valuable to the war effort. But now was the time to make a difference in real-time.

There was an urge to cough, but nothing came. One eye was half open. He could see the upstairs bathroom door. Something went by. Tension built. Was it a specter? A person? Barkley?

Noah had looked scared when Marcus announced he would be joining the Navy. Basic would be in a couple of weeks, their time was short. The three of them had grown into a family on their ghost hunts. Shannon was very much the mother, while Noah was more like an older brother.

When Basic was complete, he had a couple of weeks to himself before he would be shipping off from San Diego. Marcus opted to use the time chasing more Echoes. Grand Marais was supposed to be the last stop before some rest and relaxation. They would shoot their investigation for the documentary on the nature of Noah's Echoes.

That sounded like a good title. His mouth opened to say it aloud; he needed to tell Noah he thought of a title for the show. Violent Echo was too cryptic.

There was the sound of whimpering. Where was that coming from? He tried to take a deep breath, to clear his head. He needed to focus. His one open eye felt sticky, like when allergies strike. Springtime in the southwest is always terrible. Dogwood.

No!

The bottom of the bathroom door slid out of view and was replaced with the bottom of the bedroom door next to it. It was the room with the antique hutch. That's where the crying was coming from. It was female. Shannon? It sounded like when Shannon had gripped him tight and cried into his chest. It was a sob of dread.

Was that the smell of smoke? Something far away smelled like smoke, but also old wet cloth.

Marcus sighed. It was one of the stories about the Backlund House. Had Noah been right? Were they making it true by observing it? Marcus' own experience here on the landing—he could hear the crying, he could smell something burning, the general state of fright and thoughts of death. His own experience, *his*.

When was the last time he inhaled?

The bottom of the bedroom door seemed further away. There was a sound of voices, more sounds of fighting.

One night during Basic he had stayed out late and stared at the star—

47 - ANDREW & JOANNA NEWSTED

Andrew's knuckles were white on the wheel. The grip of the wheel creaked as he squeezed tighter. Joanna reached across and barely touched his arm. He jumped, then sighed and let go of the wheel, looking over into her concerned face.

"It's okay…" she said, but he could tell even she didn't sound convinced.

"I almost wish someone else would have seen or heard something." He reminisced about the party. "Then I would know I wasn't mad."

"I hear them, too," she responded. "But, it's our house. We can't live in fear of our own home."

She sneered at her own explanation. She couldn't stand the sights and sounds, either. She had seen enough inexplicable horror for a lifetime for all the time he had been gone. She thought *she* had gone mad, but now it was hurting them both.

"I don't feel like going home," he moaned. "I don't feel like going to bed; I don't feel like getting up; I don't feel like going to work, or hanging out, or going home…"

She frowned.

He leaned back in his seat, dropping one hand to his side between them and digging into his tear ducts with the other, staring at the house all the while. There was a small shaking *no* of the head followed by an all too familiar sigh. Without a word, he popped open his door and stepped out.

The ground crunched under his feet, drawing his attention. It was dusk, hard to tell much about the ground. There was the gravel of course, and some yellowed grass. Was the ground hard from winter frost or parched from summer heat? The disturbing realization of a loss of time made his head spin for a moment, but Joanna's exit from the car snapped him back to reality.

"The party was nice," he reassured. "I did have a good time. But I was ready to puke before anyone showed up. I loosened up when I was drunk. I don't want to live like that."

They started toward the house together.

"I don't want to live in fear."

A woman's startled shout came from the house, seemingly from their own bedroom.

Joanna had grabbed onto his arm as they were approaching, and though they had both jumped at the sound, she could feel him quivering now.

"Goddammit," he seethed.

He didn't sound scared or concerned, though. It was bitter frustration.

"When my wrist was broken," he droned, "I heard that. There's no one in there."

Standing rigid, Joanna wasn't sure what he was feeling. She felt powerless and helpless. He needed something, and she couldn't help.

"Let's not go home," she suggested. "Let's… go to a motel."

"I don't think we can afford that," he countered.

She tugged his arm, pulling him back in the direction of the truck. "Come on, we'll stay at Loretta's, then. She has a spare room and I know she'd welcome us."

"We shouldn't impose." His voice was still flat. He wasn't arguing, just not agreeing.

"I'll tell her the lock is busted, or we lost our key and can't get in. It's too late to call a locksmith. She'll take us in."

He knew he must look shut down to her, but the idea of one night's rest away from this insanity was indeed alluring.

He stopped and looked her square in the eyes. "If she resists in the slightest, we're coming back home."

Joanna nodded in agreement, to which he relented.

~

Before Joanna could even describe her made up scenario, Loretta took in Andrew's pallor. She saw shell shock, fear, anger, and desperation. If ever a man was haunted, he stood on her doorstep now.

"Huh-uh," Loretta said before Joanna could start. "Come in. I can tell when someone's beat and I've got a room I ain't usin', you come on in."

Joanna smiled and began to offer gratitude, but Loretta would have none of it. "You're welcome anytime. I'm glad to help; I'm glad you came."

Loretta was gracious and kind. She asked no questions and didn't pester them about comfort. They all watched the nightly news together in relative quiet. When Joanna stifled a yawn, Andrew seemed to finally relax.

"Thank you so much," he said. "It's been… it's been a heck of a day."

"I imagine it's been more than that," Loretta chided. "But don't mention it. I'm happy to be a friend when you needed one. I'll be turning in myself…"

"I think we'll follow," Joanna said.

They helped Loretta turn out her lights and said their goodnights. Alone, Joanna and Andrew said nothing, instead slipping out of their clothes to their undergarments and crawling into the twin bed. They didn't have much room, but it was the most relaxed they'd been in weeks.

48

Coming into the house and hearing heavy breathing and wood creaking was hilarious and nauseating all at once. She was glad her parents were still passionate, but she preferred when they sneaked around and kept things quiet. Of course, she *was* home a bit early. If they wanted to sneak in some sex, she couldn't fault them.

She paused and felt a chill. This wasn't right. There were no cars in the drive, only hers. She was home *early*; her parents wouldn't be home for a while.

Training kicked in and her stance changed. There was an intruder, and she needed to handle the situation. Backing out of the door, she reached into her pants pocket and pulled out her phone. She couldn't afford the time to be shocked by no signal. Her priority now was to get away and to safety. With no weapon and unclear the level of her threat, she needed to get away.

Making the car in only a few sprinted steps, she was halfway sitting in the driver's seat when the woman's shout came from the house. It sounded from upstairs.

She cursed under her breath. Leaving would ensure her safety, but if kids had busted into their "famed" haunted house to impress some girls and things had gone too far… She was a soldier with combat training, she could handle some punks. Running around the back of the house, she went into the toolshed and grabbed a hammer.

The backdoor in the kitchen took the same key as the front. Silent and arm raised, she crept around to the foyer and the stairs. The breathing and other sounds came from the two connected bedrooms. Keeping her back to the wall and sidling up the stairs to avoid any creaking, she kept her eye on the hall. A quick glance into her parents' room and down toward the darkroom revealed no one.

Forward along the banister then, body low and hammer ready.

There was only the sound of one male's breath and it didn't sound like rhythmic pounding against a bed or the floor. The wooden sound was that of a door swinging, thumping between the man's hands. Through the bedroom door, she could see the connecting door opening and closing, low light flashing between swings. Then she looked down and slumped against the wall, inside the bedroom door was a form—potentially of a person.

Part of her brain was telling her that something was wrong, that and it was time to go. It was dark in the room, despite it being the afternoon and light outside. She couldn't focus on the body in the doorway, though the door frame and hallway around her were clear. Inching closer, she could smell the familiar tang of blood. Adrenaline surged and her breathing became shallow. Her ears and the back of her head felt cold.

Another few inches and she could see the form of a man swinging the door between his hands. He was looking down, though she couldn't make out any details, apparently lost in thought. She forced her legs to raise her, getting ready to pounce, but the form noticed her.

The door went wide open and slammed back shut. Darting through and into the second room, she could hear heavy footfalls and the bathroom door slam across the hall. She was back into the hall and ready to attack with her hammer held high. Reaching the banister revealed no one, though. It was behind her. The second bedroom—where she had just been—burst open, and the form rushed her. She swung, felt the shock through her forearm as she landed a direct hit. She felt something in her neck, then nothing at all.

~

When her eyes opened, she had to think long and hard on where she was. She had woken up in a hospital bed before after blacking out... but this was much nicer than a field hospital. Steadying her breathing, she tried to remember how she had gotten here. A hand touched hers and she backed away and up into a sitting position.

Her mother's face was startled, *terrified*, yet also relieved. "You're awake!" she said.

"That would appear to be the case," she groaned. "What happened?"

"I was hoping you could fill some of that in," her mother said. "When I got home, you both were out cold on the balcony. I called the cops immediately—"

"Me and *who else?*"

Some of it was coming back.

Her mother gave her a worried look. "You and your dad, of course..."

She shook her head. "No... I got home and there were intruders. I heard a girl scream, so I went and got a hammer. It looked like someone was hurt, and I chased someone... I hit them... but..."

"You hit your father," her mother responded. It was in answer, but there was a tone of accusation.

She shook her head. "No, he wasn't home; I got home early and neither of you were there. That's how I knew there was an intruder. But..."

A realization struck her about as hard as her hammer-blow had been. "I came in through the back door when I came back in." She nodded her head, then slowly shook it back and forth. "He could have pulled up and went inside before I got back in."

She looked directly into her mother's eyes. "But I swear! I thought I heard someone in the house. I heard a woman shout from inside the house when I tried to leave and get help."

The worry in her mother's eyes gave away briefly to something like fear and recognition, but it was gone as soon as it had come.

"Where's Dad?"

Her mother took a deep, slow breath. "In another room. He's speaking with police."

"Police?" she cried. "Is he… are *you* pressing charges?"

"No!" her mother said waving her hands to fend off the thought. "No, he's giving his report. And he's fine, you clipped him pretty good, but it looks like he might get away with only a black eye. They took x-rays to make sure there isn't a fracture. They want to take every precaution," her mother continued. "The doctor thinks…"

The silence from her pause drew on too long for comfort. "What, Mom?"

"The doctor thinks you might have had a flashback; that you're suffering PTSD."

She slumped and leaned over into her hand. "I *know* I heard someone in the house; *before* Dad got home. Now, maybe because I thought I was going to find an intruder I lashed out at Dad, I suppose that's *possible*, but I wasn't having a flashback! Someone was *there*!"

"Okay…" her mother said. She reached out and touched her daughter's knee. "It's okay. We'll get through this."

Anger swelled up. "Don't *patronize* me."

She rolled over, putting her back to her mother. There was an instant twinge of regret, but she knew she had heard and seen things in the house that were not her father. She felt coddled like a child and she didn't have to stand for it. She could work this out on her own.

49 - ANDREW & JOANNA NEWSTED

Coming home from dinner in town, they found the house completely dark even though they'd left a porch light on and a few lights on inside.

"Power must be out," Andrew said. "I'll go around the back and check the breakers."

Joanna nodded, but was already feeling anxious.

It wasn't even two minutes and he was walking back around to the front of the house, shaking his head. He waved for her to follow him in.

As she stepped out of the truck, he called to her. "I can't see that anything's wrong, but the switches aren't doing anything. I need to make sure the fuses aren't blown; let's get some flashlights so we're not stumbling around in the dark all night."

She nodded wordlessly.

"Hey," he said, touching her shoulder, "it's okay, at least it's a nice night. If we don't have power all night, we can sleep with the windows open. It'll be kinda nice."

She smiled, but it was weak.

She followed him to the washroom where he kept a couple of flashlights. He handed her one. "I'm gonna go check it again, make sure there's nothing in the way, blocking a connection."

"Okay," Joanna said, flicking on her flashlight.

He smiled at her in the beam.

He was quick through the back door in the kitchen, right next to the breaker box on the back of the house. Everything was quiet, thankfully.

A loud *pop!* startled her, but she didn't make a sound. The lights were still off, and she began to worry that Andrew had damaged something or even electrocuted himself. She moved to check on him, but before she even crossed the space from the washroom to the door, she heard a second, quieter, though much more distinct, clicking sound upstairs. It was the same click of the closet door she had heard when she tried to switch rooms in the middle of the night.

She crossed the kitchen and stepped into the foyer from under the stairs. Soft light was coming from down the upstairs hall.

She called out to Andrew. When she looked back up, the light upstairs was gone, but the couple of lamps they had left on were now lit.

Coming in through the front door, Andrew called out to Joanna in a panic and was bounding up the stairs.

"Hey, I'm right here," she said, stopping him. "I was trying to check on you. That pop scared me a little. But also, I noticed a light upstairs had come on…"

He gave her a confused, yet knowing look, but deflected. "Well, you didn't have to *scream* like that!"

She shook her head. "I called your name out loud. I didn't scream…"

"I heard a slam, like a car door out front," he explained. "Almost as soon as I got around front, I heard you scream like you'd been startled. I didn't hear you say my name."

"I promise," she said. "I didn't scream. I was going to tell you a light had come on. I don't know what you heard, but—"

His hand shot up to silence her. She looked offended, but he put his finger to his lips and pointed to the other side of the balcony, then he motioned for her to come up the stairs quietly.

When she reached him, she asked in a whisper, "What is it?"

He shook his head. "I thought I heard someone else speaking. It was quick; a word or two."

"You think someone else is in here?"

"I don't know," he said, pulling her back toward the front door. "I want you to go sit in the truck and lock the door. I'm going to look around the house a bit. I didn't do anything to make the power come back on, and I don't know what that pop was, and I don't know if someone's in the house or not. But this is the kind of shit we put up with almost nightly over there. I'm sure I can ferret out a burglar if I need to."

They were already on the porch at this point, and she didn't hesitate to run for the truck once he had said his piece. Shining his light through the trees around the property, he saw no evidence of extra vehicles. Searching immediately around the house, he saw no signs of forced entry, and he specifically remembered unlocking the front and back doors as he had passed through them. There was nothing to suggest someone else was in the house, short of completely covering their tracks, picking the lock, and re-locking the door as they came in. That scenario suggested something nefarious.

If he could make the top of the stairs quickly, he could sneak into the bedroom and grab his pistol, then sweep the house. He calculated it in his head and knew exactly where he needed to go and how he needed to move. Swinging the front door open, he made the top of the stairs in a few bounds, skipping multiple steps. He had his gun in hand and was ready to fire before he knew what he wanted to do next.

Crossing his wrists to point the flashlight and gun in the same direction, he looked down the hall toward the windowless room and the closet, both shut tight. In the other direction where he thought the voice had come from, the bedroom doors hung slightly open as they usually did. The living room double doors were shut.

He edged along, pressed against the wall opposite the balcony railing until he could shine the light into the mostly empty room. Nothing. The door between the rooms was shut. Shining the light into the room on his other side, he could see the edge of the hutch against the wall. That could be a hiding place. He pushed the door open, checked the bulk of the room, shined his light into the closet, then opened the hutch. Empty.

Stepping back into the hall, he checked the second small bedroom at the end of the hall—also empty, save for the single bed and a nightstand. Closets were empty; nothing under the beds; upstairs living room was empty; the windowless room, the sticky closet... all perfect hiding places, all completely empty.

He was glad, but also frustrated. Why was the house picking on them now? To stay on the safe side, he wedged the gun in his belt at his back. He went downstairs, opened the front door, and waved for Joanna to come back in. She was slow to respond, but eventually made it to the stairs at the bottom of the veranda.

"Everything's okay?" she asked.

"Not a thing," he shrugged. "Maybe what I heard was a weird echo; I don't know."

She sighed, but it didn't sound relieved.

"Look, whatever it was, it seems to have stopped."

She agreed half-heartedly and stepped back into the house with him. With the lights on in the sitting room, it felt moderately safer, if only by virtue that she could see without a flashlight. She sat down in Andrew's recliner and tried to take long, deep breaths to calm herself.

Andrew rubbed her shoulder but noticed he had smudged dirt or oil of some sort on her sleeve.

"I am so sorry," he said, "it must be from the gun. Let me wash my hands and I'll gather up some laundry to throw in with that."

She gave a weak laugh, shrugged her shoulders, and shook her head. "It's no big deal..."

He stepped through the washroom and started to wash his hands. Definitely oil, probably smeared on the cloth he kept the gun folded in from the last time he cleaned it. He'd have to remember to clean it later.

As he lathered up and scraped at his skin with his fingernails, the back door popped open, startling him to jump back away from the sink and the door. He started to reach for his gun when someone quietly dragged another body in through the door.

"Hey!" Andrew yelled, drawing his pistol and leveling it at the intruder.

But the person didn't react. In fact, they maneuvered the lifeless body so that they could shut the back door and even lock it.

Joanna walked into the kitchen through the washroom, but jumped back and yelped as she walked right into the line of fire of Andrew's pistol.

"What the hell are you doing?" she called from around the corner.

"You don't see this fucker in our house?" he called, as much to the stranger as to Joanna.

But the stranger still didn't react, as if they were completely oblivious to Andrew and Joanna's presence. It was then Andrew realized he couldn't define what he was seeing. He couldn't tell if either person was male or female, what they were wearing, or if they made any sound.

Joanna peaked around the corner, as if she couldn't see the same thing he was seeing.

Was he cracking? Was this some sort of flashback? He'd seen a lot of people carry a lot of other people…

He whispered to Joanna, trying not to interrupt what he was seeing. "Go back to the truck."

"Andrew," she said, in a full voice. "You're scaring me. Can you please put the gun down?"

The stranger and its victim continued through the kitchen and turned back into the foyer. Andrew fully intended to follow them.

"Go back to the truck, Joanna," he said firmly. "Go to Loretta's."

There was no way she could leave him alone. She had no idea what he was seeing. Whether it was the house, stress, or something else, she couldn't let him hurt himself.

"Please put the gun down, Andrew," she said more forcefully.

He ignored her and followed the intruder out into the foyer, where they were now dragging the body up the stairs. He was now as oblivious to Joanna as the person on the stairs was to him. They dragged the body to the first small room, where he had heard the voice, where he had seen the door swinging, and had heard heavy breathing.

Joanna tried shouting at him, grabbing at his free hand—anything to break him out of his trance—but he didn't react at all. He was as much a ghost as any other apparition she had seen in the house. Worried for both their safety, she raced back into the kitchen to call the police, but the phone was completely dead: no dial tone and no reaction to the spinning of the dial.

Andrew snuck into the bedroom where he could see a mass of shadow, but it was mostly formless now, almost blending into the darkness of the room. It stood there, waiting for something. Then there was the faint call again, what he had heard before. He couldn't make out the word, but it was calling to someone, like saying their name. There were footsteps on the stairs, rushing. At first, he thought it was Joanna coming to try to pull him away again, but she never came through the door. No one or nothing came through the door. The shadow stranger lashed out, though, and there was a thud against the wall.

Blood began to pour from a tiny nick in the paint. Andrew shook his head. That couldn't be real. He looked hard and, indeed, dark red liquid trickled down the wall, smearing out as it seemed to come in contact with something leaning against the wall.

There were more rushing steps from out in the hall. The house seemed to shout and groan. The doors all around him slammed or banged open, then performed the opposite action. Andrew pointed the gun in every corner, ready to fire on an unseen assailant, but there was no one.

From out in the hall, deep in the upstairs living room, there was the sound of shattering glass. As he stepped out to check, he could see shadows—phantoms everywhere, elongated and distorted by a raging fire along the staircase. It must have been the fire Joanna had seen in the middle of the night.

He looked over the railing. A crying and desperate Joanna was calling out to him. Strangely, he couldn't hear her voice. He was horrified by everything he was seeing; his house on fire, blood pouring from the wall, these shadows standing everywhere—even the closet at the end of hall was flung open and he could see the creepy rhyme written on the back wall—but at the same time, he was only witnessing it.

He could feel something inside of him breaking. He looked at the gun in his hand. A thought occurred to him.

He looked back down at Joanna, even terrified she was such a pretty lady. He felt really lucky to have had her as his wife. He made the decision.

"I'm pregnant!" Joanna's voice called, finally breaking through to him.

He dropped the gun and flashlight. The fire went out, disappearing completely. Not even smoke was left behind. The shadows vanished, and the weight of the action he had been about to take began to lift off his shoulders.

"I might be." She continued. "I'm only a few days late…"

He didn't say a word. He came down the stairs and grabbed her hand. They walked out of the house—not even pausing to lock the door—and out to the truck.

Staring straight ahead, he said, "We're not raising a kid here…" then drove out to the interstate.

50 – LUCENTIO AND HELEN

Empty. A whole season passed without a guest. Not even a sightseer. Not so much as a wayward traveler asking for directions at one of the last houses before MN-61 headed into Canada. Even the wind refused to visit. The house had settled down the last couple of years. The less that people came, the bigger, quieter, and *emptier* the hulk on Lake Superior became.

"I think you're trying to tell me something," Helen said out loud as she sat on the porch, trying to will a car to come down the long drive off the highway.

Nothing. Empty driveway, empty interstate, empty house. She'd had guests all throughout the year in more lucrative times. Summers were popular, but the fall, especially the weeks around Halloween, used to see waiting lists: reservations held in hope a guest would duck out in fear before their scheduled departure. Last year, there had been two reservations. The year before that, only three. Business waned with the lack of activity. The house had gone quiet. Silence was bad for business when guests expected bumps in the night.

As if responding to her plight, a glint of headlights pulled off the interstate. Her heart leapt, and she leaned forward in her chair. Alas, the car pulled back out and retreated the way it came; someone had missed a turn.

Groaning as she stood to go back inside, she scanned the highway through the trees one last time.

"Okay," she said aloud again. "I get it. Maybe you're ready to sleep. I understand that completely."

Inside the house was the faint smell of smoke, but otherwise, it was cool and still.

"Can't you give me a shout?" she asked the empty space. "Slam a door or two?"

Her voice barely echoed off the walls. "I don't want to be alone anymore…"

The sound of crunching gravel broke the growing quiet. Spinning on the spot and reopening the door, she was greeted with a dilapidated 50s' Plymouth. The red was indistinguishable from primer and rust, but the white, where it remained, was still bright. Lucentio stepped out and flashed a smile.

His blonde hair was dusty these days, but somehow he still looked like a handsome young man. "How's business?"

"I never understood your name—Lucian, Lucio, Lucius… then your flourish of a name."

He shrugged. "Dad liked Shakespeare. You're avoiding my question, though."

Stepping up to the stairs, Helen stepped all the way out, shutting the door behind her. "I think you know the answer to that. Why else would you come around?"

"I care about local businesses and my fellow business owners," he explained with another aloof shrug. "When your business is doing good, so is mine. But it seems like I'm getting less traffic from your direction."

"You watch which direction the cars pull in from?" she asked, bemused. "I didn't think your place had windows…"

"People talk in a bar," he chided. "Ghost stories have been awfully thin of late. Thought I'd stop by and see how you were holding up."

She looked him up and down. Everyone knew Lucy's Dynamo Bay and the titular Lucies throughout the years. How could he know she was considering giving up at this moment?

"You don't have anything to do with the hauntings, do you?" she asked.

Stifling a chuckle, he pursed his lips. "That would be something."

He climbed the steps and took a seat in one of the chairs. Helen took one of the others.

"Business has been dying the last couple of years," she explained. "The house barely creaks, and *that* could be settling as much as ghosts. I think the show is over."

"Sorry to hear that. I guess that's why I'm here. Seems like I haven't had patrons talking about their stay at the haunted B&B. A week after Halloween and no nostalgic musing? I wouldn't blame you for shuttering the business. Will you stay in the house?"

"Eh, it's a bit empty," she said.

"I was afraid of that." He nodded. "It was fun while it lasted, I guess."

She turned and faced him, eyebrows knitted into a V. "We're not friends. I've been into your bar a couple of times in six years. Why are you here?"

Inhaling deeply, Lucentio folded his fingers in his lap, then slowly exhaled, saying nothing for a moment.

Letting the silence linger almost to the point of becoming awkward, he finally returned her gaze. "I like ghost stories. I'm honestly saddened I haven't had any of your guests and I thought I'd come up here and see what was up. Maybe even see if I could get a tale straight from the source, as it were."

She shrugged and stared back out at his beat up classic. "I don't have anything you wouldn't have already heard, either from my guests or from over the years."

"What about your husband?" he countered. "Is he still working nights? Has he had any daytime encounters?"

She began to huff a laugh through her nostrils. "My husband has been dead since before I moved here."

"What?" Lucentio exclaimed.

"I wanted to start a bed-and-breakfast so I wouldn't be lonely anymore," she explained. "Telling people my husband was in a room you couldn't see into from inside or out gave them a sense of security—that *maybe* that bump was him. But it was only ever me and the house. I guess *there's* your ghost story."

"Damn." He laughed. "That *is* something."

They sat in a prolonged silence again, Helen staring out to the interstate and Lucentio taking in the brief reveal.

"I guess I've been blessed with good business for a few years," she finally continued. "I moved on from Frank—my husband—and the house went quiet. I guess it did its job."

"You sound like Phoebe," he said.

"Who?"

"Phoebe Backlund… you named your B&B after her?"

She stared at him. "That was the twenties, you wouldn't know her."

He blustered. "Of course not, but my granddad told tales! *Anyway*—she found peace of mind despite the events in this place. A lot of people don't know she died happy; doesn't do a haunted house's image any good if it ends up *helping* people."

She leered at him for a moment. "*That's* why you're here. You're not checking on the business, you're making sure I've not gone a little mad. Look at the bartender with a heart of gold."

"Doing the Lord's work, I am," he joked.

He regarded the property for a while, taking in the trees, the gray sky, the faraway lapping of the lake behind the house. "I've always liked it up here. Town's not too big, but a drive up here seems to make that all that disappear. The quiet must be nice *sometimes*."

When yet another silence drew out, he looked over to see Helen's chin resting against her chest. He reached over and wrapped his fingers around her wrist and found no pulse. She had held on long enough to at least not go alone.

"You go be with Frank, now, Helen."

51 - NOAH BENJAMIN

Waking up like this had to stop.

The bedroom door was hanging open, and the bed was askew. Noah could see feet standing in the bathroom doorway from below the bed. He could hear voices—someone must be in the bathroom. Cynthia? No, he couldn't peg the voices to anyone, or even to a gender.

There was another sound catching his attention, perhaps the sound that brought him around. He tried to lie still, to avoid catching his attacker's attention. His ears still felt stuffed full of cotton, but there was a dull roaring and crackling.

Great. The staircase must be on fire.

"Fuck it," he groaned and pushed himself up. The pain was intense, but he was becoming used to it.

The voices stopped and he could hear shifting feet; his senses were coming into focus. The sound behind him was certainly fire, but he couldn't see or feel it even though his feet were even with the stairs. As he came all the way up, he looked around the corner and down the stairs. He could see the fire was burning big and bright in the sitting room.

The flames were licking at the archway. With no way to control it, it would be on the stairs, and soon. The urge to escape nagged him, but he didn't know where Cynthia was. Craning his neck further around, he saw Marcus's dead body a few feet away.

Looking back into the bedroom, he could see the figure of a man. Barely lit by the window behind him, the stranger was wrapped in shadow.

"You won't stay down, will you?" asked a man's voice.

Noah shrugged and stretched his neck. "If I'm gonna be a ghost, I'd better put on a hell of a show."

"You don't get it," the man said. "This house is more than a haunting. It's a *curse*. You can leave, but it won't leave you. You can't un-see or go deaf to this house. No matter how you explain away the ghosts, this house has destroyed all the lives that have entered it."

"And you make sure of that, I see…" Noah chided.

"I'm *ending* it."

Noah paused a moment. He squinted, wishing his eyes would adjust so he could see who this person was.

"What do you mean 'explain away the ghosts'?" Noah baited.

"Don't play stupid, now, Mr. Benjamin," the man said. "We waited for you. We knew you would come, and we knew your *theories* would make this place a target. Well, this house doesn't care about science. You fell into its trap and now you're a victim, too."

Something jumped up from the floor and tackled Noah. As they went crashing down, Noah thought, *great, this again.*

This second attacker was smaller and lighter. Noah found an opening and delivered a punch with all the upward force he could muster. A woman's voice sounded with a grunt, and he pushed her to the side. He checked the stairs again. The first step and end of the banister had caught fire. The wallpaper was peeling and burning. Escape was nearly cut off that way.

Looking back to the second attacker lying on the floor, his gut fell. "Shannon?"

"Are you expecting an apology?" Shannon coughed out, unfettered anger seething with each word.

He took a step back, the feeling of betrayal bringing his adrenaline high back down. Pain began to grip his body again. Confusion and nausea made it hard to focus.

"I don't understand…" he said, sounding crushed.

The man stepped out of the bedroom and helped Shannon up. As he bent forward, Chuck's unmistakable red hair was lit in the light of the flames.

"I don't understand," Noah said again.

"Of course you don't," Chuck said. "But we do. We waited for you. We knew you'd come in here thinking you could solve some sort of mystery, but now you're a part of it yourself."

"But why?" Noah asked, shaking his head. "You've killed people! None of this needed to happen—"

"We've been *waiting*," Shannon cut him off. "We were here when you had your traumatic encounter as a kid. When you started making the scientific journals, I got close and you had no clue. Then you set everything up perfectly. The TRAP was right—this won't go on anymore. Everything will be over tomorrow."

Noah reached his hand out for the wall to support himself. He stumbled when he didn't find it. Tripping up until his hand found the molding of the door to the upstairs living room, he shook his head, trying to put the pieces together. Then he looked at the door, over to Marcus, then back to Chuck and Shannon standing in front of the primary bedroom. They had been in there. Chuck standing where the apparition had been before. They had been talking—probably menacingly, probably looking for Cynthia.

The old ghost stories were *coming true*. Phoebe complained she couldn't stay in her own bedroom. Joanna couldn't find rest in any room. Andrew fought off invisible attackers. But all of that malice and violence… it was this group. Noah had gone out the window, had been in a fight that started a fire, ended up knocked out at the top of the stairs, right in front of that bedroom.

"You've made sure everything was reenacted," Noah said. "You pushed us in all the right directions."

"Not at all," Chuck said. "I thought you'd gather your evidence and then be on your way. We hoped you'd find something to help us bring this all to an end. But when you insisted Cynthia try and kick-start the haunting event, your *Echo*… We knew it was time."

Noah began to nod slowly. "You're the previous owners that disappeared."

"Very good, Noah," Shannon said. "You might think it didn't need to end this way, but when the Echo and the events were so close to each other, we had to see it through to the end. We had to kill this house and end this cycle."

"But Marcus was our friend!" Noah said with force. "Thom and Reggie were your friends, Chuck!"

"The house has been demanding this sacrifice, Noah," Shannon said. "This is exactly what you've been looking for. You are part of the creation of a haunting. The chronotons are going wild, but particle physics be damned, Noah, this is what has always been. You said it yourself, this has happened in real time, every time. Well, now it can end, and this house can go straight to Hell."

The poem in the closet—they couldn't escape it. From the moment they had stepped into the house, it was going to end this way. Chuck and Shannon had taken the reins from the time the lights went out and directed the whole event.

Chuck made sure Reggie didn't turn the lights back on and made sure the lights wouldn't come back on. Chuck slashed the tires during that time, too. When the group went back outside, he dragged Reggie's body upstairs. The bloody handprint in the van was a ruse to scare them, to hopefully get them back in the house.

Noah pushed himself off the wall and leaned against the railing of the balcony. Down in the foyer, the TRAP gave away the final piece. Shannon hadn't shut it down, she restarted it. The sensors hadn't been unplugged and the anti-cellular component was active. A few cables sparked and melted against the fire. She made sure they couldn't call for help.

Once the stage had been set—be it coincidence, fate, or even the predetermination of the chronotons, like Noah had *wanted* to observe—everything started to click into place.

Cynthia emerged from her hiding spot, the hutch in the extra bedroom. "And what now, Chuck? We've been friends for years, and you killed Thom and Reggie as if it was nothing.."

Chuck shook his head. "This house doesn't leave you; you can't escape it. Ten years we've been away. Ten years living in hiding, our lives torn apart by the nightmares. A small sacrifice to bring it all to an end."

"A small sacrifice?" Cynthia nearly screamed. "And us? Are we to be a part of that sacrifice?"

Noah shook his head and took another step back, pressing against Cynthia. The fire had climbed up the stairs, and Chuck and Shannon were purposefully blocking their path. This villain trope of exposition as they stalled for time to ensure no survivors… passive murder. They would sacrifice themselves to ensure the house burned down.

"You would let us leave, wouldn't you?" Noah asked. "The fire is the last thing, if we could leave, you'd let us."

They were silent.

"We're going to jump out of the window," he said to Cynthia in a quiet, but firm voice.

"What?" she whispered. He grabbed her and made to bash through the living room doors, but Chuck and Shannon lunged forward to stop them.

Noah ducked and lunged forward, counter to Chuck's movement, knocking him off balance and stumbling backwards. He'd had enough with fighting. Chuck fell down the stairs, slamming onto his back and tumbling into the flames at the bottom. No screams—he must have been knocked unconscious or snapped his neck or spine.

Grappling with Cynthia, Shannon's grip failed when she realized what had happened. Cynthia kicked her in the back and urged Noah forward into the living room.

"Don't look. Don't stop. It's going to hurt, but pain is better than dying," Noah said as they crossed the room.

He could feel her naturally begin to resist, but his own adrenaline propelled them forward and out of the broken window. Cynthia screamed, then they hit the ground hard.

"Are you okay?" Noah asked.

"I twisted my ankle, I think," she said. "Maybe it's broken. It hurts."

"We have to get to the road," Noah said. "We should be able to make a call if we can reach the road."

She nodded and forced herself up. Noah offered her support, even though he could barely hold himself up.

She gasped, but not out of pain—she was looking up. Noah followed her gaze and saw Shannon standing in the window.

"Shannon! Jump down! You don't have to die. We can get through this."

Shannon walked back into the house.

"Shannon!" Noah called, but nothing answered. He could only see a low orange glow dancing across the ceiling.

"Come on," he said, and began to help Cynthia around the house.

They hobbled their way along the rocky driveway, using their phones to light the way. Halfway down the path, Noah's signal was strong enough to call 9-1-1. He looked back over his shoulder as it rang; the fire had broken through the front door. By the time emergency crews got here, he thought, the entire house would be ablaze—dash-cams recording as they approached.

They made it to highway 61 and sat on the concrete. Noah tried his best to explain to the emergency operator the night's events.

"What if they were right?" Cynthia asked.

Noah was still on the phone but looked at her.

"Was that the end of it? Or will *we* be haunted by it?"

"It's over," he said, placing a hand on her knee.

"Your chronotons might move on," she said. "Everything is made up of smaller and smaller particles that came from bigger and bigger explosions, but none of it matters if you can't *appreciate* it."

She focused on him. "You went looking for trees, Noah, but you found a forest. Can we find our way out?" Her eyes looked far off as she pondered her own point.

But she was right—he got exactly what he was looking for. He had been seeking out the data instead of the experience. Even when he recognized the potential for danger, he was more interested in pushing the envelope to seek out that data. Even if *how* all this worked was thanks to quantum mechanics and time spun backwards as well as forwards—even *if* the data they had gathered proved that—what was the *why* of it?

52 – CRAIG & MIRIAM, AND CHARLENE RYAN

When the decision became clear, it was both daunting and a relief. A fog had lifted. Charlene had been aimless, but now she possessed clarity to make a decision. The act would be hard on her parents. There were no other choices, though. The nightmares wouldn't end; she could no longer tell where nightmares ended and hallucinations began. How long before she attacked her father again, or her mother—or friends over for a visit? It was for the best to end it.

End it. The finality of that statement made it ominous, yet somehow easier to accept. It *would* end. Even if death ended in darkness, at least it wasn't the sound of sobbing from the hutch or doors slamming and bodies chasing each other; at least it wasn't visions of dead kids in desert streets or bombs going off meant to kill her.

She slipped out from underneath her sheets and knelt at the edge of her bed, folding her hands. She prayed for forgiveness and strength to complete the task. She knew it was an oxymoron, asking for God's blessing to do this, but no other prayers had been answered. Visions of her past and the bizarre illusions of this house would not stop. She needed rest.

Stepping out into the hallway, she was greeted with the sight of the stairs and foyer engulfed in flames. That only solidified her decision. Shadows fought on the landing. She closed her eyes and took a deep breath. Opening them again, the foyer was bathed in silver morning light. Walking out onto the balcony, everything seemed normal.

She thought about her parents coming home: they would be upset. *She* would be upset if she walked in on such a thing. She needed to write them a letter, heartfelt and explanatory; making them understand would make it easier for them to accept everything and move on.

Before she could make it the few steps to the top of the stairs, the distinct click of the closet door at the end of the hall caught her attention. Light poured out into the hall, but she couldn't recall seeing any light before. She approached, squinting, and tried to rationalize. She had hallucinated flames, maybe she missed the light from beneath the door. She had *hallucinated*. She could be hallucinating now.

Throwing open the door, the light was off, but there had been no click of the chain on the light. She couldn't remember the instant it went off. It was on, then off—no noticeable transition. Had she hallucinated *this* as well? Was the house haunted, or was *she*?

She closed her eyes and leaned against the doorframe. "There's no escaping you is there?" she asked aloud. "In this house of in between…"

She opened her eyes again, only to see the dark linen closet with sheets and junk on the shelves. "I can't tell if I'm asleep or awake anymore; nothing ever seems right… I guess that doesn't matter. This is where I'll always be."

An art kit her father had bought her for Christmas years ago sat on one of the shelves. She slipped open the box and took out a piece of charcoal. On the back wall, she scrawled a poem to reflect her feelings.

Maybe it would be enough.

She put the charcoal back and noticed the scalpel in the box. It was meant for cutting paper. She brushed her thumb over the blade; it would do fine.

She took a deep, ragged breath, staring at the blade in her hand. Her mind raced as she knelt. There was a prayer in there—a call for help, half of a lyric on endless repeat from a song she'd heard yesterday, her father's face after he had been released from the hospital with some bruising, what her mother would think of her, the soldiers she had known who died, the kid she had played kickball with, her first kiss behind the church next to her middle school…

The blade was against the inside of her left forearm.

The front door burst open and slammed. Not unusual—she had heard that particular sound many times. Not even the footfalls coming up the steps gave her pause.

There was a stinging sensation as she applied pressure.

A voice called. Though it was disembodied, there was no reason to look up anymore. Her fingers felt ice cold, and there was a tingling sensation at the back of her neck. She could hear blood rushing through her ears; nausea threatened to stop her, but she had already made her decision.

When the skin finally gave way, there was a popping sensation and a rush of warmth throughout her body; she just had to drag the blade down toward her wrist.

When her mother's hand ripped the scalpel from her and tossed it aside, she was brought crashing back to reality. She looked up at her mother's face: horror, revulsion, anger, and confusion. But the nurturing nature kicked in and her mother grabbed the small wound tight and lifted her to her feet. Immediately, tears and wailing erupted from her, but it sounded alien. It was far away, as though some other thing bellowed from within her.

Her mother said it would be okay.

Despite the horror she should have been feeling, a memory of being only six years old and crying after skinning her knee, wanting her mother to console her, came to her.

Her mother's cooing continued as they rushed out of the house.

~

"It's the *house*," Miriam said.

"The doctor said she's suffering from post-traumatic stress," Craig said.

"I don't doubt that in the slightest! I read her letters from war, same as you, but you saw what she wrote in the closet."

He shook his head. "I don't know."

"I *do*. That house has been driving us mad since we moved in and now it tried to take my baby. This ends!"

"What does that even mean?" he asked. "Charlene is hurt and she needs us—not you flying off the handle, battling demons for her. She has a real condition, and we can deal with it."

"And keeping her out of that house can only be good for her," she urged. "But I can't let anyone else suffer. I've looked into it; the place has all kinds of stories around it. Well, now we've lived it, and it's gone too far. We'll keep the house… make sure no one ever suffers in there again."

"So, we're going to own an empty house…" he said more than asked. "How is that helping our daughter?"

"Until we can find out what's going on there, I'm making sure no one else suffers her fate. Someone's going to end up dead in that place. I aim to prevent that."

He buried his face in his hands. As he feared for his wife's sanity, he also worried that this event would likely tear them apart. The house had been their first step toward leading a normal family life. Granted, they had an adult daughter recently relieved of active duty. The house was meant to bring them together. From the start, it had driven a wedge between all of them.

"Fine. We'll hold onto the house. Maybe one day we can figure it out. Maybe we can put an end to it… one day."

Miriam just nodded in agreement, like it was a matter of fact and there was no contention. Her decision had already been made, it wasn't a matter to debate.

His own bruised face reminded him that violence had already manifested in the house. She was right—it would only end in death.

53 - HARRY HOUDINI

The silence that grew between them as they waited for yet something else to happen was beyond uncomfortable. Millie asked Phoebe if she could smoke, Phoebe shrugged, and everyone immediately produced cigarettes. Harry was still on the hunt and had crept upstairs, looking for more to observe, investigate, and experience. Murmurs from the group and whispers from the ghosts became difficult to distinguish. He was almost afraid they had terminated the event somehow, that they wouldn't see it to its conclusion.

All the doors had seemed to slam in quick succession when the fleeing set of feet ran up. Harry checked the small bedrooms first, musing about how easily they had become *possessed*. But now they stood silent. He crossed the hall into the room with the Backlund family hutch. He looked around for a moment, trying to open all his senses entirely, to smell something besides dust, to hear beyond human voices—and there it was. As though hiding, a soft cry; someone trying to control their overwhelming emotions.

It emanated from the hutch against the wall adjacent to the door. Looking at the floor, he could see dust on the hardwood in the moonlight. Smeared with footsteps, he couldn't distinguish his own tracks from anyone else's. He stepped in front of the hutch and leaned against the edge of the bed opposite it.

"Who are you?" he asked in a whisper. "What are you doing here? What is this thing that you're a part of?"

"Holy shit!" cried Millie downstairs.

Harry sighed; he couldn't afford to miss any detail. He stood up, thought about opening the hutch to see what he could see, but feared the act would break the action.

He stepped out into the hall and saw that same dull glow of muted fire coming from the reading room, but it was much more intense now. Donald was holding his arm out across Millie's midsection to protect her. But from what? He approached the stairs to head down, but immediately upon hitting the top of the stairs, he could see a completely different house.

It was empty, cold, and dark. The house was derelict many years. Harry could feel the thoughts of someone else; he could feel their pain. They had been in a fight and gone out a window—it was one of the presences he had felt before. Without resigning too much control, he observed from within.

He was checking for signs of fire down the stairs. He *expected* the fire to rise. Looking back into the bedroom, there was the shadow in front of the window. It started to make sense. Everything was shadows because it was nighttime and dark in this other place. The shadow at the window was someone this other person was acquainted with. They were conversing, but the words weren't making sense. All of it was raw emotion, no definition.

This was what Phoebe had shown him before, the thing that convinced him it was worth seeing the whole event in its entirety. He knew what to expect—an attack from below—but he couldn't warn this other entity, who was unaware. The conversation carried on. Meanwhile, the fire continued to grow and had reached the stairs. Was this one *stalling*?

When the attack came, Harry stepped out and let the event unfold in front of him. Knowing now what to look for, he could see the shadows produced by the flames. There were four people. Only four people left and two of them were intent on murder. What was their motivation? Why were they working so hard to kill the others? Why didn't these other people save themselves?

If the first ghost was stalling to keep his enemies upstairs, the shadow from the window was now stalling to ensure no one got out alive. The crying entity from the bedroom came into the hall and entered the fight. Somewhere in the commotion, Harry lost track of whom or what was who—it was all frenzied shadows dancing in the air. The real people at the bottom of the stairs looked on in confusion and terror. A fire was consuming the stairs, a brawl of shadows was on the landing, and there stood Harry, merely observing everything in front of him.

One of the shadows was knocked down the stairs into the flames. It was then that Harry realized everything he was watching was very far away. The sounds were there, but low; vibrations of hits were timid, if even noticeable. Harry followed as two of the figures walked into the upstairs living room. They jumped out of the window, disappearing into the night air. In their world, the window must have been broken, and that was their escape.

Footsteps sounded behind him. He fully expected to turn around and see Phoebe approaching him, indicating everything was over. Instead, an almost fully formed apparition, a woman, maybe in her fifties, stalked by. Unusually dressed, she wore straight pants and a strange blouse. He couldn't make out her face entirely, but the posture was that of someone disheartened, resigned to their fate.

This visage approached the window and looked out for a moment, most likely at the two that had escaped. There was a heavy sigh, and then she turned back into the house, striding toward the fire. He followed cautiously. He considered stepping into her path to try to learn more about her, but he wasn't positive consciously deciding to do it would work, and he couldn't risk breaking the event.

Harry could smell the fire now, but there was no heat, even though the flames were licking the top of the banister. He followed her onto the balcony where she stared at the fire-she was much clearer now against the flames.

Dr. Lawrence called from below, "What's happening?"

Harry came to the edge of the balcony and held his finger to his lips. They couldn't see her; they were all too focused on the growing flames upon the stairs.

The specter proceeded down the hall, past the master bedroom and the séance room, stopping in front of the closet door. Reaching out and gripping its handle, the door popped open with the same distinct *click* they heard earlier. She reached up and pulled on the chain and, to Harry, the light came on, as did all the other lights in the house quite suddenly. How she reacted, though, it seemed she couldn't see the lights at all. She looked back down the hall—but not at Harry— she could only see the flames. She pushed the door open wider to give herself light.

There he could see the cryptic stanza along the wall, and sure as Phoebe had mentioned, the interior of the closet was different. She placed her hand in the middle of it, then pet the wall, as though the poem had some special meaning to her. Her body shuttered, wracked with a cough from the smoke no doubt. Falling to her knees, her hand rested on the final line, *'Cause this is where you've always been*. She craned her neck one last time to look at the wall, then fell to the side and promptly vanished along with the fire on the stairs. Harry could hear the surprised gasps from below. *Now* it was over.

He walked down the hall slowly, trying to process what he had seen and experienced. It was real, but he didn't know what it was. This wasn't contact with the dead, this was watching people fight for their lives and die. It was a look into an event that did not exist. He had seen parts of it before, out of order like Phoebe explained, but the events repeated, totally dependent on the observer.

When he reached the stairs, he found himself startled to see them in pristine condition. He forced himself to accept that, despite it all being real, it wasn't real in *their* space. It was real somewhere else; they were looking in on it. He looked down the hall. The doors were resting peacefully on their hinges. The faces below stared in shock, except for Phoebe Backlund, who looked lonely.

"You've seen it all before?" he asked her.

"Multiple times."

"And the woman in the closet—and the poem?"

"She knew the poem, she had already seen it. She went to it because it was supposed to be there. It is both the beginning and the end."

"And it won't stop," Harry said. It wasn't a question. He knew it to be true.

Father Francis crossed himself and began a silent prayer. Chief Mignola and Doctor Lawrence stared as though in shock. They had both been *possessed* as well, but to them the experience may have been much darker—they had both been invaded. Donald and Millie were sighing and shaking their heads, glad the thing was over, but unsure of what they had seen.

Harry came down the stairs and looked about. It was nearly dark outside now and the few lights that had been on before the power had gone out barely lit the house. Still, having been in darkness for so long, he found them irritating. He looked at Phoebe for a long moment and she did not flinch or look away.

"What do you think it is, Mr. Houdini?" she asked. "Did you find what you were looking for? Is the spirit world real? Did you make contact with the dead?"

"No," he said firmly. "It is as you said. This is no show or set of tricks, of that I am convinced."

He turned to the group. "I think we have all seen enough. I thank you for your cooperation, friends. I invite you to draw your own conclusions. However, I am afraid I cannot offer any myself."

54 - ANDREW NEWSTED

Had it really been a handful of years? People moved after a few years all the time. There wasn't guilt at bailing on the mortgage—it was worry they'd be behind forever because of this damned house.

Andrew gripped the steering wheel tight. He knew he had sat in this exact position multiple times before, afraid to go in the house, only able to stare with a knot tightening in his gut. But this time was different. Moving day would be the last day he'd spend in this house.

Joanna was at the small two bedroom they had rented in the last month as they made the decision to get out. She understandably wanted nothing to do with it. Plus, with the pregnancy, stress was off the table. This house was nothing but stress.

Frowning, Andrew remembered when they moved in. There was hope. A family was exactly what he had hoped to start. If only the house could be as peaceful as it appeared right now, he wouldn't be gripping the wheel as tight.

His knuckles ached. He finally let go and flexed his fingers a few times. Garrett's truck and trailer pulled up alongside him. Andrew hopped out and smiled. He knew it was a smile of relief. The few times they had had guests, the house remained quiet. Hopefully this time, one last time, it would remain quiet.

"You look awfully glad to see me." Garrett chuckled as he stepped out of his truck. "Usually people hate moving."

"Getting out of this house is like getting off the boat after a huge haul in the rain," Andrew offered. "We didn't have a chance to really fill up the house, hopefully it won't take us long."

"Hey, however long it takes." Garrett shrugged. "Still don't understand how you could want out of this house so bad. You don't strike me as someone who would mind a little fixing up."

"This house needs more than fixing up," Andrew sighed.

"Is it haunted?" Garrett asked. His voice was low, almost lost in the light breeze swaying the treetops.

Andrew thought for a moment. He had joked before, telling true stories in humorous tones. If he confirmed Garrett's fears, would he be stuck moving furniture by himself?

"Yes," Andrew replied flatly. "It's where I got drafted. I'm tired of stewing in memories. It's time to move on and make new ones."

Half smiling and nodding slowly, Garrett eyed both Andrew and the house. "I grew up here. In Grand Marais, that is. I always heard stories; dumb shit really… never thought I'd set foot in this house. I guess it's the kid in me being nervous."

Andrew clapped him on the shoulder. "Honestly? The house does have some foundation issues." He lied. "There are some sounds on occasion, but we can make the record player the last thing we move, and we can be done in a few hours."

Garrett nodded and clapped his hands. "Let's do it."

They stepped into the chalky smell of dust. The house had sat mostly empty for a couple of weeks, Andrew and Joanna packing a few boxes here and there, darting in and out. All that needed to be done was to grab a few pieces of furniture they hadn't already moved to the rental house. Those, and the boxes of small trinkets that nobody remembers where they came from—or knows exactly where to put in a new place.

"Let's get the stuff upstairs out of the way," Andrew said. "It's a couple sets of small beds, tables, and dressers. That's all that's up there."

Before heading upstairs, Andrew rooted through a few boxes. He pulled out the record player and some albums. Led Zeppelin serenaded them through the tinny built-in speaker as they got to work.

Passing the large room across from the two small rooms, Garret noticed something sitting against the wall through the doorway. He stopped and pushed the door open.

"Wow," he said, taking in the hutch. "Are we moving that?"

"Huh-uh." Andrew shook his head. "It was here when we bought the house. Supposedly, it's been here since the place was built and no one can bear to dismantle it to take it out. I don't need anything reminding me of this place anyway."

Garrett shrugged and left it be.

The house remained quiet, save for music, the entire day. Andrew even relaxed and managed to push aside the horrible things he had seen, heard… and *thought*. If Garrett saw or heard anything, he didn't mention it.

Did the house think it had won? Maybe it wanted to be left alone. Regardless, Andrew was done and glad to see his last glimpse of the house through a rearview mirror.

55 - PHOEBE BACKLUND

Late at night, Lucy's Dynamo Bay was the not-so-secret speakeasy where the younger population of Grand Marais could find a drink. During the day it survived—legally and financially—as a diner frequented by fishermen and tourists. In between, when the light waned, and the boats were docked, and the young folk weren't quite brave enough—that's when it was quiet and empty. Phoebe would sneak in at such times.

The events of the evening gave way to morning and the day. People went home, disturbed and full of questions that could not be answered, but Phoebe remained with little place else to go. A drink with dinner seemed in order.

As she stepped in, Lucian came around the bar which was dressed as a diner counter. He was tall and chiseled, his blond hair disheveled from running his fingers through it too many times.

"You!" he said wagging his finger at her. "I lost one of my best girls thanks to you!"

"Oh?" Phoebe said, putting her hand to her chest. "I thought she had a stronger constitution; I had no idea a few bumps in the night would make her quit her job."

He shook his head, blowing a raspberry. "Nah, she ran off with that reporter from Duluth. I know you needed warm bodies, Phoebe, but c'mon! That girl flashed half a thigh and I sold two more ryes."

Lucian looked over his shoulder at the cook wiping down the counter. He signaled a "two" with his fingers and pointed between himself and Phoebe as he walked with her to a corner booth.

The floor had a few circular tables, but another staffer was clearing them and stacking chairs to stow in the back. In a few hours, the diner counter would convert to a bar again and the main floor would host a band and dancing feet. The big booths would serve higher paying clientele and gambling games.

"Am I interrupting anything?" Phoebe feigned concern.

"You know I like you, Phoebe," Lucian said as they sat. "I *trust* you. You know why?"

"I'm a paying customer?"

"Everyone thinks you're crazy."

"I'm flattered."

"Hey, it's to your advantage! I could tell you every dirty secret: my suppliers, my take—I could show you my inventory and where I keep it. Even if you screamed it from the roof, and even though everyone in town knows, they wouldn't pay it any mind because it's *you*. You've got free rein to do what you damn well please and people blow it off like nothin'. I ain't got nothin' to hide with you. You were a pain in the ass when you went loopy, but I get it now. I guess Millie did, too. She *was* spooked, you know. I bet that's half the reason she ran off. I think I'd want to beat it, too, if I saw blood pouring from the walls. *Anyway*, I can relax with you."

"Well," Phoebe said with a coy smile, "I guess I *am* flattered."

The cook arrived with two steaks and two glasses of red wine.

"How is he so damned fast?" Phoebe asked.

"Eh," Lucian shrugged. "I have him keep several on real low heat to keep ready."

She picked up the wine and swirled it in the glass, sniffed, then took a small sip. She gave a satisfied sigh. "You know I wasn't loopy. And I'm not crazy."

"I know it."

"You know I prayed, right?"

"I know it."

Lucian started cutting into his steak.

"I wondered and feared that I had done something truly terrible, that I deserved this for some reason." She cut into her own steak, took a bite, and chewed slowly to savor the taste.

"But it was after begging for forgiveness for so long… from God, from Handel, from the people of the town—"

"I know it… you were in here doing it."

"—I came to the realization in the brief quiet times that this was one of those situations where it feels like I've been overburdened, but it was a test of my own will."

Lucian leaned back. "You know this isn't a church, right? I mean, I got booze in the next room and I'm about to take a lot of money under the table from strangers."

Phoebe smiled and took another bite, followed by a sip of her wine. She rose the glass between them in a mock toast.

"But that's what I'm getting at," she continued. "You offer a service where it's needed. Jesus turned water to wine when the party needed it."

"Okay…" Lucian chuckled. He raised his glass and clinked it against hers.

"I realized I was in a place between worlds," she went on. "I couldn't communicate with these spirits because we're not meant to. I tried, even against my better judgment. Was I tempting fate? *Were* these demons? I realized the séance was a sham, but I needed people. I *needed people*. I became an entertainer."

"Like your *guest*?" Lucian smirked.

"Millie wasn't supposed to say anything."

"You asked a twenty-year-old girl to keep a secret?"

Phoebe chuckled in turn. "That house may belong to whatever is in there, and I'm the one shuffling between the walls. I've learned lessons, though. I'm facing death, Lucian. I'm an old widow in an empty house—well, mostly empty—and where I was desperately sad and clutching at family, I was given adventure. In turn, I can offer adventure. The house gave me purpose; it was a gift."

"I think I'd return it."

Phoebe laughed again. "Seriously, Lucian, I was terrified of life once. Now I terrify people for fun. Life is violent and cruel. I can't guarantee any sort of afterlife isn't the same. Maybe it's a vicious cycle of life and death over and over. I found a sort of peace in the insanity, though, even if the insanity is all anyone else can see. I can thank God for that."

"This still isn't a church." Lucian smiled.

"I get wine and a sympathetic ear," she said, sipping again. "Sounds like church to me."

They chitchatted over the previous night's events while finishing up their steaks. Even though Phoebe knew these things, and had run over them in her mind, and even discussed it in part with Harry, confessing her peace aloud was gratifying. Others might view her with disdain, fear, or even sympathy, but she was happy with herself. What better state of being was there?

As the light grew dim outside, they finished off a second glass of wine. When Phoebe reached into her handbag to pay for the dinner and drinks, Lucian waved her off. He insisted on offering her a ride home as well, but Chief Mignola stepped in and looked about as terrified as he had the night before.

"Ah, Chief," Lucian cheered. "How can I help you this fine evening?"

"I was, ah… I was," Mignola stumbled around his words, looking about ready to fall over himself. "I was checking in, saying hi to the local businesses before I went home for the evening."

Phoebe gave a wry laugh. "Errol, I think you can be forgiven a whiskey. You look like you might need it."

"I—I—" Mignola stammered again.

Lucian stepped up and wrapped his arm around the Chief's shoulder. "Chief, would you be willing to see Mrs. Backlund home? We've had a couple glasses of wine and I want to see her home safe. I'm sure she would be happy with a drop-off at the door. I can save your favorite spot for later."

Mignola's eyes went wide again, but instead of feigning bluster any further, he simply sighed and nodded. "Of course."

Lucian took Phoebe's hand and gave her a warm, firm shake. "A pleasure as always. And you've certainly given me some food for thought. Us service providers need to stick together. I hope to see you in again soon."

"I have to at least pick up my car…" she said with a goodbye wave.

Mignola gave them each a cockeyed stare as they stepped out of the bar. He didn't question anything as he helped Phoebe into his car. Neither did he say a word as he took her home, and there was barely a grunt of a "goodnight." His farewell consisted of taillights speeding down the drive away from the house.

56 - NOAH BENJAMIN

The TRAP was covered in soot. The mostly plastic monitors had melted, giving them a glassy appearance. The interior would be damaged, of course. Though Shannon had pulled the hard drive, the sensors were connected to their black box of sorts. Computer forensics could pull and clean up any data within the different devices. Despite the information buried within, it was a bunch of metal and plastic, like any other computer.

Noah wiped ash from the touchpad. He wasn't surprised there was no reaction, but he sighed anyway. He fell back on his haunches and looked up. The roof was gone above the stairs, blue sky and sunshine shone through. The house was wrecked worse than the computer. Both were scrap.

Without thinking, he scratched his forehead then looked at his black, dust covered hand. He shook his head and gave a disheartened laugh, then sighed again and took in the smell of burnt wood, paint, paper and... something else. He stood, purposefully sniffing the air. Sewage.

He asked one of the firemen about the smell.

"Most of the damage was right here, but it looks like heat did a lot of its own damage," he explained. "The plumbing to the primary bedroom ruptured."

With a smirk, Noah nodded. Most every haunting was easily explained away. But what about last evening? Were particle physics, spatial anomalies, and quantum mechanics sufficient to explain all the events that had led them to their fate?

A shocked whisper spoke behind Noah, *"Oh my God…"*

Noah turned to see it was Dennis Shelby, the bank officer.

"Um…" Noah searched for words and scratched his head, then rolled his eyes as he looked at his dusty hand again. "I don't even know where to start…"

Dennis shook his head. "No, I'm just glad you and Ms. Morrison are safe. The police gave me the gist."

"Did they tell you the owners were the perpetrators?"

Dennis nodded, looking up through the hole in the roof. "I'm with you on the loss of words. I guess it's over, though. No more house, no more haunting, right?"

Heavy footsteps and a dragging sound came from the balcony. Noah and Dennis both shot their gazes upward but were greeted with another fireman dragging cables that had been strung along the hall. Everything was natural and obvious now. The haunting really had come to an end when it caught up to the group and everything finally happened in order.

If they hadn't been there, though, like Cynthia asked, would it still be happening? Could it have ended before in the right circumstances? All the readings from the night before had indicated everything in the house was always happening, the same events occurring over and over in real time. Of course, that was impossible.

"It was us looking at it," Noah said.

"I'm sorry?" Dennis asked, looking back at him.

"I kept thinking something was wrong with our equipment," Noah explained. He was speaking more to himself. "It was the act of looking at it with our eyes, with the machine, and the cameras; we gave it an audience. Whatever happened last night was a possible outcome, and the night before, and the first night it ever stood. It was constantly in superposition, waiting to be collapsed."

"Superposition?" Dennis repeated.

"A state of flux," Noah said. "It could be one thing or the other, standing or burnt down. When I say collapsed, I don't mean the house collapsing, but the possibility of its physical state being determined out of an infinite number of possibilities."

"And your being here determined that?"

Here Noah sighed. His answer should be *yes*. By having the right number of people and all the cameras recording at all the different angles, the house was sufficiently observed to finally determine its state in the universe. The chronotons could determine their paths and the fabric of space molded to its ultimate position—in regards to the house, anyway. The more he clawed for the answer, though, the less meaning it seemed to carry for him.

What sense was there in knowing the *how* of it when the house had given its secrets up only with the death of five people? What was the point of diminishing the haunting in his childhood neighborhood to grooves in space when two people had died to cause the event without leaving a mark of their own?

"I don't know," Noah finally answered. "Maybe it was me. Or the group. Maybe it would have happened in some similar fashion somehow, sometime. Maybe eventually it would have gone quiet and there'd be nothing to show for it."

Plenty of metaphors jumped to mind; *staring into the abyss, opening Pandora's box*, hell even Cynthia's *seeing the forest for the trees* wasn't off the mark.

Noah bent back down in front of the machine. Was it this thing's fault? If they had only come with the cameras and recording equipment, would it have been any different? He shook his head. No point in asking what-ifs; this house had been filled with too many of them for too long. It was over. Chuck and Shannon had seen to that.

In the glossy melted monitor, he could see someone standing a few feet behind, between him and the front door. Dennis was looking at the burnt stairs to his right. Was it a fireman? He hadn't heard anyone come in or around.

Looking over his shoulder to see who it was, he quickly snapped his head back to the monitor, then fell forward into the machine.

Dennis yelped and rushed to his side. "Are you okay?"

Noah was pale and panting.

"What is it?" Dennis asked. "You look like you've seen a ghost!"

Dennis huffed as he realized what he had said.

Noah was staring at the front door, not saying a word. The confusion in his face twisted his mouth into half-formed, incoherent words.

Dennis looked up to see nothing. He shook his head. "What?"

Noah finally looked at him. "There was no one there?"

Dennis shook his head again.

"When I knelt back down," Noah went on, "I saw the reflection of someone standing behind me. I thought it was a fireman. I looked over my shoulder, and there was no one. When I looked back at the monitor, there was no one, but I distinctly saw someone. They were blocking the light and everything…"

"Too bad you can't turn your machine on and see what it was!" Dennis chuckled.

The adrenaline surging through Noah's body made it hard to think straight. He hadn't been that startled in a long time. He tried to assess all the possible explanations: trick of light considering opposing sources, state of the monitor itself being melted, or even the *Troxler Effect*—his brain playing tricks on him.

Noah shook his head. "I think maybe I'm done."

Dennis helped him up, and they both stepped out of the house.

The fireman pulling the cables in the hallway upstairs pulled another long loop to the landing, but stopped when he noticed something hit the floor. As he bent down, it was a single fresh droplet of water, splattered in the caked soot in front of the primary bedroom. He looked up, but the roof was gone there with no place it could have dropped from. When he looked back into the bedroom, he fell backward as he saw someone standing in the far corner in front of the window. When he stood, though, there was no one.

57 - PHOEBE BACKLUND

The house had remained quiet for some time now. Phoebe had no visitors, and in solitude she was able to move about the house without setting off events. One chilly morning towards the end of November, a car pulled down her private drive. She sat on the veranda in a heavy robe, sipping on coffee. She did not get up to greet her guest, and before they even got out of the car, she knew who it was.

When Harry stepped out of the passenger side of the car, he paused and looked up at the house. He shut the door and stood there for a moment. Not waiting for her, but for perhaps the house to greet him with a startled scream.

Phoebe smirked and shook her head. "She's been quiet. I think you exhausted her."

"Is that gratitude I hear in your voice, Madam Backlund?" he asked, finally coming toward the house.

He climbed the stairs and sat in the chair on the other side of the breakfast table on the porch. "I have a member of *Scientific American* with me."

As if on cue, the man stepped out of the driver's side of the car, but he didn't approach the house. Instead, he lit a cigarette and took in the view of the woods around them.

"We've offered a cash prize to any spiritualist that can prove their abilities," Harry said.

Phoebe didn't respond, instead taking another sip of coffee.

"I do not know what happened that night," he continued, "or the night previous to it that I attended. But I know, after seeing what I did, that you have something special here. It is a look into another world, one I have thought on a lot since that night."

"I notice you haven't made any announcements," she said, staring out into the yard at the smoking man. "My house hasn't been swarmed by reporters, religious leaders, or scientists."

"I figured you wanted to keep your home as your own," he said. "As interesting as this place may be, it is still where you live. I understand it's you and your husband's dream house, even if it hasn't quite lived up to it."

Phoebe let out a slow sigh. "You know I don't want your money."

"The prize is yours if you did," Harry said, expecting her answer. "But I can leave it unclaimed, and I can continue my search, leaving you be if you choose."

She sipped her coffee again. "I told you before. I built this house, but it is its own thing. It owns itself. You can offer it the prize, but I don't think you'll get much interest."

They watched the man take a long drag from his cigarette.

"You asked me that night," Harry said, "if I had contacted the dead. I said 'no' then and I still stand by that. The more I've thought about it, the more I realize you were right. The house belongs to whatever that event is. It is waiting. It is waiting for that woman to scream, and for the power to go out, and for a man to commit murder, and for that woman to read the writing on the wall."

"You think it hasn't happened yet, that these ghosts are from… the *future*?" Phoebe asked with humor sneaking into her voice.

"Not ghosts. Shadows, *echoes*, like you said. I think you've held back. I think you know far more than you're letting on."

She leaned back in her chair, continuing to stare out into the yard, but not at anything in particular. "I have followed each of their paths, from beginning to end. They came looking for something."

"Boy, did they find it." Harry chuckled.

"The murderer was following a path he thought he had to. The woman in the closet knew it was the end. If there are truly ghosts in this place—if it is really haunted—from some other plane of existence or place in time, this house is theirs."

"Have you considered having the house destroyed?" Harry asked seriously. "Wouldn't that break the cycle?"

"You don't think much about time, do you, Mr. Houdini?"

He cocked his head. "Time is all we have. I am aware of time; time is the key to suspense and the element of surprise. My whole act is based on time."

"And deception," Phoebe pointed out, looking him square in the eye. "I have considered tearing it down, burning it down, abandoning it to the forest around it. But something always stops me. Especially in the beginning, when I didn't understand. Spending all this time here, I have felt the emotions of these people, whoever they are. They came here looking for this, these events, and only in this house. This house exists for them. I cannot tear it down. It will never be torn down. Perhaps one day, though, it will *burn*."

"You agree. You *do* think it's an event that hasn't happened yet?"

Phoebe let out another long sigh, the steam of her breath lingering in the air. "It is here because these things happen, and these things happen because it is here and won't stop until this thing happens. Do you see what I mean?"

Harry nodded.

He leaned forward and looked at the front door. He conjured in his own mind the sights and sounds of his experiences. They were real, they weren't *now*.

"I am no medium. No more a medium than a doctor would be a wizard," Phoebe said. "And these are not the ghosts you're looking for. This is not contact with the deceased. You saw it, you saw them die. Can a ghost die? These are not the lingering dead; these are the as-yet dying. Your prize is safe; your reputation is safe. You found no evidence of an afterlife here, and frankly, that's how it should be. This is a trick, alright, but of nature. A trick on us who would dare to understand."

Phoebe stood and Harry followed suit. "Shall I invite you and your friend in, then? I have coffee on the stove. I'm sorry I can't make you breakfast. Honestly, I do not want to."

Harry smiled and laughed. "It is much appreciated Madam Backlund, but I'm quite sure you would rather not share your coffee, either."

"Nothing slips past you."

"I do wonder, though," he said, "the writing in the closet—where do you suppose it comes from? It is both the beginning and the end, yet we see no one write it."

"I've wondered myself," Phoebe said. "It must be important to the woman. It's the last thing she goes to. Perhaps it is truly what starts it. Perhaps once that thing is finally written, it will be the beginning of the end. This house feeds on emotions—sad ones—of loss.

"I've not told anyone, Mr. Houdini, count yourself blessed. To trigger the events, I read the insurance payout letter from my husband's death. It made my loss of him real. Perhaps the poem in the closet is her letter of loss."

Harry held out his hand and Phoebe took it. They shook firmly and exchanged cordial smiles.

"I suppose there's nothing more to say for it, then. I shall leave you to your house, Madam Backlund. If anything were to change, I would ask you to contact me," Harry said, pulling out a small card with his personal information on it.

"I will burn this," she said, not joking in the slightest.

"I don't doubt it," he said. "But I do hope you'll be careful and not burn the house down. I don't see seven people lingering around ready to see this thing through quite yet."

"Thank you for your time, Mr. Houdini. I believe we have both come to the same conclusion regarding the house and I do greatly appreciate your efforts. If it's all the same to you, I think I will retire. You can rest knowing that another spiritualist can be crossed off your list."

"There shall be an asterisk by your name, however," he said. "No fraud here, no answer either."

Harry and Phoebe shook hands again, then Phoebe retreated into the house. Harry walked out and greeted the man, who was now lighting another cigarette.

"Do we have another fraud to oust?" the man asked.

A woman's startled scream erupted, breaking the silence of the cool morning. The man jumped and made ready to run for the house, but stalled when he noticed Harry climbing into the car.

"What are you doing? Shouldn't we help?"

"No, everything is quite right," he said. "No fraud here. This is the real deal, just not what we're looking for."

The man stared him down, looked back at the house, and his shocked look grew more intense as the old woman opened the door. She said nothing, waved a friendly goodbye and shut the door. Harry laughed from the passenger seat and shut his door. The man slowly came back around and sat back down in the driver's seat.

"Not what we're looking for, *huh*?"

Harry chuckled and stared at the house.

Inside, Phoebe could see the car start up, then trundle back down the drive. She looked at Harry's card, but only for a moment. True to her word, she threw it into the fireplace where it curled and turned black against the embers of a dying fire. Upstairs, there were the sounds of feet.

IN THE HOUSE OF IN BETWEEN
BY CYNTHIA MORRISON

It has been a year since the old house off MN-61 in Grand Marais—known as the Backlund House—burned down. A year since five people lost their lives; three I worked with, one of them a murderer. We knew him as Charles "Chuck" Branson, but I would later learn his name was Craig Ryan. He and his wife—known to us at the time as Shannon, but really named Mariam—had watched and guarded the house for years, always from afar.

Mariam joined Noah Benjamin's team in search of a scientific explanation of ghosts and hauntings. Though, instead of wanting to better understand that natural world, she sought answers to questions that haunted her. Craig had become an engineer for a news outlet in Duluth, keeping his finger on the pulse of his old house. He and I had been close once, even confused for being related.

The two had a daughter, Charlene Shannon Ryan, named after each of their mothers, and the inspiration of their aliases. In the early 2000s when America was at war in the Middle East and the flow of soldiers from the armed forces could not keep up with demand,

Charlene found herself the victim of the Stop-Loss protocol and was deployed on back-to-back tours. Their family had moved into the house in upstate Minnesota before her first tour.

It's easy to get caught up in the urban legends of the house, that the supernatural activities of that place affected Charlene in chorus with her own emotional stresses, and indeed, she left her mark on the house. The truth of the matter is, though, that Charlene was suffering depression from Post-Traumatic Stress Disorder. Like many service-people before and after her, she found it hard to cope, finding no solace in people who didn't understand.

As she told it to me when I found her some months after the incident, nightmares persisted during nearly every sleep, regardless of time of day or location. She dreamt of people from different times fighting battles of their own, all within those walls; people affected by war, people considering, negotiating, and fighting with death. She said she could see that the house had taken a heavy toll on those who dared to peel back its layers to find some soul or core. She noted that the scientific facts of the space of that house did nothing to answer the questions it raised, but instead reinforced the idea that the house was a place of transition.

Charlene came to understand that the house demanded life. Writing the infamous stanza within the upstairs closet as a warning to any who would come later, she attempted to take her own life. Whether it was luck, force of nature, or divine intervention, her life was saved when Mariam came home before it went too far.

Three days later, she was released back into the care of her parents and taken home, back to the supposedly "haunted house." But an attempted suicide and dreams of ghosts were not what did the family in. In fact, Charlene explains, the stanza was the only reminder of that event. There were no more phantom entities, no more inexplicable sounds; the house had gone quiet.

But Charlene would not let her parents remove her work from the closet. For her, it was a reminder of how bad things had gotten. No matter where anyone was in life, physically or spiritually, they were always in a constant state of change. For Craig and Mariam, however, it was a reminder of weakness. Not on the part of their daughter, but of their own, in their inability to protect their child. From war, from fear.

In only a few months' time, Charlene was on her own feet—working, seeing friends, and looking to strike it out on her own. It's difficult for her to say—as it is with any child moving out on their own—when things went silent; time and distance alleviated the pain of the past, but also the distance between conversations with her parents. Sometimes, a letter would come from her mother after she had moved out of the state. Old fashioned, but a tangible thing they shared. Texts and e-mails were even more rare.

"A suicide attempt might bring some families closer," Charlene told me. "Maybe to learn about the problems that arose, or holding each other closer when the inevitability of time has dawned on you. For us, though, it tore us apart. I can't say it was for the worst. I had hit rock bottom but rose back up. Somewhere along the way, we passed each other as they in turn descended."

I couldn't blame her. Once Chuck and Shannon shed those personas in the rising fire that night, I saw two people inconsolably broken, driven by an obsession their daughter had toed and escaped. The house was an allegory for transition. It didn't matter if Noah had been there with his team or that I had gone along hoping for my big break; anyone who has ever been in that house came away changed.

Now, for posterity's sake, Noah made major and significant discoveries with the recovered data from his machine. The haunting *was* us. The cameras we set up and the machine analyzing the data—it always looked like time was in flux because we were directly affecting the space around us. The ghost stories throughout the years were the events of that night, played on an infinite loop in that single space. Once a device could track the chronoton particle, the Observer Effect theory and the notion that time is nonlinear were proven. We could, and can, affect the events of the past. It made huge impacts that are still being studied today and will be, no doubt, for a long time from now.

Many other scientific studies over the centuries have taken their tolls; this one came at a heavy cost. Charlene was understandably devastated by the loss of her parents, but it had been some years since she had even spoken to them. Noah dropped out of the public eye shortly after the events, but predicting I would hunt down Charlene to close the story once and for all, he asked that I deliver a letter to her. I did not read it, but when Charlene opened it, I could see the simple "I'm sorry" handwritten on the single page, with his flourish of a signature written considerably smaller than normal.

She had it with her today when she came to visit the memorial recently erected at the site of the burned house. Nothing remains of the house today; nothing could stop the bulldozers this time. Now all that stands in that space is a bronze pedestal with a replica ledger book, much like Phoebe Backlund used to sign in her séance guests. It has the signatures of those that died that night. Charlene set the letter at the foot of the pedestal, suspecting the apology was as much to any of them as it was to her.

Now those of us who survived the fire, or the years, have a greater understanding of our notions of time and our place in the universe. Not so much thanks to the experiment that night—though it helps in understanding the mechanics—but because we were privy to a place in the universe that exposed the transition of life and time. We saw the unfathomable and beheld both ourselves, yet nothing at all. We are all merely ghosts, waiting to be observed.

Acknowledgements

I owe a debt of gratitude to a number of people who challenged and guided me along the journey from idea to something tangible. Authors, editors, readers, reviewers, and podcasters from across genres have helped and supported me and this book. I want to thank the writing and horror community for every encouragement. Also, Harry Houdini, who wanted so much for there to be a connection to the other side that he was willing to tear the belief apart looking for the truth. And finally, my wife and daughter, Amber and Autumn, who supported me through writing, editing, rewriting, and re-editing IN THE HOUSE OF IN BETWEEN. Without you two, I would not be.

About the Author

J.D. Buffington lives in Tulsa, Oklahoma with his wife, daughter, a capricious cat and two devious dogs. He seamlessly weaves vivid nightmares and haunting anxiety together to immerse readers into a state of fright and wonder. He can be found on most social networks.